Dear Little Black Dress Reader,

T... for picking up this Little Black Dress book, one
... reat new titles from our series of fun, page-turning
... e novels. Lucky you — you're about to have a fantastic
... ic read that we know you won't be able to put down!

...n't you make your Little Black Dress experience
...tter by logging on to

www.littleblackdressbooks.com

where you can:

...ter our **monthly competitions** to win
...geous prizes

...et **hot-off-the-press** news about our latest titles

...ead **exclusive** preview chapters both from
...ur **favourite** authors and from brilliant new
...iting talent

...y **up-and-coming** books online

...n up for an essential slice of romance via
...r **fortnightly email** newsletter

...nothing more than to curl up and indulge in an
...e romance, and so we're delighted to welcome you
...e Little Black Dress club!

...ith love from,

The *little black dress* team

Five interesting things about Jessica Fox:

1. I can't resist stopping to look at newly married couples emerging from churches.

2. My palm-reader told me I have a lifeline that is shorter than my heart line. I assume this means I will be with my husband Rob in this life and the next. I just hope he will have learned to pick up his socks by then.

3. I have a phobia of elevators. On our honeymoon, the Eiffel Tower was definitely worth it. Until I realised I'd left my camera at the top.

4. I was once on a hen night where the groom appeared in the early hours and started chatting me up!

5. If my house was on fire, and I could only rescue one thing, it would be my antique tarot cards. Sorry, Rob.

By Jessica Fox

The Hen Night Prophecies: Always the Bride

Jessica Fox

little black dress

First published in Great Britain in 2011 by
LITTLE BLACK DRESS
An imprint of HEADLINE PUBLISHING GROUP

A LITTLE BLACK DRESS paperback

1

Cataloguing in Publication Data is available from the British Library

ISBN 978 0 7553 4961 6

Typeset in Transit511BT by Avon DataSet Ltd,
Bidford-on-Avon, Warwickshire

Printed and bound in Great Britain by
Clays Ltd, St Ives plc

Headline's policy is to use papers that are natural, renewable and
recyclable products and made from wood grown in sustainable forests.
The logging and manufacturing processes are expected to conform to the

With special thanks to Ruth Saberton

Acknowledgements

To my lovely mother-in-law, Brenda Thomas. She is always there for me and a great coffee drinking partner!

Prologue

May 2010

I *have got to be the luckiest girl in the world!*

Zoe Kent rested her elbows on the cool stone window ledge and gazed out of the villa window towards the lush Apennine Mountains. Sunshine flooded the scene in which cyclamen and myrtle jostled for pole position, while the air was heavy with the intense scents of rosemary and wild fennel. The soft breeze, which played with her blonde hair, was already filled with the warmth of the day.

Zoe smiled and her whole body fizzed with excitement. In under an hour she would be married, and she was in absolutely no doubt that she was marrying the right man.

Unlike last time.

This time she knew in every cell of her being that she was doing the right thing. This time everything was going to be perfect!

It's the most beautiful setting imaginable, Zoe thought with pleasure. Her dressing-room vantage point had a bird's-eye view of the arbour threaded with plump ivory roses and green ribbons. She could watch the villa staff scuttle about as they set out elegant white chairs and tables across the smooth lawns, carried bottles of champagne into the billowing white marquee, and arranged the white carpet aisle that she would be walking along before marrying the man she loved.

How could it be anything *but* perfect when her fiancé was the most generous, wonderful and thoughtful man on the planet? Just look at the amazing location he'd picked for their special day. There were all the thoughtful touches too: the stunning ivory Vera Wang sheath dress that fitted her perfectly; the beauticians and hairstylists, who'd transformed her into a radiant bride. It was the complete opposite of her first wedding, which she'd planned with military precision. This time she hadn't had to lift a finger.

'Come! Your hair no good in wind! You sit!'

The hairdresser, tutting at the strands of hair that the breeze had prised from Zoe's headdress, propelled the bride away from the window. Seating her firmly back at the dressing table, she began to tease the golden curls back into order. It seemed like hours had been spent tonging and pinning Zoe's thick hair up with pink roses, and for once she had been given no choice but to sit back and let herself be pampered. Her nails had been manicured while another beautician had given her the most blissful shoulder massage. It was heavenly, but rather strange not to be in control.

However, Zoe couldn't help reverting to type. 'Have the caterers arrived?' she asked. 'Is the seating taken care of? And where's my bouquet? The florist does know the wedding's at three, doesn't she?'

The hairdresser's sloe-dark eyes met Zoe's in the age-speckled mirror and she patted her shoulder soothingly.

'You shush now! Just relax and enjoy! Your fiancé, he take care of everything!'

Zoe opened her mouth to argue but shut it again quickly because the hairdresser was right. New man, new relationship and a whole new start!

With a smile Zoe raised her champagne flute to her reflection. Today really did feel like the happiest day of her life. She just wished her closest girlfriends could be here to share it. But her fiancé would have to be a miracle-worker to organise flying all of them to Italy.

There was a knock on the door. Actually, more like a thundering!

'Lemme in lemme in lemme in!' came the voice behind the door. It was a voice that Zoe knew well, but she must be imagining it.

She got up and had barely even twisted the handle when she was hugged by a tall blonde whirlwind.

'Libby!' she cried in surprise. 'But how . . . ?'

Once Zoe was released from Libby's strong embrace (goodness, her sister had been upping the ante at the gym!) she saw another familiar face waiting behind.

'Congratulations,' Priya whispered. 'Your man moved heaven and earth to fly us out here for today. He's absolutely perfect for you, Zoe.'

Zoe nodded and grinned. 'I know.'

'I can't believe you're really getting married again! And so soon!' cried Libby, helping herself to a glass of Moët.

'This time it's different,' Zoe told her sister.

Priya squeezed Zoe's hand. 'You deserve it after all you've been through.'

'The weird thing is, we should have seen this coming,' Libby said thoughtfully. 'Angela's predictions at your hen night have come true for all of us so we shouldn't be surprised she was right about you as well.'

'Even if you didn't tell us for ages what it was she said,' chided Priya.

'Are you surprised I kept it to myself?' Zoe shook her head. 'It was hardly the kind of news a girl wants to hear just before she ties the knot for the first time.'

'Angela's never wrong,' said Libby, nodding sagely.

'Wish I'd asked her for the lottery numbers!' joked Priya.

Zoe laughed. 'Talking of that famous hen night,' the

laughter stopped and she paused, 'I don't suppose any of the other hens were able to make it as well?'

Priya and Libby glanced at each other for a split second but it was long enough for Zoe to know that they'd already had this discussion. Her heart sank into her glittery sandals. That was a *no* then. It seemed not everyone was excited about her second marriage.

'Sorry, babes, but it's just us,' Priya said gently. 'It's not easy for everyone to make it. And I'm sure you understand why Charlotte hasn't flown out.'

Zoe nodded. Of course she understood, but all the same it would have been lovely to see her.

What about Fern, her zany, platform-booted, curly-headed best friend? They'd been through so much together over the years, from uni to working together on countless screenplays. Zoe could hardly imagine herself getting married without Fern being around. For her best friend not to have made the effort really hurt and could only mean one thing: Fern was still really angry.

In spite of the glorious sunshine, the stunningly romantic setting and the certain knowledge that in less than an hour she'd be marrying the man who truly was her soul mate, Zoe felt desperately, desperately sad. She turned away from the others so they didn't see the tears pooling in her eyes, and stared bleakly down at the garden. Without her best friend to share in her happiness, everything felt off key and out of balance.

Zoe swallowed the lump that suddenly filled her throat and, despite the honeyed sunshine dancing across her skin, she felt icy cold.

Would Fern ever forgive Zoe for what she'd done?

June 2009

'Steven Kent! That's enough; I don't care how much you beg!'

Trying her hardest to ignore her fiancé's pleas and his delicious kisses, Zoe Forster placed her hands on Steve's chest and gave him a shove onto the pavement. 'You'll be late to your own stag do if you don't get your skates on.'

'So cruel,' Steve sighed, his hazel eyes twinkling from behind his trendy wire-framed glasses. 'All I want to do is stay in with my beautiful fiancée, but no. She insists on kicking me out into the cold.'

Zoe laughed. 'It's June and twenty degrees! You just want to stay here and keep an eye on me.'

He held up his hands. 'Guilty as charged. I've heard all about what goes on at these hen parties. The minute I turn my back, the strippers will be knocking down the door.'

'We're not having strippers!' Zoe insisted, crossing

her fingers behind her back. Although she'd been absolutely adamant on this score her nutty sister, Libby, was in charge of tonight and you could never be *quite* sure what she would get up to. She swallowed nervously as a policeman walked past on the opposite side of the street. She really hoped his uniform wasn't held together by Velcro with a waxed chest hiding beneath the shirt and tie.

'A hen night without a stripper? Sacrilege!' Steve pulled a mock-horrified face. 'I can stand in: I've seen *The Full Monty* enough times to know exactly what to do.'

He started to whistle 'You Can Leave Your Hat On' while flexing his biceps and thrusting his groin about in true stripper style. Zoe giggled. She adored her fiancé but with his slender frame and glasses he was about as far from a Tango-tanned muscle-bound stripper as it was possible to get.

'Can I just remind you that it's my friends who are coming over tonight?' she pointed out. 'One of whom happens to be your sister? I really don't think Charlotte would want to watch your naked dance steps!'

'And on that happy note, I'm off,' Steve said hastily. 'Good luck with Lottie, by the way. The way she feels about marriage lately I'm amazed she's even agreed to come.'

Their eyes met and mutual understanding flowed between them. Steve's recently divorced sister was certainly bitter when it came to all things romantic. Zoe had invited Charlotte in the hope that a night in with the girls might cheer her up and she hoped it wasn't going to prove to be a big mistake.

'Libby's promised to make this a night to remember so I'm sure it'll make even Charlotte crack a smile,' she assured him. 'Now you'd better get going or Rufus and the boys will think you've stood them up.'

'I'm going, I'm going!' Steve blew her a kiss. 'Have a wonderful time, Zo. And don't wait up for me. Pole-dancing clubs don't close until the small hours – or so I hear!'

'Idiot,' said Zoe fondly. She knew he was going to Brick Lane for a curry with some of his colleagues. One of them, a film producer called Rufus, was a bit wild, but she knew Steve inside out and trusted him totally. There wouldn't be any silly shenanigans at his stag do.

So what if her friends thought they were dull and predictable? There was a lot to be said for peace of mind. Let her dad get married more times than she'd ordered a skinny latte, she'd rather stay with the same, faithful man for ever. That was just the way that their relationship was. They had no secrets.

She watched Steve climb into his sleek new BMW and waved him off, blowing kisses back until the car turned left at the junction of their road and was lost in the traffic of Richmond High Street.

Smiling, Zoe wandered around their Victorian terrace,

checking that everything was in place for the evening ahead. Wine was cooling, bowls overflowing with crisps and nachos were positioned around the sitting room, and in the kitchen a delicious selection of canapés were cooking slowly in the Aga while dishes of the ingredients to make an Eton mess in seconds chilled in the fridge. Candles were flickering, Michael Bublé was crooning from the iPod and the French doors were flung open onto the garden allowing the scents of stocks and rosemary to drift into the house on the warm evening breeze.

Perfect, thought Zoe. Now all I need are my hens!

An hour later the party was in full swing and Zoe's favourite women had well and truly raised her spirits so high that she practically needed oxygen. She hadn't laughed this hard in a long time. Zoe was adorned with numerous L-plates, brandishing a giant vibrator like Luke Skywalker's light sabre (thanks a lot, Priya!) and wearing a veil and Fern's glittery tiara.

The girls were sitting at Zoe's kitchen island and busily hoovering up Priya's Bombay Mix while telling wedding anecdotes. Steve's sister, Charlotte, had been reprimanded several times for being negative about marriage and Libby had personally threatened to drown her in the guacamole if she so much as breathed the words 'cheating bastards' again. Fern, meanwhile, had just finished recounting a story where the bride decided at the altar she was actually in love with the maid of honour and all hell had broken loose.

'Well, don't go trying that on Saturday,' Libby said. 'I love you, Zoe, but you're not my type!'

'What is your type?' Priya asked.

Libby shrugged. 'Tall, sporty, fit?'

'Basically, if it's male and has its own teeth she'll jump its bones,' grinned Fern.

'Whereas Fern isn't even bothered about them having their own teeth!' shot back Libby. 'Didn't you once pull a pensioner?'

'Zoe!' Fern's tiny ring-covered hands flew to her mouth. 'I can't believe you told them! He didn't look that old, I swear. I thought he was fifty at the most.'

'Until bedtime came and he took his dentures out,' said Libby, and they all screeched with laughter while poor Fern did a beetroot impression.

'To be fair, she did call it a day at that point,' Zoe said, wiping tears from her eyes. 'And never dated a lecturer again.'

'I didn't need to,' Fern tossed her bright blonde curls defiantly. 'I was with Luke Scottman after that, wasn't I? He was in my drama society at uni.'

'Luke Scottman!' breathed Charlotte, and for a split second her cynical mask slipped. 'I've watched *Buddhist Assassin* about a million times just for the naked butt scene. Is he really that fit in real life?'

Fern considered this for a moment then she shrugged. 'Yep, 'fraid so! And I'll tell you something else too . . .'

The hens all leaned forward, eyes wide as they waited to hear some first-hand information on Hollywood's hottest A-lister. If anyone would know it would be Fern; she'd dated him for nearly three years.

When she was certain that she had their undivided attention Fern said slowly, 'When it comes to Luke, believe me, girls, he really does have . . .' she paused and held her hands a foot apart, waiting to make sure they were all hanging on her every word, '. . . his own teeth!'

'You really had us going there!' Libby grinned as they all dissolved into gales of laughter.

Fern's eyes were big blue circles of innocence. 'What did you think I was going to say? Anyway, enough tales of woe and silliness! At least we know that Zoe's wedding is going to be perfect!'

All the girls had raised their glasses and were smiling at her.

'Zoe and Steve have always been the perfect couple,' Fern continued with a broad grin. 'They are a true match made in heaven, and the rest of us can only hope that one day we find a relationship that comes anywhere close. They are everything that a couple should be. And so I say, to Zoe and Steve!'

'Zoe and Steve!' the girls echoed, chinking their glasses together.

Zoe joined in too but her smile felt a bit too tight across her face.

'We're not *that* perfect,' she replied. Dare she admit her doubts and fears about Steve?

'Of course you are!' the other chorused.

Zoe bit her lip. There were things about her and Steve that they didn't know, things she'd kept back. Was it right for her friends to think everything was flawless, when they had their troubles too? They were measuring their own relationships against something that just wasn't real. Was it any wonder Fern thought her boyfriends always fell short?

Steve was no saint. He had more in common with her father than any of them knew. But then again, she was no saint either.

It wasn't fair. She had to say something . . .

'Guys, you know I love Steve—' Zoe began nervously, only to be interrupted by the girls all chorusing *ahhhh*, with the marked exception of Charlotte, who looked like she was sucking a particularly acidy acid drop. 'No, seriously, listen to me,' Zoe continued. 'You're all always going on about how perfect Steve and I are but there are things you don't know—'

Just as she was on the brink of telling her friends the one thing she'd never dared share with anyone, the shrilling of the doorbell interrupted her hesitant words.

Libby beamed and jumped from her seat. 'That'll be my present, babes!'

Fern, Priya, and even Charlotte looked gleeful. 'Strippers!' squealed Priya.

Zoe buried her face in her hands. 'Oh God, Libs. You didn't get me a stripper?'

'Of course not! How clichéd would that be?' said Libby. 'Girls, please prepare to meet our very own fortune-teller!'

2

Zoe soon discovered that one of the perks of being a bride, along with the stress of organising a wedding and having to convince an outraged Libby that the bridesmaids' dresses weren't really pink but *cerise*, was that she was also afforded the dubious honour of being the first in line for a tarot reading.

I hope this doesn't take too long, thought Zoe as she walked through her dark kitchen and into the conservatory. Psychics were Libby's thing, not Zoe's. She wanted to spend the time with her friends, not Richmond's answer to Mystic Meg!

'Come in, sweetheart. Don't look so nervous! This is supposed to be fun,' beamed Angela as Zoe hovered in the doorway. 'Take a seat.'

Zoe paused. Although Angela, in her comfy M&S slacks and with her round smiley face, looked more like someone's nan than a psychic, there was something about the atmosphere in the conservatory that halted Zoe in her tracks and made the hair on her arms prickle.

Behind Angela the garden was smothered by inky darkness and the house seemed filled with a peculiar tense silence, almost as though it was holding its breath. The soft lamps that usually cast a soothing buttery glow into the conservatory had been switched off, and instead candles threw strange leaping shadows against the walls while the low driftwood coffee table that she and Steve had found on a long-ago holiday in Fowey was shrouded in a blood-red throw. Disconcerted by this strange change to her home, and cross with herself for being so irrationally spooked, Zoe took a deep breath and forced herself to sit in the seat opposite Angela.

Get a grip! she told herself. It's not as though you believe in any of this mumbo jumbo. And she doesn't even look like a psychic. More like a pub landlady!

With these stern thoughts she instantly felt better. She'd let Angela do her stuff and be back with the hens before you could say 'Peggy Mitchell'!

'Welcome, bride-to-be,' said Angela warmly as she handed Zoe the tarot deck.

For a split second Zoe was taken aback. How on earth did Angela know that she was the bride? Then she remembered that she was wearing the veil and L-plates, so coming to the right conclusion had hardly required the detecting skills of Miss Marple.

'Now, I'd like you to shuffle the cards, please, and

split them into three piles,' Angela directed, and Zoe did as she was told.

Angela laid the cards out in an intricate pattern on the red velvet and stared at them for a while with her fingers steepled beneath her chin and her brow furrowed. She sighed heavily.

'What a burden you carry, my love. Being married is something you really fear, isn't it?'

Zoe laughed. 'Hardly! I've thought of nothing else for weeks.'

Angela's eyes narrowed. 'I didn't say *getting* married, my love, I said *being* married. You're desperately afraid that taking marriage lightly might run in the family and that you might not be able to honour the promises that you'll make next week. Although you'd never voice it to anyone, your deepest, darkest fear is that your fiancé doesn't take marriage particularly seriously. You're afraid he's cut from the same cloth as your father, aren't you?'

Zoe felt her mouth swing open. How on earth could this total stranger know about her father? Zoe had hardly told anyone about Michael Forster's history. Why would she? Having a father who compared to Henry the Eighth in terms of marital restraint wasn't exactly something she was proud of.

'It plays on your mind,' Angela continued thoughtfully. 'You want everything to be ordered to outweigh the disorder he caused you. You work so hard to keep up

appearances and make everything perfect that sometimes you're quite frazzled by it all. Aren't you, my love?
Yet still you carry on because that's what everyone's
come to expect from you and you'd hate anybody to be
disappointed.' Her eyes narrowed. 'More than that.
You're afraid of disillusioning them.'

Zoe was stunned. It had taken her cognitive therapist
months to draw these conclusions, and cost a small
fortune too. How on earth had a total stranger managed
to find all this out in just a matter of minutes? For a
second she teetered on the brink of believing totally in
the woman seated opposite. Then Zoe reminded herself
sharply that Libby had booked this reading and since her
sister was to discretion what Jordan was to modest
dressing Angela probably already knew every sordid
detail of their family history.

'Well, that's all very interesting and I'll certainly bear
it in mind,' she said politely.

Angela shrugged her plump shoulders. 'I can see
you're not a believer, my love! Still, that doesn't matter
a fig to my spirit guides. Right now they're asking me
to let you know that you *must* tell your best friend the
thing you fear telling her the most. They know how
frightened you are, sweetheart, and how you're afraid it
will mean the end of your friendship but they promise
she will get over it. Eventually.'

Her mouth dry, and feeling cold to her bones, Zoe

gaped at Angela. What? How? There was no way this total stranger could possibly know about *that*! Zoe had never breathed a word of that huge secret to anyone. There was only one other soul on the planet that knew the truth and she would bet everything she owned – in fact, she'd even wager her life on it – *he'd* never said anything. And as for him coming into contact with Angela, well, that was quite simply impossible!

'How do you know that?' she whispered.

Angela reached forward and patted Zoe's cold slim hand with her pudgy warm fingers.

'*I* don't know,' she said softly. 'It's my guides who see all.'

Zoe wasn't so sure she liked the idea of these nosy all-seeing spirit guides! Flustered and shaken, she slipped her fingers away and swiftly changed the subject to her wedding day. The other subject was off limits, stored away in the darkest corners of her mind where guilty shadows lurked, and she really didn't want to go there. Tonight was supposed to be a happy occasion.

'What about my wedding day?' she asked quickly. 'Do your guides see it going smoothly?'

'Which wedding day?' Angela looked confused.

'What? I don't understand.'

'The one next week or the other one?' Angela asked plainly.

'*What!?!*'

'You'll be married twice, you see, so which one do you mean?' Angela asked. 'Actually, it doesn't really matter; I see both going perfectly.'

'That's total nonsense!' Zoe cried. 'I'm only ever getting married once. I totally believe that marriage is for life. You said as much yourself, remember?'

But Angela was looking at her with something close to pity. 'No, my love, I said you were afraid of being like your father. I never said you'd only marry the once. It's here in the cards and there's no mistaking it. You will get married twice.'

I bloody won't get married twice! Zoe thought furiously. Absolutely no way was she going to become the Liz Taylor of Southwest London!

'My guides are never wrong,' insisted Angela, fixing her with a bright-eyed gaze.

Zoe told herself she didn't believe a word of it, but, never one to be impolite, she just smiled. 'Thank you, Angela. That was . . . fun. However, I have something in the oven and I better check on it. Can't trust that lot to do it!'

As far as she was concerned the evening had taken a turn for the worse. How could Angela spoil her special day by insisting that her marriage wasn't going to last? She loved Steve and they were the perfect couple! Everyone said so. Angela had been talking total nonsense.

But what about all the things she got right? said a small voice deep down inside her. She knew about your deepest, darkest secret. And if she was right about that then she could be right about your being married twice.

She felt sick. In seven days' time she would be making vows to the man she adored in front of all their family and friends. It should be the happiest day of her life but now, thanks to this hen-night prophecy, she was filled with a terrible sense of foreboding.

Zoe never thought she'd say it but she was starting to wish that Libby had booked a stripper after all.

Valentine's Day 2010

Slices of tentative sunshine stole through the blinds and danced across the duvet until Zoe could no longer ignore them. It was time to get up. Yawning widely she stretched out beneath her Egyptian cotton sheets.

My first Valentine's Day as a married woman.

She reached out for Steve, but her hand just met thin air. Opening her eyes Zoe glanced over to the alarm clock and saw that it was seven a.m. Goodness! Steve would be long gone: he had a breakfast meeting on set at half-past. He must have slipped out so as not to disturb her, which was typical of him. Her husband had to be the most considerate man on the planet. Still, she couldn't help thinking it might have been nice to have been awoken for some early morning Valentine's Day passion. They were still newlyweds, after all!

It was warm in bed, the duck-down duvet heavy

against her legs, and for a moment Zoe was sorely tempted to close her eyes and drift back off to sleep. Although she and Steve were both working on the BBC's latest adaptation of Henry James's *The Portrait of a Lady*, Zoe wasn't needed on set until later. In fact, she only had a couple of short meetings about the script pencilled in for this morning, which should leave her plenty of time to meet up with Steve for their traditional VD lunch, as they laughingly referred to it.

Pushing back the covers, Zoe padded across the reclaimed floorboards, headed into the bathroom and opened the cabinet above the basin. Even before the door swung outward Zoe already knew what she'd find inside – and all this without possessing Angela's psychic talents! Tucking her thick waves of golden hair behind her ears and going onto tiptoe, she rummaged inside the cabinet until her fingers closed around a heart-shaped Post-it note. Peeling it away from the tube of Colgate, Zoe knew without looking that it would read 'Happy'. There'd be another one stuck to her shampoo in the shower, Zoe thought fondly, as she shrugged off her nightdress and stepped into the wet room. She was right. This note read 'Valentine's', and unless her husband had suffered a sudden attack of spontaneity 'Day' would be somewhere in the fridge and 'Darling' on the front door. Such was the reassuring familiarity of their life together!

After a tinglingly powerful shower (where she

discovered that Libby had used up her Jo Malone Lime and Basil shower gel . . . again) Zoe dressed in her favourite dark plum Jasper Conran trouser suit and wandered downstairs collecting 'Darling' from the front door as she picked up the post. Hey, why not live life dangerously for once and read the notes out of sequence?

She walked to the fridge to pick up 'Day' from where it would be magneted to the front. But when she got there she saw nothing. That's odd, she thought. Has Steve decided to mix it up for once? There was no note inside the fridge either. It was only when she saw something pink fluttering on the floor that she sighed. She'd been right all along. The note had just fallen off.

Hurrah, thought Zoe as she tipped Special K into a bowl. Another Valentine's Post-it trail completed and, even if it didn't require the brain power of Stephen Hawking to figure it out, it was nice to know Steve cared enough to make the effort.

Although it might be more fun if he found some new hiding places . . .

Zoe's treasure hunt trail of clues was far from over, though, and, as she left the house, she was already trying to work out what restaurant Steve had decided to book for their special lunch. He always kept this part of their day a surprise, and Zoe knew that he'd have been busy laying a series of clues that she would have to follow throughout the morning. The chiming of her BlackBerry's text signalled a picture message from Steve. A clock face showing one p.m. Hmm . . . If she made an effort to power through her meetings and didn't allow herself to become distracted when she visited the costume department then she'd definitely be there in time. Wherever *there* was, of course!

'These are gorgeous, Lila,' said Zoe, running her fingers over the soft fabric of the costumes.

'Thanks, hon,' replied Lila with a smile. 'And don't worry, everything's all set for tomorrow.'

'Thanks.'

'Don't thank me! You organised everything!'

How many times had someone said that to Zoe? She'd lost count after a hundred.

'It makes me wonder,' said Lila with a lopsided grin, 'in your house, does Steve have to organise anything?'

Steve! It was half twelve already. Steve would be so hurt if she didn't make it on time. 'Sorry, Lila, I have to go!' Zoe said, and ran for the door.

Switching on her BlackBerry, she was soon greeted by a flurry of picture messages, the first of which was a blank screen. The second was an aerial shot of London.

White City! Zoe turned on her heel and strode as quickly as she could along Wood Lane. Once at the station she laughed aloud when she saw that Steve had taped several clues to a series of trees. That man had way too much time on his hands!

Closer inspection of these new clues revealed an elephant painted blue, a tie, a football fan wearing a blue scarf, a shot of a shocking-pink gerbera and finally the words 'Head here' scrawled in Steve's distinctive loopy handwriting.

That was pretty easy, Zoe decided as she retrieved them. The restaurant must be in Chelsea, home of Steve's beloved football team and of the famous flower show. Steve had chosen the trendy Thai restaurant on Fulham Broadway, which went by the rather strange name of Blue Elephant. He'd been wanting to try it ever since Charlotte had raved about the place, so she shouldn't really be surprised. Both Steve and Zoe adored Thai food and at just the thought of Thai green curry and fragrant jasmine rice her stomach started to rumble.

Taking the tube to Fulham Broadway would mean more clues but would take too long. She'd no doubt be instructed to go thirty steps in one direction and then twenty in another. She didn't have time.

She decided to catch a cab straight to her destination. Steve would never need to know she'd cheated. Anyway, she told herself firmly, it's not cheating – I just know my husband really well!

By the time Zoe's cab drew up outside Blue Elephant she was nearly twenty minutes late and the restaurant was buzzing with trendy young Londoners, all brandishing chopsticks and drinking scarily expensive wine. She scanned the place several times, but she couldn't see any sign of Steve at all. Odd. Maybe I ought to have looked at those other clues after all, she thought. Perhaps she'd got it wrong. But past experience had taught her that Steve's clues were never the subtlest and he'd dropped enough hints about wanting to try this place. Something must have held him up. She hoped he was all right. Steve was never late anywhere. Greenwich Mean Time could use him to set the clocks.

When another five minutes had passed Zoe could bear it no longer. She'd have to ask one of the waiters if Steve had made a booking.

'One p.m., reservation for two for Mr Kent.' The maitre d' looked up from his ledger and gave Zoe a broad smile.

Zoe was relieved. She hadn't got it wrong; she knew what her husband was doing and guessed perfectly. But then she felt a pang of something else. Disappointment? Part of her was hoping to be surprised.

'Happy Valentine's Day, Mrs Kent. Shall I show you to your table? Or would you like a drink at the bar while you wait?'

Zoe was just about to plump for a glass of Pinot Grigio at the bar while she called her husband, when her BlackBerry chimed, announcing a message from Steve.

So sorry sweetheart but I have to cancel – have a casting crisis. Will make it up to u. Promise xxx

Blimey! Zoe was so taken aback after reading this that she needed that drink. Steve cancelling their special VD lunch? He'd never done that before, not in seven years. And what was even more out of character was that he always called and spoke to her if there was a change of plan. He never texted because he thought it was rude. This was unusual in the extreme.

Whatever this casting crisis was it must be big. She'd better get back to TV Centre!

'Wow, Fern! You look amazing!' Priya cried, clapping her hands with delight. 'That dress was made for you!'

'You think?' Fern twirled in front of the mirror, white silk, ribbons and acres of tulle flying out around her while her corkscrew curls boinged in excited agreement.

'Definitely. Unlike this,' said Priya, who was struggling to get into a tight green velvet day dress, complete with leg-o'-mutton sleeves and a bustle. 'I think you should speak very nicely to Zoe and ask her if you can keep it.'

Zoe laughed. 'You can be as nice to me as you like but that dress is staying put! It cost thousands to make and we need it for the scene where Isabel marries Osmond. So don't even think of trying to smuggle it out in your handbag!'

'As if I would ever do that!' Fern's sparkling blue eyes widened. 'That would crush it – I'd have to use a carrier bag at least!'

It was the day after Valentine's and the girls were in the Beeb's costume department and having a whale of a time as they tried on Lila's fabulous creations for *The Portrait of a Lady*. Zoe and Fern had to stay on late for a night shoot anyway so Zoe decided that rather than twiddle their thumbs for a few hours, she'd get their friends over. This evening they were being Edwardian ladies, or rather Zoe, Fern, Charlotte and Priya were, while Libby was far more interested in munching her way through the buffet Zoe had laid on.

'Go on, Zo,' Fern was wheedling. 'They'd never miss it once filming's over! And it'd make the perfect wedding dress.'

'You're thinking about weddings?' Zoe's eyebrows shot into her blonde fringe. She'd known that Fern was really happy with her new man (which was a *huge* relief, given the traumas and shenanigans it had taken her to find him) but she'd no idea things were that serious.

Fern blushed. 'Just . . . hypothetically. If I were to ever get married – which I'm not saying I am, by the way – this dress is just the kind of thing I'd want. That's all.'

'Right,' Zoe said slowly. 'So nothing could be further from your mind then?'

She caught Priya's eye and the two of them burst out laughing.

'Carry on, tease away,' huffed Fern. 'But I'm really

happy for once. He's amazing. In fact, even though we're working apart, he still flew to London and took me out for a Valentine's dinner. How romantic is that?'

'Very, babes, and I'm glad. You deserve to be spoiled,' Zoe told her warmly. 'He's lucky to have you.'

Fern smiled. 'I think we're both pretty lucky. And just think! I nearly let him get away, like the muppet I am. This has to have been my best Valentine's ever.'

Priya nodded, her dark eyes shining. 'Mine too. My man isn't here, obviously, but he sent the most amazing bouquet of flowers. Jasmine, hibiscus, myrtle – all the ones he knew I'd recognise from my time in India. And we're going away for a romantic break tomorrow morning.'

Zoe smiled. It was great to see her friends loved up and happy after so many useless men!

'We went white-water rafting up north,' Libby chimed in, returning from the buffet with her plate piled sky high. 'It was awesome and I'm bloody starving now!'

Priya raised a neat eyebrow. 'White-water rafting? That's hardly very romantic.'

'The sex we had afterwards was,' Libby said cheerfully. 'There's nothing like a good rush of adrenalin to make you horny.'

Zoe winced. 'Too much information, hon.'

'You're just jealous.' Libby grinned. 'Being an old married woman you probably haven't had sex for months.'

Zoe bit her lip because her sister had hit a nerve. It wasn't months exactly, but she and Steve were so busy at the moment they hardly saw each other. If Steve was at home then Zoe was in the production office, and when she was in he was often out on location. When they did finally tumble into bed they were both so exhausted that making love was the last thing on their minds. Still, there was more to a marriage than sex, she reminded herself sharply, and when they did have time and could keep their eyes open long enough, the sex was always amazing. Quality, not quantity!

'Where did you and Steve go for your traditional VD lunch?' Priya was asking as she wriggled out of her tight dress. 'Was it the Thai restaurant he'd been hinting about?'

Zoe laughed. 'Of course! But actually I was on my own because Steve got called away on a full-blown casting crisis.'

'Bloody hell!' exclaimed Libby, with her mouth full. 'That must have been some crisis if it made Steady Steve change his plans.'

'It was, and don't call him that,' Zoe said automatically. 'I may as well tell you guys – it won't be a secret for much longer – but both the male and female leads of *The Portrait of a Lady* have pulled out at the eleventh hour. It was something to do with a disagreement about contracts, according to Steve.'

Libby shook her head. 'Bloody film stars. There probably weren't enough blue M&Ms in their selection pack.'

Zoe shrugged. 'Who knows? But to recast now when we've already started shooting is really going to hold us up and will cost thousands. It might even mean that the Beeb pulls the plug on this shoot. Finances are pretty tough at the minute.'

'Bollocks,' said Fern.

'Bollocks indeed,' Zoe agreed. 'So poor old Steve got all this dumped on him at lunchtime yesterday and as you can imagine he's seriously stressed now.'

Libby munched thoughtfully while Fern and Priya, both of whom worked in film, looked sympathetic. Suddenly conscious that any negative rumours could sound the death knell for her production, Zoe pasted a cheery smile onto her face and said brightly, 'He's working on something now so I'm sure it'll all be OK. And my Valentine's wasn't totally ruined because he brought a takeaway home and a lovely bunch of flowers.'

'Pink tulips!' chorused the others.

'Surprise, surprise,' said Libby, rolling her eyes. 'Honestly, sis, doesn't it drive you mad? He's so flipping predictable.'

'Don't be mean,' said Fern sharply. 'There's a lot to be said for loyal and dependable.'

'Loyal and dependable?' snorted Libby. 'You make him sound like a Labrador! Seriously, Zo! The day Steve takes you by surprise will be the day Madonna wins an Oscar!'

'Steve isn't predictable,' Zoe protested, fighting the urge to cross her fingers as she said this. 'Remember how surprised I was when he gave me an engagement ring with emeralds set in it?'

'But you weren't surprised at all that he proposed, just surprised that he'd chosen an unusual ring,' pointed out Libby. 'We'd been expecting him to pop the question all day, seeing as it was your fifth anniversary.'

'It was very romantic!' Zoe said, stung.

'Trail of Post-it notes leading you to a ring maybe?' Libby wondered. 'With a couple of clues thrown in for good measure?'

'Steve has ways he likes to do things, that's all,' Zoe told her sister, hotly.

Libby held up her hands. 'Sorry! Sorry! It's just that I like to live my life on the edge, that's all. I can't bear the thought of things getting routine. I'd rather chop my head off.'

'Zoe and Steve have been together forever, so of course things get a bit . . . um . . . mundane,' Priya told Libby firmly.

She meant it kindly but her words irritated Zoe. For so long she'd been fêted by her friends as the only one who could sustain a long-term relationship and they'd envied her as they'd had their hearts trampled on by a variety of wildly unsuitable men. She and Steve had been the Monica and Chandler of their group, the rock that held them all together for the past seven years. Now that they were all in relationships, they didn't need her and Steve to be quite so solid anymore. Suddenly they all felt stable enough themselves to mock her and Steve for being up on the very pedestal they'd put them on.

'Zoe, you don't like surprises,' Libby was saying, 'so Steve really suits you. I didn't mean to take the piss. You guys are perfect together.'

'I do like surprises,' Zoe said, but nobody was listening to her, they were all far too busy discussing how stable and organised and thorough she was, never taking risks and always doing the right thing. They made her sound as exciting as a test card, and although she knew they were only trying to be kind, Zoe started to get cross. When Priya remarked that even Zoe's work was sensible and lacked risk because she adapted other people's novels rather than write her own, something inside her snapped.

'I *am* writing my own stuff, actually!' she burst out. 'I've been working on my own screenplay for about six months now.'

So there! she felt like adding.

But no one heard her.

'You could have saved your money on the psychic, Lib,' said Fern. 'There's no surprises coming in Zoe's life.'

'Marriage, glittering careers, kids somewhere down the line,' said Libby.

'Summer holidays in the same cottage in Cornwall every year,' said Priya, and the girls laughed.

'What *did* the fortune-teller say to you?' Fern's brow crinkled. 'Do you know, I was so caught up in my own prediction that I don't think I ever found out what she said to you.'

'That's easy!' Libby chimed in. 'She would have said that Zoe will live happily ever after, reading Post-it notes from Steve!'

The others were all nodding and suddenly Zoe found that she was really annoyed. Before her brain could stop her, Zoe's mouth was engaged. 'You guys don't know anything about me and Steve,' she blurted out. All eyes were on her. 'You don't know that Steve once eloped to Las Vegas!'

Libby's face was a picture, her mouth hanging open on its hinges. Priya's eyes were molasses-dark circles of surprise and Fern's silver-ringed fingers had flown to her lips. For a moment they were all stunned into silence before the questions started to flow like cheap Chardonnay.

'My God!' Fern exclaimed. 'That is just so crazy. Steve was married before?'

'No. Way,' breathed Libby, and then, 'Who did he marry? When?'

'How on earth did that happen?' said Charlotte with a frown. Clearly she had no idea.

'You're not winding us up?' Priya wanted to know. 'You're telling us the truth?'

Zoe sank onto a chair, scooping a mound of bustles and hats out of the way before nodding Churchill-style at her friends.

'He was only nineteen and on a boozy holiday with a load of his uni mates,' she told them, consciously echoing almost word for word what an embarrassed Steve had told her. 'To cut a long story short he got pretty tanked up in the casino and ended up marrying some girl he met there who was working as a croupier. Jane Smith, he said she was called. Anyway, they were married for about twelve hours before they both sobered up and Steve said they filed for annulment just as their hangovers kicked in.'

'Bloody hell,' breathed Fern. 'I get pissed but not so pissed I end up marrying a stranger!'

'Does he still have contact with her?' asked Charlotte.

'The annulment went through and Steve never heard from her again. It's ancient history and just a silly drunken teenage prank. It didn't mean anything.'

'Why didn't you tell us?' Fern twirled a lock of hair around her forefinger and looked hurt. 'I'm your friend. I was there when you met Steve and I had no idea about any of this. How come you've kept it quiet all these years?'

Zoe swallowed. A little part of her was honest enough to admit that she'd liked everyone thinking she and Steve were the perfect couple. She'd always held back, not wanting to shatter their illusions, and there had never felt like a right time to come clean. Just thinking about all this made Zoe want to reach for the Nurofen.

'I guess I didn't know quite how to tell you,' she said slowly. 'I wanted to but by then you all thought Steve and I were perfect. I suppose I didn't want to spoil everything and let you down.'

'I don't know about let down,' said Fern slowly, 'but I'm certainly stunned.'

The others nodded, lost for words, and Zoe felt terrible. She could have told them in a nicer way rather than deliberately choosing to shock them.

'I'm sorry,' she said, her head hanging and her thick blonde hair falling across her face as though trying to shield her from their surprised faces. 'I should have told you before, shouldn't I?'

'We wouldn't have thought any less of you,' Priya told her gently. 'We're your friends.'

'I'd have been relieved to think you and Steve were

human after all,' Libby teased. 'It would've been nice for once not to be the only one who cocks things up.'

But Fern said nothing and Zoe felt terrible. As Zoe's closest and dearest friend she was probably really hurt to have been kept from her confidence. I'll make it up to you, Zoe promised her silently. I'll explain everything.

'I can't believe you kept this to yourself for so long,' Fern said finally.

'I didn't even know,' cried Charlotte. 'And he's my brother!'

Zoe bit her lip. 'I know and I'm sorry. And I'm even sorrier for springing it on you like this. I didn't exactly pick a good time, did I? The evening's ruined.'

The girls all chorused 'No' and 'Don't be silly', but Zoe knew they were just being kind. She couldn't have killed the atmosphere more successfully if she'd lobbed a few hand grenades at it. The girls stuck it out for half an hour more but no one was in the mood to try on frocks and giggle anymore, so they took their leave and only Fern was left with Zoe to clear away. As Zoe hung the dresses back up and packed the barely touched buffet away she felt terrible. She'd never hosted a bad party in her life and knowing that she'd ruined a fun night made her feel awful.

Their friendship was far too important to risk by keeping secrets. But did Fern really want to know all of Zoe's secrets? Or was it better that some things stayed buried in the past? Did she tell Fern *everything* and risk losing her friendship, like Angela's ridiculous spirits had suggested?

Perhaps some things were just better left unsaid.

5

Deep in thought, Zoe and Fern made their way from the costume department across to the studio where a late rehearsal test shoot was being held. As they entered the studio Zoe's heart sank when the producer, Rufus, spotted her.

'Hey! Here she is! My old mate's ball and chain!' he boomed, making a beeline for Zoe and Fern, scattering cast and crew members like ninepins as he strode over. 'Where's Steve tonight, babe? Doing a bit of cleaning? Or is it ironing tonight?'

Fern gave Zoe a pitiful look and Zoe gritted her teeth, something she'd been doing for so long around him that it was amazing she didn't just have a mouthful of gnawed stumps. Rufus was Steve's oldest friend, a smoking, drinking, strip-clubbing, arms-dripping-with-skinny-big-boobed-blondes kind of friend and he drove her round so many bends she could have won the Monaco Grand Prix.

When he kissed her hello those moist red lips strayed

far too close to hers for comfort and his hand lingered longer than was strictly necessary on her waist. And the way his glittering dark eyes slipped to her chest made her very uncomfortable. Zoe supposed all husbands had to have one party-animal laddish friend but she really wished that Rufus wasn't Steve's.

And she wished even more that she didn't have to work with him on this production.

'Steve's flat out trying to solve our casting problems,' she told Rufus, kissing him hello and dodging those lips with a skill born of seven years' acquaintance.

'Good old Steve, we can always rely on him to come good in a crisis,' said Rufus. 'Did I ever tell you about that time we went on a bender in Amsterdam and I stole a barge? Only Steve was sober enough to stop us crashing it!'

Zoe did a mental eye roll. Rufus had told this story so many times she could write the screenplay.

'Still, no trips to Amsterdam for Stevie anymore.' He grabbed Zoe round the waist and shook her. 'Not when this hen is pecking him all the time!'

Argh! Rufus's constant comments about Steve being 'under the thumb' made her skin itch with irritation. How on earth was she going to manage to work closely with him for months on end? It was going to drive her crazy!

'Anyway, I'll have to leave the story about Steve and

the donkey for another time,' Rufus guffawed, but when his eyes fell on Fern he stopped laughing, and by the way they lit up Zoe could tell he liked what he saw. 'The set looks great. Fern Moss again, I presume?'

'That's me,' Fern said, with a weak smile.

Zoe nodded. 'She's the best in the business.'

'Mmm, and she's pretty hot too,' Rufus agreed.

Fern grimaced and Zoe could see that she was ready to thump him, so she stepped in to save Fern from a criminal record.

'She's taken,' Zoe said. Over her dead body would she let Rufus near one of her friends – she and Steve had comforted enough broken-hearted exes over the years to know that he ought to come with a government health warning.

'And I'm busy.' Fern scurried away to escape the I-could-gobble-you-up gaze he was undressing her with.

'She's a great set designer, though,' Zoe continued. 'Maybe we could promote her to production designer?'

'Calm down, love, don't get ahead of yourself,' said Rufus dismissively. 'I said she was hot, not that I wanted to pay her more.'

'But she's a great—'

But Rufus was no longer listening. In front of them a light bulb had exploded and showered the set with shards of glass. Uttering a string of expletives that would have made Gordon Ramsay blush he strode off to deal with whatever unfortunate crew member was to blame, leaving Zoe clenching her fists in rage.

Lord, as much as she loved her husband, his taste in best friends left a lot to be desired!

Taking a deep breath, Zoe rejoined Fern where she was dressing the set.

'Remind me why we put up with him again?' Zoe asked, motioning to Rufus.

'Rufus is a nightmare,' said Fern, 'but it's hard to argue with his collection of BAFTAs.' With a deft flick of the wrist Fern draped a green muslin scarf across the chaise longue, smiling with satisfaction at the result. 'There,' she said. 'That's what we needed. A splash of jade to accentuate the dark tones of the rest of the drawing room.'

'You're a genius, hon,' Zoe told her warmly. 'This set looks amazing. It's everything I described to you.'

'Well, your description was written so clearly it was simple to visualise.'

Zoe put her arm round Fern and gave her a quick squeeze. 'We make a good team.'

'We certainly do.' Fern smoothed the scarf, then straightened up to look Zoe in the eye. 'Zo, do you trust me?'

'Of course!' Zoe cried. 'Fern, you're my best friend. You know I do.'

Fern shrugged. 'Do I? I'm not sure any more. I can't believe you didn't tell me about Steve being married before. That's a major secret to have kept.'

Zoe sighed. 'It was Steve's secret. He didn't tell anyone.'

'OK, I understand. I can see that you have to keep his confidence.' Then Fern gestured to Rufus. 'So the walking groin doesn't know, then?'

Both girls glanced across at their producer, who was deep in conversation with one of the minor actresses, one arm braced above her against the wall as he prevented the poor soul from making an escape.

'Rufus knows because he was there,' Zoe said wearily. 'It was probably all his fault Steve got married in the first place. That's just the kind of thing Rufus would think is a laugh.'

'I can see that.' Fern looked over to Rufus again. He was now in real danger of falling into a Grand Canyon cleavage. 'But I don't buy the not-wanting-to-disillusion-us story, I'm afraid. What's the real reason you kept it to yourself?'

Zoe sank onto the chaise longue and placed her head in her hands.

'I didn't know about it myself for ages,' she told Fern. 'Steve and I had just bought the Richmond house and I was so excited about us moving in together. I wanted to get engaged and move things to the next level but every time I mentioned it he got really cagey and changed the subject.'

'I bet he did,' said Fern. Perching next to Zoe, she placed her arm around her friend's shoulders and gave her an encouraging squeeze. 'So what happened?'

Zoe closed her eyes. It was all so long ago but the pain was still fresh. Even now it made her heartbeat quicken and her skin prickle.

'In the end I asked him outright; did he want to be with me or not? After my dad's shining example Steve knew how I felt about men who didn't commit and I told him I had to know where I stood. Otherwise it was over.'

'That's fair enough.'

'And that was when he confessed that he'd already been married.'

'I bet you were gutted,' said Fern, never one for an understatement.

Gutted? Having your heart ripped out without anaesthetic and then run over by a steamroller was more like it. For a moment she'd just stared at Steve, shocked beyond belief, before betrayal had swamped her like a tsunami.

'I told him I didn't want to be with a man who was already shaping up to be like my father,' she told Fern shakily. 'A man who lived on a rollercoaster of marriage and divorce. So I broke it off with him and went away for a few months to get some head space.'

'Oh my God, I remember that!' Fern said. 'None of us understood why you'd broken up.' She furrowed her brow like a detective working on a crime. 'And then you went working abroad, when you had never been the backpack and dreadlock type. It just didn't make sense.'

'Well, it does now, I expect.' A headache started to beat at her temples and Zoe massaged them with her fingers. 'I worked on a film set in Australia for a while, hoping it would take my mind off things.'

'That's right!' Fern's eyes widened. 'Weren't you shooting with Luke? It was the first *Buddhist Assassin* movie, wasn't it? The one that made him famous?'

Zoe felt her face flame. She really, really didn't want to be having this conversation right now. Or in fact at any time.

Fortunately Fern wasn't really paying attention; she was far too busy gazing at the sky and meandering down an imaginary path.

'Oh my God, Zo, isn't it mental to think that Luke's a major film star now? I mean, just imagine if I'd never broken up with him. I could be living in a mansion in Hollywood now and everything. I'd be best friends with Cameron Diaz, *obviously*, and go to parties with Spielberg.' Fern sighed. 'If I'd known all that was coming I'd have thought twice about finishing with him!'

Zoe was concerned. 'You don't regret letting Luke go, do you?'

Fern shook her head, golden springs of curls bouncing vehemently. 'No way! I'm much happier as I am. Besides, we all know that Luke wasn't my one-that-got-away. I'm with my perfect man now and, gorgeous as Luke is, and as much as I loved him once, he's not the one. Anyway, never mind me,' said Fern, rather too hastily. 'We're talking about you, Mrs Kent! What made you come back from down under and forgive Steve?'

'I guess I came to my senses,' Zoe said quickly. 'One stupid drunken mistake didn't mean Steve was turning into my father. Nobody's perfect, after all.'

'Except you,' teased Fern, she hugged her close and gave her a kiss on the forehead. 'You're the exception that proves that rule, babes!'

'I'm far from perfect!' protested Zoe, but Fern just laughed and reminded her about her beautiful house, starry career and – even though Steve was a divorcee – her wonderful marriage. It seemed no matter what Zoe did, her friends would carry on thinking she was perfect. She wished Fern hadn't bought into the 'Perfect Zoe' myth. If she knew the truth about what Zoe had done to her Fern would think she was anything but. In fact she'd probably never speak to her again.

Which was why Fern must never, ever find out the truth: that perfect Zoe had had a perfect fling with her beloved Luke.

'Steve! Come on! The cab's here!'

As the doorbell chimed for the second time Zoe shouted up the stairs for her husband and shrugged on her favourite Stella McCartney jacket. It was a delicate white linen creation and maybe not the wisest choice for a late Valentine's meal at their favourite Indian restaurant. Just as she was swapping it for a warmer soft leather one, the bell shrilled again and Steve came thundering down the stairs, grinning from ear to ear.

'Let's go!' he said.

'Since when was curry so exciting?' laughed Zoe. 'I think I need to dress myself up as a tandoori chicken if this is the kind of reaction I'd get!'

'It's not the curry I'm excited about. It's the Valentine's surprise I've booked for you! Ta-da!'

He flung the front door wide open to reveal a groom in full livery standing on the doorstep, while pulled up by the garden gate was a shiny black trap harnessed to an equally shiny black horse.

'Your carriage awaits, my lady,' Steve said with a bow.

A blast of chilly night air swirled into the hall.

'Surprised?' asked Steve, and he looked so proud and hopeful that Zoe didn't have the heart to tell him she'd already guessed what he was up to. Earlier on he'd nearly gone into orbit when she'd gone to book a cab, snatching the phone from her hand and insisting that everything was taken care of.

'I don't believe it! I couldn't have guessed in all the world! You really are . . .' But she couldn't keep it up.

'You guessed, didn't you?' Steve said sadly.

'OK, I may have kind of guessed when you asked me about if I had a horse allergy.' She smiled and stroked his arm. 'And leaving the leaflet from the carriage company on the kitchen table was also a bit of a giveaway.'

Steve laughed. 'Oh, and there was me thinking I'd been really cunning.'

Zoe stood on tiptoes and kissed him tenderly. 'I'm your ball and chain, remember; there's not much gets past me. I've wrapped up warmly and packed a blanket too, just in case.'

'Organised, as always,' Steve said with a weak smile.

'There's nothing wrong with being prepared,' Zoe told him.

Steve's smile faded to nothing. 'But it's hardly romantic.'

'Neither is freezing to death on a bitter February

night,' she retorted, threading her fingers through his and squeezing his hand reassuringly. 'Now let's get going. And maybe if I haven't got frostbite we can get romantic under the blanket!'

'Blanket sounds pretty good!' he said, and hauled her towards the carriage.

The cold ride through the streets of Richmond turned out to be very romantic. As they held hands and kissed to a background soundtrack of clip-clopping hoofs and jangling bridles, Zoe thought how lucky she was to have Steve. He might be a bit on the predictable side but his kindness and generosity more than made up for it. And anyway, excitement was overrated. Fern's love life was certainly exciting but she seemed to spend an awful lot of time either as high as a kite or in the depths of despair. It is much better to be on an even keel, Zoe decided as she snuggled up to Steve beneath the blanket. She could always rely on him to be there and never to let her down, which was surely worth a lot more than all the extremes? And unlike some of her girlfriends' partners, she knew she could trust Steve one hundred percent: he'd never cheat on her. Libby might roll her eyes like a dying dog and mutter, 'Bor-ring,' but Zoe didn't care. Boring had a lot to be said for it!

Twenty minutes later, and with a nose numb from the chilly night air, Zoe was very pleased when the carriage came to a halt outside their favourite Indian restaurant. Situated outside the trendy part of town, the Kohi Noor was pretty shabby and firmly stuck in nineteen eighties red velour hell.

The owner of the restaurant, who insisted they'd called him Prem from their very first visit, greeted them at the door. He was a round Indian man with a bushy beard and a glint in his eye. 'Mr Steve, Mrs Zoe. How are my two favourite customers?' he asked, shaking their hands in turn, then laughing like it was the funniest joke in the world. Prem was one spice short of a jalfrezi: it was pretty much pot luck whether you actually got the dish you ordered, but the food was so amazing and the atmosphere so welcoming that the place was always packed.

'Your usual table?' Prem offered.

'Yes, please,' said Zoe.

He walked them in and sat them at a table in the back of the restaurant.

'Just nipping to the bathroom,' said Steve.

The owner handed Zoe a menu but she waved it away. 'Thanks, Prem, but I know what we're having: chicken korma for me and a tandoori chicken for Steve, aloo gobi, mushroom rice and a naan to share.' They always ate the same thing here, which would probably cue more eye-rolling and 'Bor-ring's from her sister, but why change seven years of habit when the food was so good and she knew that she loved it?

Hmm. That was a bit metaphorical if she really thought about it . . .

'This is nice, isn't it?' Steve said, joining her at the table. 'Our first Valentine's meal as a married couple. I'm so sorry I missed our lunch.'

'Babe, don't worry about it.' She leaned forward and kissed him on the lips. 'We've got plenty more to come.'

Steve smiled, his merry eyes crinkling. 'Do you remember when we first met?'

Zoe tilted her head to one side, feigning forget-fulness. 'Er . . .'

'Don't give me that,' he said, reaching across the gold brocade tablecloth to take her hand. 'You remember it as well as I do. You looked so sweet and scared on your first day at the BBC. I think I fell in love with you from the moment you walked into my office.'

'Isn't there a law against that sort of thing? You were supposed to be my mentor!' Zoe reminded him, shaking her head in mock disapproval.

'And haven't I mentored you every day since?' he teased. 'You were so cute, always scribbling away with that precious Parker pen of yours.'

'I loved that pen,' sighed Zoe. 'I wonder where it went.'

'No idea, but the same place as our waiter, I think.' Turning in his seat Steve peered round the restaurant.

'I'd like him to take our order before we're celebrating our golden anniversary.'

'I've already ordered,' said Zoe.

Steve frowned. 'I wanted to get us some champagne, babe, and I was going to try something different too.'

'But you always have tandoori chicken.'

'Maybe I felt like a change.'

Right on cue the waiter appeared with two Cobra beers and their food. Steve smiled politely as the man put down his food, but he didn't look happy.

Zoe hated upsetting Steve. Maybe she could turn this crisis into an opportunity? After all, the restaurant frequently got orders wrong.

'Excuse me,' said Zoe, interrupting the family at the next table, 'what did you order?'

The mother smiled and sighed. 'I ordered a matar paneer, but we got a lamb saag.'

'I ordered a lamb saag,' said the man on another table. 'But I got a prawn vindaloo.'

'I ordered a biryani,' said a woman at another table. 'But I don't fancy it now; I'd much prefer pilau rice.'

'I've got some pilau rice!' an old man called from three tables away.

Minutes later Zoe was chatting with all the customers in the restaurant and dancing round delivering dishes. With a few swaps and trades everyone was even happier with their order than they were originally.

Everyone except Steve, that was. As Zoe tipped her newly acquired dish of saag aloo onto her plate he said quietly, 'Why do you always have to do that?'

'Do what? Take all the saag aloo? But you don't like it.'

'I don't mean the food,' said Steve, sounding frustrated. 'I mean the whole organising thing. Why can't you leave people alone to sort things out for themselves? Why do you always have to go wading in and fix everyone's problems?'

'You know me,' said Zoe, and tucked into her food. 'It makes me happy to help. Everyone's got what they want now.'

'And you know that for a fact, do you?'

What on earth had got into him? Zoe frowned. 'Nobody's complaining. Apart from you, that is.'

'I'm not complaining. I'm just pointing out that you've got a controlling streak a mile wide. If you stopped always taking charge of situations maybe you'd find that actually life is full of fun surprises.'

Ah. So that was it. He was hurt that she'd guessed about the horse and carriage and had packed a blanket.

'I just like to be organised. Sorry if that spoils things,' she said.

'Part of the fun of this restaurant is that you never know what you're going to get. That's why everyone comes here. The mistakes are what gives this place its charm.'

Clearly Steve wasn't prepared to back down on this one so with a sigh Zoe set her spoon down.

'I just wanted to make sure things were right.'

'Because you're obsessed with perfection!' Steve accused. 'Everything has to be perfect for you, Zoe. There's no margin for error or good old human mistakes in your world, are there?'

'That's rubbish!' Zoe said, offended. 'I am not *obsessed* with perfection!' but her protestations were cut short by her mobile ringing.

It's got to be-e-e-e-e-e perrrrfect.

Her ringtone didn't exactly help her cause. Steve started waggling his eyebrows like a demented version of Frankie Howerd. Zoe had to laugh in spite of her annoyance.

'OK, maybe you have a point!' she admitted, as she pressed End on her phone to send the call to voicemail. 'But maybe my being a perfectionist is a good thing.'

'How exactly do you figure that out?' Steve asked.

Zoe reached out and took his hand, her fingers tracing the cool metal of his wedding band.

'Because I chose you,' she said softly. 'And you are perfect for me.'

Leaning across the table Steve kissed her tenderly and traced the curve of her cheek with his thumb.

'Nice try, Mrs Kent,' he grinned. 'I'm hugely flattered, and of course in total agreement, but the bottom line here is that you know I'm right. It's time you started to relax a little and just see what life has to offer.'

'OK, you win.' As his sparkling eyes held hers, all furnace-hot intensity, Zoe couldn't argue a second longer. Besides, the food was getting cold and she wanted their Valentine's meal to be perfect.

Oops!

7

If anyone thinks working for the BBC is glamorous
then they ought to come and check out my office,
thought Zoe ruefully as she struggled to clear a space in
the tiny cubbyhole. It had once been a broom cupboard,
but as it was adjacent to the studio where they were
shooting the interiors for *The Portrait of a Lady* she'd
commandeered it, chucking out the tatty mops and
rusting buckets, and now the six-by-five space was her
small windowless refuge from Rufus.

If ever so slightly claustrophobic!

Sweeping a sheaf of folders onto the floor, Zoe
perched on the small desk she'd dragged in and hunched
over the latest copy of her script, brow furrowing when
she saw that yet again Rufus had scrawled notes across
it in violent purple ink. Skimming over the changes
he'd suggested, Zoe felt herself growing equally
aggressive, and after a few minutes she slammed the
pages down, seething.

Bloody, bloody Rufus! Never mind that they already

had the mother of all casting crises on their hands, now he had changed all the appearances of the characters. Suddenly Isabel Archer was a blonde rather than a red-head – not the end of the world as the hair and makeup department could sort this – but this Gilbert Osmond had to be a good foot taller than his predecessor, which was going to create havoc for the wardrobe crew. They'd have to start from scratch! Which meant Zoe was due an ear-bashing from Lila.

Overcome with weariness, Zoe ground her knuckles into her eyes until star bursts flared and jumped in front of her vision. How on earth would they ever keep the production on time and to budget if Rufus insisted on pulling stunts like this? He was making her job impossible. And as for poor Steve, who was away for a few days in a desperate attempt to cast new leads, he was probably wasting his time as, judging from Rufus's latest instructions, the producer already had actors in mind.

She was just on the verge of calling Steve to warn him when a sharp rap on the door announced the arrival of Susannah Middlemarch, the fifty-year-old co-producer on *Portrait*. Instantly Zoe's heart lifted. Although brusque Susannah, with her jet-black bob and razor-sharp suits, was a tough cookie, her impressive professional reputation went before her. She'd been involved with just about every successful period drama that the Beeb had produced in the last ten years and Zoe was in complete awe of her. Zoe almost turned down the job when she heard Rufus was producing it, but knowing that she'd be working closely with Susannah Middlemarch had been a big plus point and had finally tipped the balance. Zoe also had a strong suspicion that the controller of programmes had drafted Susannah in to keep Rufus's famously erratic ways in check. With Susannah in charge there was less chance Zoe would do time for murder.

She'll have her work cut out there! Zoe thought wryly as she looked down at the ink-covered script.

'God, what a hovel. Is this the best they could get you?' Susannah was saying, wrinkling her nose as she glanced around the makeshift office.

'I'm just grateful to have any space,' said Zoe. The words 'away from Rufus' hung in the air.

'There's no room to swing a gerbil in here, never mind a cat,' Susannah snorted bluntly. 'Still, writers always get the crappy end of the deal, I suppose. I can't see any of our stars settling for a broom cupboard instead of a plush dressing room.'

'If we ever get any stars,' said Zoe bleakly, and, showing Susannah Rufus's hastily amended script, added, 'unless he's already got somebody in mind?'

The older woman took the script from Zoe and as she glanced over it she shook her head.

'The little shit! So that's what he's up to. I swear to

God if he's done something stupid I'll have his bollocks for earrings!'

'What's going on?' Zoe asked.

'Rufus has just called a major press conference and hasn't deigned to enlighten the rest of us as to what it might be about,' said Susannah, who was clearly fuming beneath her groomed exterior and crisp power suit. 'Although now I've seen his latest *improvements* to our script I have a good idea exactly what he's up to.'

So did Zoe, and she didn't much like the sinking feeling it gave her. She followed Susannah into the main studio, which was almost the size of an airport hangar. The crew had already gathered, the press had arrived and the security guys were holding back a crowd of onlookers. Outside the studio Zoe could hear a strange chanting but although she strained her ears she couldn't quite make out what they were saying. It sounded like 'Who's what man?' but that just didn't make any sense. It was a bit weird too. Jonathan Ross's A-lister was female this Friday and *The One Show* hadn't booked Robert Pattinson for at least another week, so Zoe was mystified as to what was causing the excitement.

'What the hell's he up to?' hissed Susannah, her mouth pursed up like a cat's bottom. 'He's whipped up a media frenzy, the idiot!'

'Great publicity for the production, though,' pointed out Fern, who was elbowing her way through the crew to join them. 'It'll drum up interest, and God knows we need it. Henry James is hardly sexy stuff.'

Susannah shot her a look that ought to have given Fern frostbite but fortunately Fern was far too busy trying to see what was going on to notice. Even if she had, Fern's nature was so warm and sunny that she'd have melted their boss's icy stares in moments.

'Maybe you should speak to Rufus quickly,' Zoe suggested to Susannah. 'Before he does anything rash.'

'Good thinking,' said Susannah with a nod.

But just as Susannah took a step forward there was a blast of feedback from the PA system and the man himself leaped onto a makeshift podium. Dressed from head to foot in black, and with his wild mane of curly black hair standing on end, Rufus looked like a chunkier version of Russell Brand, and Zoe knew from bitter experience that he was every bit as unpredictable but not nearly as likely to make her laugh.

'I'm not going to keep you good people in suspense for much longer,' Rufus said, taking the mic from its stand and speaking into it in the style of Bono playing the O2. 'The excitement and suspense are probably killing you! Do you want to know what's going on?'

'Yes!' cried everyone in the room.

'Get on with it, you little twerp,' muttered Susannah.

Rufus paused dramatically, relishing the undivided attention. Then he smiled. 'Guys and girls, your worries are over! Thanks to the good old Rufus magic we've managed to cast the most amazing new male lead for *Portrait of a Lady*! You're going to love this! Hell, the whole of the UK is going to love it!'

Fern could contain herself no longer; she was practically bouncing with excitement. 'Who is it?' she called.

Rufus tapped the side of his nose with his forefinger. 'Patience, angel! He's due to arrive any sec!'

Right on cue the screaming outside crescendoed and there was an explosion of camera flashes. Doors slammed, the shrieking rose to ear-piercing levels, and press and crew alike went wild. Suddenly the chant became crystal clear. Zoe and Fern stared at each other as the penny dropped.

The crowd wasn't chanting 'Who's what man?' at all.

'Luke Scott Man! Luke Scott Man!'

'Luke!' Fern squeezed Zoe's hand so hard that Zoe yelped and snatched it away. Those silver rings were painful biting into your skin! But Fern was oblivious. Bug-eyed with excitement she gasped, 'Zoe! Luke's coming! This has to be Fate!'

It did? Right now, with screaming fans and an overexcited crew, Zoe felt that the only thing fated would be the future of this production. Luke wasn't just their old uni buddy any more; he was a Hollywood star right up there with Brad and George. The thought of how much he'd demand to take part in their small-scale BBC film made her feel faint. The budget wasn't huge to begin with, and had been trimmed even further in recent months due to economic pressures. Hiring an A-lister was hardly in keeping with the BBC's directive to implement austerity measures. The Director-General would flip and probably pull the plug on the whole thing.

'Zoe! Did you hear me?' Fern tugged on her sleeve. 'Do you think it's fate that Luke's here? It must mean we're meant to be together after all!'

'How exactly have you figured that one out?' Zoe asked, perplexed. 'You guys broke up years ago. Anyway, I thought you were blissfully happy with your new man? You told me he's your soul mate.'

'Yes, yes. Of course! He's amazing!', Fern flapped her hand dismissively. 'But remember my prophecy? *You had him but you let him go?* What if it *was* Luke after all?'

Zoe closed her eyes wearily. If Fern actually thought about this for a second she'd know that she wasn't meant to be with Luke. Her new partner was perfect for her and Zoe had never seen Fern so settled and so happy. This sudden wobble was just an expression of Fern's romantic tendencies. She hoped.

Zoe tried to hide the panic in her voice. 'We've been through this a thousand times.'

'But I loved him so much. I never wanted us to split up. I just thought our lives were going to be too different for us to make it work. You must remember how heartbroken I was when it ended.'

Zoe did remember. Fern had sobbed herself sick and lost so much weight that they'd all been terrified. Her grief had been awful and genuine – not the usual over-the-top Fern Moss dramatics.

Which was why, even all these years on, Zoe still felt hideously guilty that she'd enjoyed a fling with Luke. Things had been over with him and Fern, and Fern had told everyone how she was over him. It wasn't as though she'd deliberately set out to seduce her best friend's ex, but she'd known how Fern felt about him in the past. No matter how hard Zoe had tried to convince herself otherwise, she knew Fern would see her behaviour as the worst kind of betrayal. Zoe could only pray that she'd never find out. Having Luke here made the odds of that plummet.

'I've told you before, all that prophecy stuff was total nonsense!' she told Fern sternly. 'Besides you've found The One now, remember?'

Fern giggled. 'I know, I know! But it's still exciting! Our Luke is a world-famous movie star and we're working with him!'

The limo doors had opened and, judging by the fevered screaming, the man himself was outside. After a few minutes of autograph signing and chatting with his adoring fans, Luke Scottman entered the studio surrounded by security and looking every inch the film star in his wraparound shades.

Zoe hadn't seen Luke since those long-ago weeks in Australia, a period in her life that she'd tried very hard to put behind her. But seeing him now, even through the crowds of people that blocked the way between her and him, she was whizzed back in time with a speed that the Tardis in *Doctor Who* would struggle to match. Just the merest glimpse of that thick mane of sunshine hair and those shoulders, broad and muscular beneath the simple white T-shirt, was enough to transport her back to Queensland. That relentless daytime heat and those long, hot nights making love. The quiet only punctuated by the chirp of crickets and whirr of the ceiling fan. The dusty Land Rover journeys across the bush to the film set when Luke's hand held hers. It was still as vivid as though it had happened yesterday. She could even hear his voice whispering into her ear, the tender words as sweet as warmed honey, and feel again the way the sensation of his hard body against hers had turned her bones to water. Suddenly the studio felt far too small and Zoe wanted to turn and run away. There was too much left unsaid, too many secrets floating far too close to the surface, for things to be comfortable. How could she possibly work with Luke when the last time they'd met had been as lovers? And never mind what might happen if Fern or Steve ever found out . . .

'Are you OK?' Fern was asking. 'You've gone ever such a funny colour.'

'I'm hot,' said Zoe, which wasn't a fib. Her face suddenly felt as though it was on fire. Maybe she was about to spontaneously combust? It could only be a mercy if she were because she suddenly had a horrible feeling things were about to get very complicated.

'You're blushing. Get a grip, Zo! It's only pukey Lukey,' teased Fern. 'Although I must admit he's looking seriously buff these days!'

But Zoe wasn't listening. How could she concentrate on anything when Luke Scottman had met her gaze, despite the hundreds of people there, and was staring at her across the room just like something out of a corny Mills & Boon novel? As his sapphire-blue eyes locked with hers she felt that old familiar fizz of desire and her heart began to race. It's just a reaction to the past, Zoe told herself firmly. It doesn't mean anything! Besides, Luke was one of the hottest men on the planet – *Empire* magazine had just crowned him Hollywood's sexiest star – and she wouldn't be human or female if she didn't find him attractive. This quickening of her pulse and the sensation that the world was spinning on its axis was just down to shock and surprise, and not because she still had any feelings for Luke. Of course not.

She was married to Steve, for heaven's sake!

'Zoe!' Luke called, waving at her. 'Hey, Zoe! It's me!'

Now all eyes in the place swivelled to Zoe. He couldn't have drawn more attention to her if he'd asked her to paint her bottom blue and dance the cancan across the room. Rufus raised an eyebrow and his eyes glittered with something like amusement while Susannah looked seriously impressed.

'You know him?' she asked. 'You're friends with Luke Scottman?'

'We were at uni together,' admitted Zoe.

'He was *my* boyfriend!' said Fern. 'Damn, I hate being so short! I knew I should've worn my platforms today. He can't see me down here, can he?'

Since Luke was making a beeline for her across the studio, Zoe's first instinct was to run, but run where? To her broom cupboard where she'd be well and truly cornered? Luckily at this point Fern had had enough of going unnoticed and, shrieking at the top of her voice, she breaststroked her way through the crowd and launched herself at Luke like a small blonde weapon of mass destruction.

'Luke! Luke!' she squealed. 'Oh my God! I can't believe you're here! It's amazing!'

Luke's eyes tore from Zoe's and he looked down to see Fern. His face made a different kind of smile – a warm and impulsive one – and he laughed and hugged Fern.

'Fern! Long time, no see!' he said.

'It's not that long since Prague; you can't have missed

me that much!' Fern was saying. 'But hey, Zoe's here too and you guys haven't seen each other in years! Come and say hi!'

Grabbing Luke's hand, Fern tugged him away from his crew of PAs and minders and towed him towards Zoe. There was no backing out now and Zoe stepped forward, away from Susannah. For a split second Luke and Zoe just stared at each other, drinking in features once so dear and so familiar, before Luke folded her into a bear hug.

'Hello, you,' he said.

Just the sensation of those strong arms pulling her against his broad chest was enough to unlock Zoe's personal Pandora's box. The fresh lemony tang of his skin and those warm lips pressed against her cheek unleashed a thousand similar memories so overwhelming that Zoe felt giddy.

'It's good to see you,' Luke breathed against the top of her head. Zoe tried not to tremble.

'Isn't it fab that Luke's working with us?' Fern squealed at Zoe. 'All the gang together again! It'll be just like old times!'

Zoe swallowed. Not if she could help it.

'Not quite,' she said firmly, stepping out of Luke's embrace. 'I'm an old married woman now, remember?'

Her message to Luke couldn't have been any clearer but his chiselled face remained just as open and as sunny.

Maybe she was just being paranoid? Luke was a movie star now and he'd dated some of the most beautiful women on the planet. As if he would still carry a torch for her! She was in danger of becoming as much of a drama queen as Fern.

'Hey, that's right! I forgot that congratulations were in order!' Luke said with smile. 'How's married life?'

'Fantastic!' Zoe gushed. 'Wonderful. We're so happy.'

'Well, then, I'm pleased for you,' Luke said. His eyes held hers again for a split second longer than was strictly necessary as he added, 'I hope he deserves you. He's a lucky man.'

'He bloody isn't,' boomed Rufus, who'd fought his way through a throng of journalists to join them. 'The lovely Zoe never lets poor old Steve out to play with the boys. When you meet him have a good look at the dent he's got in his forehead. It's made by her thumb!' He roared with laughter at his own joke.

'I'm sure Steve would much rather be spending time with Zoe than going out on the lash with you,' Fern said sharply, and Luke nodded in agreement.

Sensing that he was outnumbered, and that the new alpha male was not necessarily going to side with him, Rufus just shrugged the comment off and started to talk loudly about his new plans for the shoot. The man was like Teflon, Zoe thought. Nothing stuck to or bothered him.

'So how come you took this part?' Fern asked Luke when Rufus finally paused to draw a breath.

'Rufus called my agent up and asked if I'd be interested,' Luke explained. 'I wasn't sure at first because I usually spend all my time these days blasting things with guns but it seemed like a great way to stretch my range as an actor. Then I found out that I'd get to hang out with my oldest pals too. So of course I said yes!'

'How did you know we were working on this shoot?' Fern wondered.

'Through my spy network,' Luke deadpanned. 'I've had you all followed for years.'

They goggled at him.

'Not really! I read it on Zoe's Facebook, of course!' Luke laughed. 'It's not all awards ceremonies and glamorous parties, you know! I spend most of my spare time in hotel rooms surfing the Internet and tweeting.'

Of course Zoe had accepted Luke's friend request on Facebook, but she never thought he'd actually take the time to look at her page.

'And watching *Star Trek* movies!' Fern teased, poking Luke in the ribs, and he held his hands up saying that he was guilty as charged.

Rufus grimaced. 'You need to get out more, man. I'm going to make it my personal mission to show you round London, take you to some hot clubs and show you some of the classiest women you've ever seen. A notorious womaniser like you will be in his element!'

'Thanks, but I think I'll be far too busy learning my lines and catching up with my friends and family for that kind of thing,' Luke told him politely.

'OK, how about I introduce you to the unclassiest women you've ever seen?' scoffed Rufus. 'Plenty of time to hang out with your rellies when you're old!'

'Not tonight, yeah, Rufus.' Luke's eyes danced from Zoe to Fern and back.

'What this film needs is some serious publicity,' continued Rufus, undeterred. 'I won't bullshit you, things were looking pretty ropy when the original leads pulled out so we need as many column inches as we can get. You in a club with some fit bird is just what we need. I've got the editor of Zoo on speed dial; one call to him and we'll have all the page-three stunners you could ever dream of. I won't promise, but I reckon even Jordan would join us for a night on the town.'

Luke really was a fantastic actor because his benign facial expression didn't flicker as he looked at the producer. Only Zoe saw how tightly he clenched his fist behind his back.

'Tempting, Rufus, but I'm afraid my days of drunken debauchery are long over. It's all wheatgrass drinks, yoga and macrobiotic diets for me these days. Much as I hate to disappoint you, the only women I plan on hanging out with are Zoe and Fern.'

Rufus's top lip curled. 'Jesus wept! Not another red-blooded man tamed by you, Zoe? Anyone else's bollocks for the chop?'

'Believe me, Rufus, your testicles are safe from me,' said Zoe coolly. 'Now I think you'd better go: Susannah wants a word.'

'Bloody hell, I'm surrounded by feminists. Oestrogen alert!' grumbled Rufus, glancing across to Susannah, who was indeed beckoning him over to her. 'If you change your mind, Luke mate, I'll be in Chinawhite from ten!'

'Good Lord!' breathed Luke, raking a strong tanned hand through his golden hair and watching as Rufus strode through the studio barking orders at all and sundry. 'He's certainly a character.'

'He's certainly something,' said Fern, drily, and the three of them fell about laughing, just as they used to do at uni. This broke the ice, and the awkwardness that Zoe had felt between her and Luke totally vanished, leaving her wondering if it had all been in her imagination.

'So if you're not going out on the pull with Neanderthal man tonight what are you planning to do?' Fern asked Luke casually.

He shrugged. 'Sit in my suite at Claridge's all alone and watch a *Star Trek* movie like the sad git that I am?'

'No way! We can't leave you alone with the Klingons,

Luke!' Fern gasped, hands flying to her mouth. 'You'll have to come over to Zoe's for the evening. She'll cook dinner.'

Luke raised an eyebrow. 'I hate to be a spoilsport, but don't you think Zoe should be issuing that invitation, Ms Moss?'

'Oh, Zoe doesn't mind,' Fern said airily.

Zoe was lost for words. Normally she didn't mind at all. She and Steve adored entertaining and their house was always full of their friends, either having casual kitchen suppers or sitting around the huge dining table for a four-course meal. She loved cooking and it was generally accepted amongst their friends that it was open house at Zoe and Steve's so for Fern to invite Luke was nothing unusual – except that of course it was. Zoe had never invited an ex-lover back to her marital home for dinner before.

But how could she say no without arousing Fern's suspicions?

'I've not been shopping—' she began but Fern wasn't worried about such trivialities.

'I'm sure you'll rustle something up,' said Fern. 'I'll get some nice wine to go with it.' Since Fern was to cooking what Gordon Ramsay was to polite language, this was their usual arrangement, and try as she might Zoe couldn't think of a way to get out of it that wouldn't seem odd now.

'Steve's away for a few days,' she said. 'The numbers will be odd.'

'Bummer! Never mind, I'll bring *my boyfriend*,' Fern said, placing a heavy emphasis on the title and glancing at Luke Princess Di style from beneath heavily mascaraed lashes. 'Or maybe you can give Priya a call? She's always a hoot.'

'Priya's on her romantic getaway, remember?' said Zoe. Unfortunately, she added silently.

'Oh, well, it'll just be the four of us then,' said Fern cheerfully. 'Is that OK with you, Luke?'

Luke considered. 'If that's all right with you, Zoe?'

Zoe swallowed back her protestations. She was just being silly. What happened between her and Luke was ancient history and both of them had moved on. What else could she do but agree?

'I'm looking forward to it,' she said brightly. 'I'll even make a chocolate mousse in celebration.'

As soon as the words were out of her mouth Zoe could have cheerfully ripped her tongue out.

'That's Luke's favourite dessert!' Fern clapped her hands together with delight. 'How clever of you to remember!'

But the question was really how could Zoe forget? Suddenly her mind's eye was flooded with images of Luke playfully smoothing rich chocolate mousse across her breasts and stomach before his blond head bent forward as he licked and teased every last morsel from her trembling body. Looking up, she met Luke's bright gaze and knew instantly he remembered too. Her face flamed. Bloody subconscious! Perhaps she should go for hypnotherapy or something? Dinner would be bad enough, but how could she possibly work closely with this man when he'd made her cry out like that?

She'd have to find a way of quitting. Maybe she could use Rufus as a reason? After all, everybody knew how impossible he was to work with.

Arranging that her guests should arrive for half seven Zoe made her excuses and returned to her broom cupboard where she shut the door and bashed her head several times against its hard wood. How on earth had life suddenly become so complicated? She couldn't believe that only the day before she'd been wishing that her life was more exciting and unpredictable. She must have been crazy!

Alone in her office Zoe wished with all her heart that Steve hadn't gone away. She didn't think she'd ever needed her husband's calm presence more.

8

By seven o'clock that night, after giving herself a stern talking-to and drinking a glass of Merlot, Zoe was feeling much more like her usual, in-control self. The lights were dimmed in the kitchen, Florence and the Machine were playing through Steve's beloved Bose stereo speakers and the food was all prepared.

Zoe had decided that they'd eat in the kitchen. She loved her kitchen; with its Delabole slate floor, huge island in the middle and big squishy sofas by the conservatory, it was the perfect place for chilling out and informal entertaining. Steve had installed a giant flat-screen TV in the alcove opposite the Aga, and most evenings both he and Libby were to be found lounging on beanbags, Xbox controls in hand, as they blasted hapless aliens to smithereens.

Actually, not Libby so much these days, Zoe thought wistfully as she placed a bottle of white Burgundy to chill in the huge American-style fridge. Since she'd found a new man and a new career, Libby was a busy girl and her

Xbox marathons had started to dwindle. But Zoe wished that her sister could have been here tonight. There was something very reassuring about her down-to-earth attitude. Libby had also worked with Luke recently on a film set in Thailand, so they'd have had loads to chat about, whereas with her and Luke there was a giant elephant in the room that it would be pretty hard to ignore. She could only hope and pray that Fern wouldn't spot it.

Maybe it wouldn't be that bad. She was sure he'd have forgotten all the letters and emails he'd sent after she fled from Australia – after all, his love life had hardly been out of the papers since. He'd hooked up with the stunning actress Trinity Duval and they'd become one of the most famous celebrity couples in the world, second only to Brangelina.

He probably hadn't given me a second thought until he spotted me this afternoon, Zoe told herself.

Six years had passed since she'd packed her bag and slipped away in the small hours, six years in which Luke had become one of the biggest stars in the world. She'd only seen him for a few minutes today but Zoe was struck right away by the polish of the man. Gone were the slightly crooked teeth and in their place a perfect set of bright white gnashers that Simon Cowell would envy. His body, always good, was now gym-honed to perfection and his skin glowed with vitality while his hair was thick and glossy. Even Luke's nails were buffed, his complexion perfect *café au lait* scattered with golden stubble. She'd have bet anything that even his simple white T-shirt and faded blue jeans had expensive labels on the inside. He looked like a perfected version of the handsome, slightly scruffy boy she'd known all those years ago.

Zoe couldn't help but wonder what Luke had thought when he'd caught sight of her. She didn't have the benefit of personal trainers, dieticians and designers and, unlike him, she seriously doubted that she looked better at twenty-eight than she had at twenty-two. Catching sight of herself in a burnished copper pan, Zoe sighed at the slight creasing around her eyes and wished she'd bothered to do her hair that morning rather than just scraping it back into a high ponytail. Even her work clothes had been frumpy: plain black trousers, pumps and a dark green top. No wonder he'd stared. He'd probably wondered what had happened to the carefree, sun-kissed girl he'd last seen, the girl who'd worn tiny shorts and jewel-bright tops, and whose golden hair had rippled down to the small of her back.

Oh dear, Zoe thought, I must make more of an effort! As Libby liked to point out, she was married, not dead!

Then she laughed out loud for being so vain. What did it matter what Luke Scottman thought when she had Steve, who loved and adored her just the way she was?

How did the saying go? 'The past is a foreign country: they do things differently there.' Well, that was certainly true, and the Zoe from those days felt like a stranger now. It was time to stop fretting and look forward to catching up with one of her oldest friends.

The food was all prepared and ready to go. Tonight Zoe had shunned M&S for the small deli up the road. She'd spent a relaxing twenty minutes selecting the perfect ingredients for a meal she'd cooked from scratch. Now the three-cheese soufflé, walnut salad, creamy fish pie and chocolate mousse were just waiting for the final touches, which shouldn't be a problem because, being a perfectionist, Zoe had it all down to an art. She poured the mousse mixture into the dessert bowls and carried the tray to the island. Everything needed precision timing, and if one thing went wr—

The shrilling of the doorbell made her jump. It was lucky that the mousse had already set, otherwise the slate floor would have been a right old mess. Zoe glanced at the clock, frowning when she saw it was only seven p.m. She hoped it wasn't an early arrival because, hot and sticky from cooking, she'd been hoping to go upstairs and take a quick shower. Day-old makeup and your husband's tatty old jogging bottoms was so not a good look, unless of course you wanted to channel your inner Vicky Pollard!

'Hey, hope I'm not too early but I can't hang around a

moment longer. It's bloody cold out here and I'm starting to really miss LA,' called a deep and cheerful voice through the door.

Zoe's heart plummeted. Sure enough, there was Luke standing on the doorstep and looking ridiculously handsome in a black cashmere coat and periwinkle-blue scarf the exact hue of his merry eyes. Mrs Patel next door was staring in disbelief and one of the hoodied teenagers from across the road had his chin practically in the kerb.

Oh God. If she didn't get Luke inside soon the paps would arrive!

'Come in, come in!' Zoe said, practically dragging Luke in the door and slamming it behind him. Hopefully the neighbours would just think they'd imagined the arrival of a Hollywood star and would leave her in peace. Rufus might be over the moon at all the free publicity but Zoe was fine without it. The last thing she wanted was a tabloid exposé of her brief fling with Luke Scottman.

'These are for you,' Luke said once inside, handing her a delicate hand-tied posy of freesias. 'They're still your favourite, right?'

Zoe was taken aback. 'Luke! They're lovely and yes, they are very definitely still my favourite. Fancy you remembering that!'

'I remember lots of things,' said Luke. 'I also remember that you used to love Jacobs Creek so I've brought a bottle of that too. I thought we could have a glass before dinner. Just like when we were students and Jacobs Creek was the height of sophistication.'

Zoe smiled at the memory. 'Drinking this will be a nasty shock for you, I should imagine! Don't film stars practically live on Cristal?'

'Darling, we bathe in it!' he laughed, and Zoe felt easier. This was still Luke, Zoe realised as he followed her along the hall and into the sitting room. So he was more polished, and seriously successful, but he was still the guy who used to pinch her spot concealer and could belch 'God Save the Queen'! Getting nervous and feeling awkward with him was just silly!

'You have a lovely home,' Luke told her as he sank onto one of the squidgy sofas in the living room.

'Thanks, we like it.' Zoe uncorked the wine, sloshing it into two large glasses, and handed him one. 'Shame that the owner hasn't had a chance to clean herself up, though! Sorry if I'm a state.'

'You look fine,' he said.

She sat on the sofa opposite and they chinked glasses. 'To catching up with old friends,' she said.

'I'll drink to that,' he agreed with a smile.

While they waited for Fern, laughing as they remembered numerous occasions where she'd been late, Zoe and Luke chatted about everything, from the renovations she and Steve had done to the house to the huge success of Luke's *Buddhist Assassin* movies. At some point she knew that they'd have to talk about the past because it was there as a delicate subtext beneath every 'do you remember when' and 'do you still like' uttered, but Zoe would really rather not wander down memory lane with an old lover in her marital home and while her husband was away.

When her BlackBerry started to shrill and the word 'Fern' flashed across the screen she pounced on it with relief. Safety in numbers and all that!

'How long are you going to be, hon? I've made cheese soufflé and I need to pop it into the oven.'

There was a pause and Zoe's heart sank. Please, Fern, she pleaded silently, don't let me down now!

'I'm really sorry, Zo, but I've been a total Muppet and lost my keys again!' wailed Fern. 'We're locked out the house and waiting for a locksmith. It could take ages so I don't think we'll be able to make it.'

'Oh, Fern! How many times have you lost your keys?' Zoe raised her eyes to the ceiling in exasperation while Luke started to chuckle.

'She had the locksmith on speed dial when we were at uni,' he reminded her.

'Too many times,' sighed Fern. 'What did you cook for dinner?'

Zoe told her and Fern wailed even louder. 'That sounds yummy! God, I'm starving! It sounds like you've really pulled the stops out too for this one. I hope our celebrity guest is impressed.'

'Mmm,' said Zoe. She supposed she had made an extra special effort because Luke was coming, but only because he must eat at some of the best restaurants in the world and she didn't want to disappoint him.

'Don't tell me – Fern can't make it?' Luke said as Zoe ended the call.

'She's locked herself out again for the millionth time.'

He laughed. 'It's kinda nice to know that some things never change.'

'Unlike your accent! When did you go all mid-Atlantic on us? And those teeth are certainly new!'

Luke blushed. 'Guilty as charged. The Americans are genuinely horrified by British teeth and my Austin Powers snaggleteeth were one of the first casualties of my move to the States.'

'And the tan? And the muscles?' Zoe teased. 'And maybe even Botox?'

'Hey, I resent that! I always had muscles!'

Zoe laughed. 'OK, so what's this about you being, as Rufus so delicately put it, a "notorious womaniser"?' she asked. 'I thought you were practically married to Trinity Duval? The last I heard you guys were really loved up and you'd even brainwashed the poor woman into liking *Star Trek*.'

Luke was so taken aback by this he practically choked

on his wine. 'Where the hell did you hear that? *Heat* magazine?'

'No.'

'Facebook?'

'Better than that!' said Zoe, feeling triumphant. 'Libby told me. You can't go on a shoot with my sister and not expect her to tell your friends all the juicy gossip! I thought you and Trinity were practically at the aisle.'

He put his wine glass down and placed his head in his hands. 'The problem was that Trin thought that too.'

'But you didn't feel the same way?' Zoe was on familiar turf now. Comforting her broken-hearted friends was something she used to do on a regular basis. Granted they weren't usually drop-dead gorgeous ex-lover Hollywood movie stars but the principle was the same.

Luke shrugged his broad shoulders. 'I guess not or we'd have already done the deal with *OK!*, wouldn't we? Anyway, if you read any of the gossip magazines you'd know that Trinity's dumped me for not committing and is all loved up with Bobby Roberts.'

'Bobby Roberts? That old hairy rocker from *Death Slayer*? But why?' Zoe was taken aback. Ancient tattooed Bobby Roberts made Ronnie Wood look like a clean-living, fresh-faced teenager. How Trinity could have ditched the gorgeous Luke for *that* was beyond her!

Luke looked up slowly. 'You know why,' he said hoarsely, and once again Zoe felt the burning intensity of that blue-eyed gaze. 'Trin knows I'll never marry her because I'm in love with someone else. I can't get over the one amazing woman who blew my mind and then left me without a word of explanation.'

Zoe stared at him, aghast. Somewhere she thought she could hear the flapping wings of all her chickens coming home to roost.

'I couldn't get over her,' Luke continued, his eyes never leaving Zoe's. 'No matter how hard I tried to distract myself by seeing other people. She loves somebody else, and she married him . . . but if she ever gave me so much as a hint that she was unhappy . . .'

That elephant was stampeding right through the room now. Luke's voice trailed off and for a moment they just stared at each other. The atmosphere was concrete heavy and Zoe was horrified. Surely Luke wasn't trying to tell her that he was in love with *her*? No way. He couldn't be!

Luke exhaled slowly. 'Zoe, I'm sorry if I've spoken out of turn or upset you but you have to know the truth. I—'

'Goodness! I've totally forgotten the food!' Zoe cried, leaping to her feet and almost knocking the wine over in her haste to escape. 'The fish pie's been in the oven for over an hour! It's going to be ruined!'

She fled to the kitchen and right on cue the smoke detector began to wail. The kitchen was thick with fumes and instead of the delicious aroma of creamy tarragon and sole, it was filled with the choking stench of burning.

'Quick, open the back door!' ordered Luke as, hot on her heels, he grabbed a tea towel and yanked open the oven. Moments later the charred remains of Zoe's masterpiece sat forlornly on the terrace while ice-sharp air flooded into the kitchen.

'Er, dinner is served,' said Zoe with a shrug.

Luke smiled. 'Have you got a takeaway menu?'

'I'll see what I have in the freezer.' Zoe smiled back.

She popped a frozen pizza in the oven and they both retreated to the living room again.

The confessional mood had been well and truly shattered, and before long they were chomping through one of Tesco's Finest margaritas and reminiscing about their student days. The Jacobs Creek was finished and they were the best part down a bottle of Chablis when Luke jokingly remarked that he was glad he'd come over for pizza.

'I'm so sorry,' Zoe said. 'I'm normally a much better hostess than this – just ask Fern.'

'Hey, I'm not complaining.' Luke said softly, looking into her eyes. 'I love pizza and I love . . . hanging out with you.'

Zoe gulped. Flattering as it was to have a Hollywood superstar flirting with her she knew she had to put a stop to it right now.

'It's really late and I've got an early start tomorrow. How about I call you a cab?' she offered.

Luke took the hint and played along. 'Good Lord! I had no idea it was nearly midnight. You're right as usual! We can't have Gilbert Osmond looking wan and baggy-eyed. Let me ring my driver.'

Wow. Luke had gone up in the world. Fancy having his own driver! She supposed that she had Steve to drive her to the shops but it was hardly the same thing.

But after a short phone call Luke snapped his phone shut and turned to Zoe with a really worried expression on his sculpted features.

'I hate to be the bearer of bad tidings but I think you may be stuck with me,' he said. 'My driver says there's no way he can get across London tonight. The roads are impassable, apparently.'

'What do you mean?' Zoe was confused. 'What's happened?'

Gently Luke placed his strong hand in the small of her back and propelled her towards the living-room window. Pulling the curtains open with a flourish he revealed that the world outside was transformed into Narnia as snowflakes whirled around the lampposts and drifted against the low garden walls. The cars outside were iced like birthday cakes and suddenly Zoe realised that all was silent. In true British style a snowfall had brought the city to a grinding halt.

'How on earth did we miss this?' she breathed.

'Too busy gossiping and eating junk food,' Luke replied. 'I'm sorry, Zoe, but it looks like you're not going to get rid of me. If that's OK?'

Being stuck all alone with Luke Scottman had to be right up there in the list of most women's dreams, thought Zoe. What a pity then that having Luke stay over was actually her idea of a nightmare. Still, what choice did she have? She could hardly turn the poor man out into a blizzard.

She took a deep breath. 'Of course it's OK. Let me show you to the spare room. We've just finished doing it up actually so you should be really comfortable.'

'I'm sure I've heard that you're supposed to share body heat in arctic conditions!'

Zoe raised her eyebrows. 'We're in Richmond, not Siberia. I think we'll be fine.'

'You can't blame a guy for trying!' Luke grinned. 'You'd better show me this spare room then.'

So they went upstairs, trying to ignore the intimacy of climbing the steps together. 'Here you go,' Zoe said, opening the door to the pretty yellow and white bedroom, which until very recently had housed Libby's gym equipment and skateboards. 'It's not Claridge's I'm afraid, but hopefully it'll do.'

'It looks great to me. Besides, I've slept in worse. Remember that shack in Australia?'

Zoe remembered perfectly. The place was basic and the bed little more than a mattress on the floor. But that hadn't bothered them. They'd been so wrapped up in one another that the last thing they'd been worried about was the lack of luxury. Her face flamed at the memory.

'You *do* remember,' Luke said softly.

Zoe closed her eyes in defeat. 'Of course I do. But we were different people, Luke.'

He shook his head. 'I haven't changed. Sure, I might have all that Hollywood nonsense going on, but underneath it all I'm still the same guy.'

For a moment they stood awkwardly in the doorway while the atmosphere grew heavier than the snowfall.

Luke sighed. 'I'm not being fair, am I? Here's you, all happily settled, and I come charging in. Just ignore me, Zoe. I've had far too much Jacobs Creek, that's all.'

The lines were well rehearsed, but they both knew that the wine had nothing to do with what Luke was saying. Years of words unsaid hung between them like tangled film cables, and much as she wanted to put things right Zoe didn't know where to start. What she did know, though, was that tonight, woozy from drink and with her husband away, was not the time to start unravelling the past.

'Well, good night then, and thanks for a great evening,' Luke said finally.

'It's been lovely to catch up,' Zoe said, and meant it

too. The last few hours had been spent wandering down memory lane – or at least her edited version of it – and it had been a lot of fun.

Luke dipped his head to kiss her on the cheek just as Zoe turned to kiss his. Accidentally their lips touched for the briefest of moments and they both jumped backwards as though scalded.

'Good night!' Zoe squeaked and, heart thudding, fled to the sanctuary of her bedroom. She shut the door behind her and sagged against it. Moments later she heard the answering click of the spare-room door and then all was silent.

Zoe woke up with a breakdance troupe flick-flacking around her skull as though practising an audition for *Britain's Got Talent*, and a mouth drier than Jack Dee. She opened her eyes, winced at the glaring sunshine, and closed them hastily. Bloody Luke! He'd always been a bad influence. Just how many lectures had she missed because of him and his penchant for midweek benders? But it was one thing to skive a class on medieval literature and quite another to miss work. She'd just have to hope that a hot shower and a pint of Resolve did the job.

At this thought she sat bolt upright, her brain swivelling horribly in her skull. Luke was still in her flat. They'd done nothing to be ashamed of, so why did she feel so embarrassed?

Dressing gown firmly belted around her waist, she padded along the corridor to the spare room. Forcing a smile she rapped her knuckles against the door.

'Luke? Are you awake?'

When no answer was forthcoming Zoe opened the door and peeped inside. Oh, the relief when she saw he wasn't there! The duvet was straightened, the curtains drawn back – a dent in the pillow was the only clue he'd been there at all. He must have skipped out early to save face, Zoe realised. Sobering up, Luke must know he'd said far too much and that he'd seriously overstepped the mark. Besides, if he'd felt a fraction as rough as she did this morning, he wouldn't want to start analysing last night's accidental almost kiss. Hopefully he wanted to forget about the evening's weird events just as much as she did.

I'll catch him later on set and draw a line under last night, Zoe decided as she made her way down the stairs *en route* for the kitchen and a huge mug full of coffee. If they had to work together she would make sure that everything was on a strictly professional footing. That was the best and most appropriate way to handle this awkward situation.

Zoe was just spooning espresso beans in the Gaggia when movement from the garden caught her eye.

What was that? Was she being burgled?

She reached for the phone and was about to dial the police when she saw someone else drop into her garden. Then another. All carrying cameras.

Several photographers had scaled the red-brick wall dividing her house from a small service alley and were merrily snapping away. With a cry of horror Zoe stepped away from the conservatory, pulling her robe tight across her chest, and yanked the curtains shut. Seconds later the doorbell began to shrill and the brass knocker thundered like something from *Macbeth*. What on earth was going on?

Taking a deep breath and tucking her long blonde hair behind her ears, Zoe went to investigate, gasping when she opened the door and discovered that most of Britain's press was camped outside. Camera flashes dazzled her and for a split second she was too stunned to react.

'What's your relationship with Luke Scottman?' shouted somebody, thrusting a mic under her nose.

'Is it true he spent the night with you?' demanded someone else.

Click! Flash! Pop!

Zoe's hands rose to her mouth in horror.

'What's your name, love?' asked a burly-looking pap, stepping forward and practically chinning her with his camera. 'How long have you been seeing Luke?'

'I'm not seeing Luke!' Zoe protested, when she was sufficiently recovered from her shock to get the power of speech back.

'Come on, love! We saw him leave in the small hours!' called somebody else.

'You can't fool us! Creeping out at dawn – one of his favourite tricks, that is!'

'You've been spying on Luke? That's outrageous!' Zoe was furious on her friend's behalf.

'The *Dagger*'s readers want to know what Luke Scottman's like in bed. Does he really have an enormous—'

Zoe wasn't hanging around to hear any more of this. Spinning on her heel, she slammed the door in their faces and then leaned against it while her heart played squash against her ribcage. Oh Lord, this was a nightmare. She didn't need to log on to her computer to know that already grainy images of a clueless Luke sauntering down her garden path would be zooming all over cyberspace, followed now by pictures of her in her robe with bed-head hair and smudged makeup. If it looked incriminating to her – and she *knew* it was all totally innocent – then what on earth would it look like to the rest of the world?

Zoe tore up the stairs and back into her bedroom, where she quickly drew the curtains before snatching up her mobile phone from the bedside table. She had to speak to Steve before he bought a paper or checked the news!

'You have reached the voicemail of . . .'

Argh!

Steve wasn't answering. How could she leave a message saying that although it looked as if she'd just spent the night with another man she hadn't really?

Steve was honest and trusted her, but even so, that wasn't the kind of news that any husband wanted to hear. He'd been away and she'd been so looking forward to seeing him – but this was definitely not the homecoming she'd had in mind.

Taking a deep breath, Zoe dialled the taxi company and ordered a cab. There was no way she was walking to the station with the world's tabloid press in tow. She'd have to run the gauntlet, leap into the cab and pray she reached the studio before Steve did. How did celebrities cope with living like this day in day out, she wondered as she peeked through a crack in the curtains and leaped backwards when hundreds of camera flashes lit the early morning gloom like lightning. She shook her head in disbelief. She'd never thought she'd say it but she took her hat off to the rich and famous. Paparazzi attention was bloody hard work!

By the time she arrived on set Zoe's mild hangover had turned into a pounding headache, which even a dose of Nurofen didn't touch. Fighting her way through the press had been hideous and the bumpy taxi ride had made her insides curdle. She hadn't dared to stop for a paper; she was just hoping against hope that the story hadn't broken yet. Luckily the crew had been at work since seven and probably hadn't had a chance to check the up-to-the-minute online news. Nobody was gossiping about her so-called night of passion with their leading man . . . yet.

Glancing down at her shooting schedule Zoe learned that today the production team was recreating a street scene from the 1800s. A frown pleated her brow as she looked up and saw that the designer had coated the road with tarmac. Tarmac! Why not give Isabel an iPad and a hybrid car?

'Hey! What on earth is going on?' Zoe asked Marc, the production designer. 'This is supposed to be a nineteenth-century city street, not the fast lane of the M25!'

Marc sighed heavily. 'I'm well aware there's a problem, thanks.'

The thudding in Zoe's temples went up a gear. 'I think this is slightly more than a *problem*, Marc! It's a disaster! You're going to have to change this. There's no way we can shoot now.'

'It's all taken care of,' said Marc shortly.

'How?' Zoe felt herself slide closer to hysteria. 'We're behind schedule as it is!'

Marc slammed his shooting schedule against his fist. 'For God's sake, Zoe! Stop being such a control freak! The set design has nothing to do with you! You're only the writer, so leave the rest of us to get on with our jobs.'

Only the writer! Zoe was fuming now.

'If I thought you were capable of doing your job properly I'd happily leave you to get on with it,' she told him through clenched teeth. 'But I think you've proved that's not the case. Where's Fern? This wouldn't have happened if *she* was in charge.'

'Fern's gone to order some manure. We thought that if we covered the tarmac in muck it might look a bit more authentic.'

Zoe wasn't convinced that Isabel Archer walking through cattle dung was quite what she'd had in mind when she'd written the scene but she supposed it was preferable to having her stroll along a freshly laid tarmac street. Clearly her headache and the stress of this morning were wreaking havoc on Zoe's professionalism.

'Sorry, Marc, I shouldn't have blamed you,' she said. 'I've just been having a really rough morning.' And she backed into something hard and metallic.

'Ow!'

She turned to see that she was up close and personal with a delivery truck and she had just bumped into the metal hatch. Her eyes widened in time to see the hatch fall open and the contents of the truck pour out.

The manure delivery truck delivered its load . . . right on top of Zoe!

It came thick and fast at first, then slowing to a heavy drizzle of muck. She squeezed her eyes shut. When she dared to open them again she saw her cream suit was freckled with pungent manure and her beautiful suede boots were ruined.

From a metaphorical crap day to a literal one in less than ten seconds!

'Argh!' she screamed, and the whole studio turned to stare at her.

Frantically trying to dab the muck from her jacket Zoe staggered towards the dressing rooms. The smell of farmyard was so strong it made her gag, but it had the effect of parting the crowd of crew and extras in a way that Moses would have envied. Zoe didn't blame them one bit. She wasn't sure where Fern had sourced this manure from but whatever those animals had been eating they needed to change their diet. And *she* needed to grab a shower fast and then borrow some clothes from the wardrobe department.

'My God, you look a state!' Floor manager Celina drained of colour as Zoe walked past her, *en route* to the dressing rooms. She pursed her gore-red lips. 'What happened?'

Zoe sighed. Since Celina's on-set nickname was Rottweiler getting past her without undergoing the third degree had been a slim hope. The woman guarded the dressing rooms with a savage intensity.

'It's a long story – can I tell you later? I'm just going to wash up in the dressing room.'

Celina wrinkled her nose. 'Sorry, Zoe, but I really don't think so! These dressing rooms are only for stars!'

Zoe stared at her. 'You've got to be kidding? Look at

the state of me! I can't work like this.'

But Celina shook her head. 'Sorry, but I can't let you in. That dressing room is strictly reserved for our leading lady.'

Zoe, normally very easy-going, felt her blood begin to boil.

'We don't have a leading lady,' she reminded Celina through gritted teeth. 'So nobody is going to feel insulted or put upon if I just sneak inside and clean myself off.'

Celina folded her arms across her ample chest. 'Just because you're married to the director and sleeping with the male lead doesn't mean you can swan around here doing whatever you like.'

'I beg your pardon?' boomed a voice from behind them.

Zoe and Celina spun round so fast that it was a miracle neither of them suffered whiplash. Celina's mouth looked like a livid gash when she saw that Steve was standing behind them and had heard every word of their conversation. Uttering a mortified apology Celina scuttled off as fast as her plump legs could carry her while Zoe went cold to the marrow.

'Babe, what she just said is rubbish! This is all a ridiculous misunderstanding. 'What happened was that Fern—' she began, but Steve held his hands up, a signal for her to stop talking.

'Sweetheart, please don't look so worried. I'm not

about to do the whole jealous husband act,' he said. 'I know you and Luke go way back. And I saw the snow last night. The paps must have seen him leave our place and put two and two together to make sex.'

'That's exactly what happened!' Zoe cried in relief. 'Oh, Steve, I was so worried you'd think something had gone on.'

Steve smiled at her with such a tender smile that her heart twisted with love. 'Hey, I trust you, Zoe. You'd never cheat on me.'

'Of course I wouldn't!'

'I know,' Steve said, 'so don't be upset.' He stepped forward to hug her but stopped dead in his tracks when he caught the stench of the manure.

'Oh God!' He retched. 'I love you, babe, but your new perfume leaves a lot to be desired! As director of this production, and the man you are sleeping with, I'm going to march you into that dressing room this instant and wash whatever that is off!'

'Sir! Yes, sir!' laughed Zoe.

Zoe and Steve walked together towards the dressing room and Steve continued, 'I know you've never felt anything for Luke besides friendship.'

Zoe looked at the floor. 'That's right,' she muttered, and swallowed hard.

'And I also know you'd never hurt Fern by getting together with Luke.'

Her chest felt so heavy she found it hard to breathe, let alone speak.

'God, remember how she fell apart when they broke up. It was awful, wasn't it?' he said. 'You could never be so cruel.'

If guilt was made of calories Zoe would have been the size of an elephant at that precise moment.

'And these are for you.' Steve produced a bunch of pink tulips from behind his back. 'They're to say I'm sorry I've been so busy the last few days. It's been a nightmare trying to find a female lead.'

The tulips were the remorse cherry on the guilt cake. 'Any luck?' she whispered.

'Yeah, I think so. Somehow Rufus managed to get Trinity Duval interested. I had to go and schmoose her and get her to sign on the dotted line. Which she did, thank God.'

Zoe frowned. 'You do know Trinity is Luke's ex, don't you? What on earth is Rufus thinking?'

'The same thing he always thinks: that it'll be great publicity,' shrugged Steve. 'And he's right. The press will love it.'

'But why send you to persuade her? Why not do it himself?' Zoe was confused. Rufus loved hobnobbing with the stars; it wasn't like him to step aside willingly.

Steve was just about to answer when, through the plate-glass windows at the front of the studio, they saw a limo draw up, all shiny black paintwork and tinted windows. The chauffeur skipped round to open the door and stood to attention as a pair of long slim legs swung out, followed by the slim body and impossibly large breasts of none other than Trinity Duval. Clad in a crimson DVF wrap dress that clung lovingly to her sensational curves, and with her mane of honey-blonde hair tumbling to her tiny waist, Trin looked every inch the film star. Zoe could practically see Steve melting like Häagen-Dazs on a hot day. She couldn't blame him; Trinity was gorgeous – especially when compared to the creature from the black lagoon that he was married to!

Aware of how she looked and smelled, Zoe hung back while Steve greeted Trinity with the ubiquitous air kisses and chatted easily to her. One of Steve's gifts was putting people at their ease, Zoe thought fondly. Look at how Trinity was smiling and laughing up at him! The actress was notorious for her demands and temperamental behaviour, yet here she was, chatting and joking with Steve as though they were old friends. Maybe this production wasn't going to be such a disaster after all.

'Hey, Zoe!' called Steve, beckoning her over. 'Come and meet our leading lady. Trinity, this is my wife, Zoe. She's the genius who's adapted and written our script.' He turned to Zoe. 'Trinity's an amazing actress. She's going to make Isabel Archer come alive.'

Trinity must be an amazing actress, Zoe thought with

a smile. She'd managed to look really pleased to meet her even though she smelled worse than an exploded stink bomb factory! One beautifully manicured hand was offered for Zoe to shake, although the actress drew the line at kissing her cheek, and Trinity said warmly that she was delighted to put a face to the name at long last.

'You have a wonderful husband,' she purred. 'We had such fun together last night.'

'Oh, really?' Zoe shot Steve a sharp look but her husband was suddenly fascinated by the toes of his Timberlands and couldn't meet her eye. A cold finger ran down her spine. Trinity was stunning, the stuff that male fantasies were made of. Just what sort of fun had they had, exactly? She trusted Steve, but even so . . .

'It looks like you've had an accident?' Trinity was saying, her gaze settling on Zoe's ruined suit. 'Why don't you use my dressing room and freshen up? I'm sure my PA can sort you out some clothes too.'

The thought of jumping in a shower and getting rid of the muck was such a welcome one that it was all Zoe could do not to weep with gratitude. But she couldn't help wondering if Trinity was just being kind or whether there was something else. Was she paranoid or was there a distinct whiff of guilt beneath the generous offer? And as for lending her clothes, well, even if Zoe never ate again she'd never be a size zero! She was quite happy being a healthy size eight, thanks all the same.

Well, OK then, size ten.

But she was in no position to decline her offer. 'Thank you, Trinity,' she said, and sprinted to the dressing room.

Zoe was just toying with the idea of going for a third lathering – that manure was super stinky, after all – when above the hissing of the power jets and gurgling of the water she heard a voice.

'Hello? Trin? Is that you in there, babes?'

Hang on a minute! Zoe knew that voice, it was the same one she usually heard asking where the ketchup was or whether she could borrow a tenner. Quickly turning off the shower and pulling on the fluffy bathrobe Trinity had left for her, Zoe stepped into the dressing room and saw Libby raiding the fruit bowl.

'What are you doing here?' she demanded.

'Bloody hell, Zoe!' Libby exclaimed, leaping into the air and spraying her sister with apple. 'Don't creep up on me like that!'

'I'm not creeping; I borrowed the shower. What are you doing here?' Zoe asked. 'And do you think you ought to be helping yourself to Trinity's fruit?'

'Oh, Trin won't mind that. She doesn't eat,' said Libby airily, pocketing a peach. 'Anyway, we're old friends, remember? We met in Thailand last year. Luke was there too.'

Zoe did remember. Libby had sung Trinity's praises for weeks.

'So, how does it feel to hit the headlines?' asked Libby with a grin.

Zoe rolled her eyes and slumped into the overstuffed sofa. 'Not great.'

'We saw it on the Internet,' said Libby nonchalantly through a mouthful of fruit. 'I shouldn't worry, sis. Nobody with half a brain would believe Luke Scottman's bonking *you*.'

Zoe wasn't sure she liked being dismissed like this. 'Why shouldn't I be "bonking Luke", as you so delicately put it? In a hypothetical sense. And if I wasn't married, of course.'

'Like, duh! Because he's a world-famous film star and could have anyone!' Libby explained. 'Besides, you *are* married, and you'd never cheat on Steve.' Her bright blue eyes narrowed suspiciously and Zoe felt her cheeks grow warm under her sister's scrutiny. 'Why are you blushing? Did something happen between you guys last night?'

'Don't be ridiculous! Of course not!' said Zoe, while her cheeks did an impression of a blast furance. 'I can't believe you'd even ask me that!'

'Hmm,' said Libby. 'Must just be a coincidence that you look guilty then.'

'I do not look guilty!' Zoe said, and stood up in exasperation. 'I have nothing to be guilty about! If there is anyone who believes in the sanctity of marriage, it's me. You know how much—'

'Whatever you say, big sis. Whatever you say!' Libby lobbed her apple core at the bin, whooping when she scored a direct hit. 'Oh, don't look at me like that, I'm only teasing you. Of course you wouldn't cheat on Steve. As if!'

And with this parting shot Libby blew Zoe a kiss and sauntered off in search of Trinity. Zoe sighed and, sitting down at Trinity's dressing table, regarded her reflection thoughtfully. Her sister would be shocked if she knew about the two passion-filled weeks she and Luke had shared in Australia; in fact, everybody would be disappointed and horrified. Especially Fern and Steve.

Placing her chin in her hands Zoe gave herself the steely look that normally worked wonders with extras and tricky crew members.

There's nothing else for it, she told herself sternly. You are going to have to talk to Luke!

10

Zoe pulled on a pair of Trinity's ridiculously skinny jeans and a glittery off-the-shoulder sweater and, scraping her damp hair back from her face and into a high ponytail, made her way to Luke's dressing room. Annoyed with herself for feeling nervous – this was still just Luke, after all – she rapped on the door and resisted the urge to chew her nails while she waited for him to answer.

Zoe grimaced; she hated it when her private and personal lives collided. This was one of the reasons why she had thought long and hard about working with Steve on *Portrait*. But Steve wasn't proving to be the complication, and as much as she was a creative writer, even in her wildest imaginings she'd never dreamed Luke Scottman would be cast as the leading man.

'Zoe!' Luke looked taken aback to see her when he opened the dressing room door. His hyacinth-blue eyes swept her body, darkening in appreciation at her fresh-from-the-shower glow. 'This is a nice surprise.'

Suddenly very aware of her skintight jeans and bare shoulders Zoe yanked up the neck of the sweater and ducked beneath his arm into the dressing room.

'Luke, this isn't a social visit. Have you seen the news?'

Luke pushed the door shut and, leaning against it, crossed his arms and gave her a slow heart-stopping smile. In his faded jeans and plain white T-shirt he looked every inch the heart-throb.

'My night of passion, you mean? With a stunning mystery blonde?'

Zoe rolled her eyes. 'It's not funny! Luke, everyone must be talking about it by now.'

'Welcome to my world,' Luke sighed. 'Take my advice and just ignore it. Fish-and-chip paper and all that.'

'Maybe.' Zoe started to pace the room, worrying her lower lip with her teeth. 'I felt terrible for Steve, though. That can't have been a very nice thing to hear.'

'Do you want me to speak to him?' offered Luke. 'I'm happy to tell him that there's nothing going on, if you like?'

'No, no, Steve's fine. He knows that I'd never cheat on him.'

'Shame,' said Luke, and Zoe shot him a look. 'Just joking!' he added with his hands raised in surrender. 'Seriously, though, I'm really sorry for leaving this morning without saying goodbye. I guess I felt kind of awkward about . . .'

At the memory of that almost kiss, innocent though it was, Zoe felt her face flame.

'It's fine, so please don't feel awkward,' she told him. 'We'd both had a lot to drink.'

'It had nothing to do with drink,' Luke said softly. 'Spending time with you last night was really special to me. It reminded me of those weeks we had in Australia. They really were the happiest of my life.'

Zoe felt the ground shift beneath her feet. 'Oh, come on, Luke! You've had Oscar nominations since then, and even been Rear of the Year!'

Luke's mouth set in the stubborn line she remembered so well. It was the same expression she'd seen when he'd argued with her about the interpretation of lines when they were in the uni drama society.

'I mean it,' he said. 'Nothing has ever compared to those two weeks, before or since.'

Zoe swallowed. This was so not the way she wanted this conversation to go. If they were going to manage working together then Australia had to be left in the past where it belonged.

'Luke, those two weeks were very nice,' she said gently, 'but it was a long time ago. I'm married to Steve now – *happily* married. I'm really pleased to be working with you but I'd rather we put the past behind us.'

Luke sighed. 'Yes. OK. I'm sorry.' He looked up at her from beneath his soot-dark lashes and then smiled the smile that melted millions of female hearts across the globe. 'Friends?'

Zoe laughed. 'That look isn't going to work on me! I've heard you burp "God Save the Queen", remember?' She picked up a cushion and chucked it at him. 'Of course we're friends. I never thought for a minute we wouldn't be. In fact, I'm hoping you're friendly with all your exes.'

'What do you mean by that? Me and Fern are—'

'Not Fern,' said Zoe, shaking her head and grimacing. 'Rufus has just hired Trinity Duval as your leading lady.'

Luke pulled a face. 'Great.'

'I can only apologise. It's typical Rufus behaviour, I'm afraid. He isn't exactly known for his sensitivity.'

He laughed. 'That's one way of putting it. I've yet to meet anyone in the business he hasn't upset. If the guy wasn't such a genius, I don't think he'd have lived this long. Rufus will find the mixture of publicity and aggressive chemistry totally irresistible.'

Zoe nodded. He was spot-on.

'Anyway, don't worry about it,' Luke shrugged. 'Trin and I broke up amicably and we've both moved on.'

'Well, that's a relief.'

'Besides, in spite of what you may have read in the papers, things between us were never serious.' Luke gave Zoe an intense look and the atmosphere became so thick you could have cut it with a chisel. 'I couldn't commit to her when I was always thinking about someone else.'

Time to beat a hasty retreat, thought Zoe as she headed for the door.

'Please don't go,' Luke stepped forward and, catching her arm, pulled her round to face him. 'I really need you.'

'Luke, I've already told you! That's all in the past.' She shook his hand away. 'How many times do I have to say it?'

'Zoe, you've totally got the wrong end of the stick. I'm not after your body – gorgeous as it is – I need some help with this annoying wig.' He gestured at a long, dark mass of horsehair draped across the dressing table in a tangle that would send the wardrobe department into a panic.

'What on earth have you been doing to that?' she gasped. 'Wrestling it?'

'Pretty much! I've been trying to fix it with wig glue and tie it back. I didn't want to be a diva and call the makeup girls but I'm finally admitting defeat. I can't even tie a bow!'

Zoe giggled and the atmosphere was gone. 'I remember the Grad Ball. Fern had to sort your bow tie out, didn't she?'

'Good old Fern,' said Luke fondly, sitting down at the dressing table. His reflection fixed Zoe with big pleading eyes. 'Come on, Zoe. Please help me fix this thing! You always were good at fixing stuff.'

'Libby calls it an obsessive compulsive disorder,' Zoe sighed.

'Well, whatever it is I'd certainly appreciate a dose right now,' Luke said, handing her the wig. 'I'm due on set in twenty minutes and I'm supposed to look like a nineteenth-century dilettante, not Brian May!'

Zoe brandished the wig glue and ribbon. 'I'll see what I can do. I've seen the girls do this loads of times.'

'So you're practically an expert,' said Luke, looking relieved. 'How hard can it be?'

The answer was: very hard. Soon there was tape, glue and wig hair stuck to pretty much everything.

'Oh dear!' cried Zoe in frustration. 'Edward Scissorhands could have done a better job.'

'At last!' Luke was almost weeping with mirth as he tried to remove a clump of tape from his cheek. 'I've finally discovered the one thing that you are rubbish at!'

'No, wait,' said Zoe. 'Let me try one more time.'

She leaned in close and applied the glue carefully to his scalp, then smoothed the horsehair on to the glue. 'There!' she said. 'Now don't ever say that—'

But as she straightened up she realised she'd succeeded in gluing her own hair to his head. She tried to pull it off but her fingers were coated with glue and she was now attached to him. No matter how hard she tried to untangle them both it seemed they were well and truly stuck together.

'Ow!' yelped Luke.

'Sorry!'

She twisted round to the side to attack the problem from a different angle and suddenly their faces were only inches apart.

They looked into each other's eyes. Talk about too close for comfort! Zoe swiftly tried to pull away.

'Ouch!' Luke cried again. 'That hurts!'

Zoe winced. Her real hair was pulled so tight that she was in danger of scalping herself if she wiggled too much. The more she tried to tug herself away from Luke the more it hurt.

'Zoe, stop!' pleaded Luke. 'Brute force is not the answer! This wig glue needs a solvent to remove it. The only thing we can do is try and get into a comfortable position and then buzz Celina for help.'

'Please, no,' sighed Zoe. But what choice did she have? Reluctantly letting Luke shift her round so that she was sitting on his lap she resigned herself to the humiliation that was bound to follow.

Luke leaned them both forward, reached round Zoe and pressed the button for the intercom. 'Hi, Celina?' he said. 'It's Luke, Luke Scottman?'

As if she needed reminding.

'Er, Zoe and I are in a bit of a sticky situation and we could really do with your help. And something to dissolve wig glue?'

The excited squeaking from the other end of the phone suggested that Celina was only too happy to dash over and oblige a famous movie star.

And there Zoe was, practically giving him a lap dance. This was awkward. 'Sooooo,' she said, desperately thinking of something to say.

From the look on Luke's up-close-and-personal face, he didn't know what to say either. He started humming a tune – a Coldplay song that always reminded her of their time together. Was he doing this on purpose? His light breath on her face made her whole body tingle.

'Can you stop that, please?' she asked in a whisper, her lips almost brushing his as she moved them.

'Why?' he asked. 'I thought it was your favourite.'

'Not anymore.'

They sat in silence for a moment and let the awkwardness work its magic.

A minute later, Celina came flying into Luke's dressing room, and hot on her heels were Trinity, Fern, Libby, Rufus and Steve, all of whom stared open-mouthed at the spectacle of their writer glued to their star's lap, their lips so close they were practically kissing.

'What the hell's been going on in here?' demanded Rufus, waggling his eyebrows. 'Or maybe I shouldn't ask? Shall we go and leave you guys in peace?'

'We're stuck together with wig glue,' she hissed.

'Whatever turns you on, darling,' drawled Rufus.

'Although I must say I'd take handcuffs over glue any day.'

'Enough of the jokes already,' Luke said, unintentionally whispering into Zoe's ear.

'Why have you brought the entire crew with you?' Zoe asked Celina, scarlet with embarrassment at being caught in such a ridiculous predicament.

'Sorry!' Celina looked anything but, she was obviously still bristling from their earlier encounter and enjoying every minute of Zoe's dismay. 'When Luke said he was in a sticky situation I assumed he must be in real trouble so I called everyone I thought might be able to help.'

'It was my hairpiece,' Luke said, turning a little towards Celina and the others, and taking Zoe with him.

'So I see,' she replied. 'You seem to have Zoe Kent stuck to it.'

'We don't seem to be able to keep you two apart,' said Trinity. Her voice was feather light as she said this but the look she gave them both was as warm as the Ben and Jerry's warehouse. Zoe shivered. She really hoped Luke hadn't ever mentioned Australia to Trinity.

Celina started applying the solvent, her fingers working away in the millimetres between Zoe and Luke's heads. 'This wig is wrecked.' Celina looked pained. 'We'll have to start again with it.'

'I'm sorry. I thought I could fix it, but I was wrong,' Zoe said in a small voice.

Steve laughed. 'That's my wife! Always trying to fix things and sort everybody out. Babe, you're just not cut out to be a hairdresser. Admit it!'

'I admit it,' Zoe said. 'Now please, will somebody free me!'

'I'm never letting you near my hair,' shuddered Fern.

'No wonder Steve's so bald,' added Rufus. 'It's safer that way, eh, mate?'

Everyone started to laugh as they looked from Zoe to the matted mass of what had been an expensive glossy wig, and in spite of feeling like a prime candidate for Prat of the Year she couldn't help seeing the funny side. But while Celina dabbed her face with the glue solvent, she was still uncomfortably aware that Luke's full sexy mouth was only a kiss away from her own and from the twinkle in his eye she knew that Luke was thinking exactly the same thought. Unless she was very careful this comedy had every chance of turning into a tragedy, something that Zoe had absolutely no intention of allowing to happen.

From now on she was going to have to make every effort to ensure that she kept a very healthy distance from Luke Scottman.

A few days and much teasing about wigs and glue later, the shoot was well and truly underway and Zoe no longer had the time to fret about Luke Scottman. Apart from the fact that she was being kept ridiculously busy by Rufus's constant demand for eleventh-hour changes to the script, they'd been so far behind schedule that there'd been no choice but to just have the briefest of rehearsals before plunging straight into filming. Trinity had about fifty nervous breakdowns a day and was constantly flouncing off the set in tears, while Luke had a habit of vanishing, only to be discovered hidden away in his dressing room watching *Star Trek* and frantically trying to mug up on his lines. Talk about high-maintenance A-listers!

Trin and Luke might add glamour to the production, thought Zoe as she drew a line through Rufus's latest script change, but they also add an awful lot of stress.

When this shoot was over, she was dragging Steve on holiday somewhere hot and sunny, stuff the expense.

She'd hardly seem him for days and they badly needed some quality time together. As things stood they weren't so much ships that passed in the night as ships that fell into bed exhausted before munching cornflakes the next morning and sailing off in their different directions. They hadn't had a decent conversation for days, Zoe realised with a jolt. 'Is there any milk?' and, 'Night, babe,' hardly counted. And as for making love . . . well, that was almost a distant memory.

Making a mental note to visit some holiday websites that evening, Zoe dragged her attention back to her script. Moments later, she was interrupted by a harassed young runner called Melody, who'd been sent to summon her to Rufus.

Zoe sighed. 'Is it urgent? Only I'm really busy with these rewrites.' . . . that bloody Rufus thinks we need, she added under her breath.

Melody's face was as pink as her velour top. In her early twenties and in her first job on a film set, she was in awe of everyone and desperate to get things right. Which was easier said than done when Rufus had her running backwards and forwards changing plans, upsetting actors and generally doing his dirty work.

'I'm really sorry, Mrs Kent, but he said he wanted you *pronto*,' she said breathlessly, 'and then he snapped his fingers!'

'Oh, he did, did he?' said Zoe grimly. *Of all the bloody*

cheek. Then catching sight of the worried expression on the runner's face she sighed and said more gently, 'It's OK, Melody. It's not your fault. I'll go and find out what he wants.'

Rufus was in his office puffing away on one of his evil-smelling cigars when Zoe arrived. The room was filled with a cloud of blue smoke and just walking in made her eyes water. For a brief second Zoe considered mentioning the smoking ban but seeing the way his mouth was twisted into a scowl as he paced up and down she decided against it. Rufus was clearly in one of his infamous bad moods.

'Hi, Rufus, you wanted—'

'This shoot is a heap of shit,' were his charming opening words. 'These so-called fucking superstars can't act to save their lives. Trinity's more wooden than Pinocchio. And as for your precious Luke Scottman – someone please tell him he's playing Osmond, not Captain sodding Kirk.'

Zoe sighed inwardly. This was typical of Rufus, acting first and thinking later. Luke and Trinity were Hollywood film actors. They specialised in big-budget blockbusters in which script and acting generally came second to special effects. Neither was an RSC actor or RADA trained, yet Rufus suddenly expected them to exhibit acting skills that Kenneth Branagh would envy.

'Where there's a name there's a blame,' Rufus was

saying, each word uttered in time with his pacing. 'If this production's a flop I'll sue their bloody arses to kingdom come!'

'You're being really hasty,' Zoe told him, perching on the corner of his desk. Rufus's circles round the room were starting to make her feel giddy. 'It's not Luke and Trin's fault there's been no time to rehearse. And besides, Henry James is hardly an easy taskmaster.'

'Who the hell is Henry James? The director of photography?' Rufus crushed the stub of his cigar beneath his cowboy boot. 'If he's giving them crap then I need to know about it.'

Zoe counted to ten then said, 'Henry James wrote *Portrait of a Lady*. He's the author, Rufus.'

Rufus looked unimpressed. 'Well, he should have made a better job of it. Can we call him up? Get him on set as a script supervisor?'

Lord give me strength, thought Zoe. 'Unfortunately, he died in 1916.'

Rufus shrugged his burly shoulders. 'Whatever. Well, if we can't have him then it's your job to sort this.'

'My job? How exactly do you figure that out?'

'You wrote the bloody script! If the actors can't understand it then you've done something wrong!'

Zoe was usually very calm and rational, but Rufus would have driven the Dalai Lama to violence. How dare he question her professionalism?

'There was nothing wrong with my script until you started to meddle with it,' she flared. 'And the only problem with the actors is that you've made so many changes they don't know whether they're coming or going!'

Rufus looked at her in surprise. 'Blimey. What's got into you? PMT?'

Argh! The man was more annoying than a tight G-string! Gritting her teeth so hard that she was amazed they didn't shatter, Zoe just about managed to stop herself from throttling him. Rufus, though, was totally oblivious.

'Birds,' he said, shaking his head. 'So hormonal. You lot should never have got the vote.'

This was Rufus's standard wind-up patter and Zoe had heard it a hundred times. She knew he wanted nothing more than to provoke an emotional reaction that would prove his point, so taking a deep breath and choosing to ignore his provocative comments she said calmly, 'If you're not happy with the rushes then we'll need to change things. How about we pause filming and give the actors today as rehearsal time. I'm sure that will make all the difference.'

'Just what I'm thinking,' Rufus agreed, his wicked sloe-black eyes narrowing thoughtfully. 'Seeing as you're so intimate with this Henry James I suggest you make a beeline for Luke Scottman and help him go through his lines.'

Zoe couldn't think of anything she wanted to do less than having to be alone with Luke for hours on end. Offering to sit with Luke and read his lines was asking for trouble: it was doing exactly this that had led to their brief relationship in Australia. He was bound to think she was trying to recreate the past and that would open an entire worm-canning plant.

'Can't somebody else do it?' she pleaded. 'Melody would jump at the chance.'

Rufus shook his dark curly head. 'No. You wrote this crap so it needs to be you.'

Zoe decided to level with him. Maybe he had a better nature she could appeal to. 'Rufus, since Luke was caught leaving my house in the small hours the press have been all over us. I think it would be much better if Luke Scottman and I had as little to do with one another as possible, otherwise somebody's bound to leak a story to the media!'

Rufus guffawed. 'They'd have to wait in line.'

Zoe goggled at him. 'Excuse me?'

'I'd be the first to tip them off. I *want* the press to get the wrong idea! It's brilliant publicity. Imagine the column inches we'd get. The sexy male lead having an affair with the director's wife. Bloody brilliant!'

Zoe's mouth was so wide open that Trin's limo could have parked in it.

'Oh, come on, you surely can't be this naïve?' scoffed

Rufus. 'Who do you think let the press know that Luke was at your house in the first place?'

Her blood whooshed through her body. 'That was you? How could you do that to me? And to Steve? You're supposed to be his best friend!'

'For Christ's sake, relax! There's no harm done. I knew good old Steve wouldn't mind. He knows the production comes first. Besides,' he added, those dark eyes sweeping her body scornfully, 'it's not as though anyone would really believe it. Why would Luke Scottman want to be with a Richmond housewife? He can have anyone.'

It was on the tip of Zoe's tongue to set Rufus straight but luckily she stopped herself in time. Rufus was a wind-up merchant, and there was no way she'd give him the satisfaction and, heaven forbid, any more ammunition.

'So be a good girl and run along and help lover-boy learn his lines,' Rufus said icily. 'Or do I need to find myself a new writer?'

Zoe swallowed her fury. She knew she was good at her job but at the end of the day she was still 'only the writer', and in the film business writers were as easy to pick up as germs on the Northern Line. Gathering what shreds of her dignity were left, she raised her chin and left his office, but with every step she took she felt Rufus's gaze burning into her back. She didn't trust

Rufus one inch and she had a hideous feeling that he knew far more than he was letting on. This thought made her very uneasy indeed.

'That scene is perfect!' Zoe placed her script on the table and smiled at Luke. 'You've totally nailed Osmond. He's hopelessly cold and repressed because that's the way he's been shaped by society but underneath he has such a depth of emotion. I can really see that in the way you play him.'

'He really does love Isabel Archer,' nodded Luke. 'The poor sod just doesn't know how to express it. Typical useless bloke, I suppose!'

Luke and Zoe had been working on his lines for the past two hours and in spite of her misgivings, it had been absolutely fine. Luke had been grateful for the help. She'd spent the three years they were in the drama society at uni soothing his artistic temperament and coaxing the best from him, so she was an old hand.

'There's just one more scene I'm stuck on,' Luke was saying, flipping through his script. 'I've tried and tried but I just don't seem to know how to play it. It's the section that starts on page 48.'

'OK.' Zoe leafed through her script but on reaching page 48 she frowned and looked up at him. 'Are you trying to be funny?' It was the kiss scene.

Luke held up his hands. 'No! No! Definitely not! I

just can't get to grips with how a cold fish like Osmond would kiss the woman he secretly adores. Seriously, Zoe, I'm not taking the mickey!'

'Hmm,' said Zoe doubtfully. There was a twinkle in his eye and however flattering it was to have the gorgeous Luke Scottman offering to kiss her, there was no way she was falling for that old ruse. 'Well, we can't have you messing this one up, it's a key scene.'

'Exactly,' said Luke, taking a step towards her.

Zoe smiled and took a step back. 'How about I send Melody to fetch Trin and I direct you both through it?'

Luke placed his chin in his hand and his denim-blue eyes narrowed thoughtfully. 'It's not so much the acting as the text,' he said slowly. 'I just can't understand why Isabel Archer would be interested in kissing Osmond. How does she feel at the moment of the kiss? Is she excited? Perplexed? Filled with pity? And why the hell does she go back to him at the end of the film when she never seems to be that enthusiastic about him in the first place? It's a kinda lukewarm love affair, isn't it? And what's the point of being with somebody unless everything about them makes you burn with longing?'

As he said this Luke looked at her and Zoe knew he was no longer talking about Osmond and Isabel. Swallowing nervously, she did the only thing she could: she focused one hundred percent on the job in hand –

explaining the script to their star actor. *That* was why she was here. Not to justify her life choices to an ex-lover!

'The main theme of this novel is freedom versus responsibility,' Zoe explained, purposely sounding like a prim schoolmarm. 'Isabel's committed to sticking with Osmond because he's the man she's chosen to spend her life with. Her sense of responsibility means that she has to give up her soul mate because she has already committed herself to another man. What she wants and longs for simply can't come into it.'

Luke snorted. 'What bollocks! Sounds to me like she's just being stubborn. If she's giving up her chance of happiness because of some misguided sense of duty then she's an idiot.'

'Isabel's married. Believe it or not some people believe in the sanctity of marriage,' countered Zoe.

'But not when you're supposed to be with someone else,' argued Luke. 'That's just stupid.'

'It's not stupid; it's called commitment!' snapped Zoe. 'Something you film stars don't know the first thing about!'

Luke glared at her. 'And what's that supposed to mean? We're not all like Elizabeth Taylor, you know.'

'My God, what are you two shouting about?'

Zoe and Luke spun round to see Trinity in the doorway, a vision of beauty in a flowing sapphire maxi dress with her golden ringlets tumbling over her bare shoulders. She looked at them in alarm. 'I could hear you rowing from next door!'

'We're not rowing!' said Zoe, then realised she had said it rather more sharply than she'd intended.

'We're not rowing,' Luke told her, 'we're debating literature.'

'Really? My, you are going up in the world,' said Trin. 'I didn't even know you could read, darling.'

Luke and Trinity glowered at each other, bristling like two alley cats squaring up for a scrap. Seeing her golden opportunity Zoe cleared her throat and tactfully suggested that now Trin was here she could direct them through the scene. Luke looked pained but Trin was touchingly grateful and before long they were galloping apace to the kiss.

'No, no! Not like that!' Zoe exclaimed when Luke dropped a chaste peck onto Trinity's collagen-filled mouth. 'You look like you're kissing your granny! This is the woman you adore; the woman you've secretly loved for years. That's what the audience needs to see. And, Trinity, you need to look as though you're filled with wonder.'

Trinity fluffed her hair sulkily. 'When a woman's kissed by a real man she can't help but look that way, honey. When I kiss my Bobby, believe me, I hear fireworks going off.'

'That'll be his arthritic hips,' muttered Luke.

'Darling, being jealous doesn't suit you,' scolded Trinity. 'When I kiss my Bobby I'm trembling for the rest of the day. That's what happens when a couple are as deeply in love as we are.'

'Since when were you in love with Bobby Roberts?' asked Luke, looking amused. 'The last time we spoke you said you'd rather drown in a vat of Botox than be with someone who has albums older than you.'

'Oh, that was before I slept with him, angel,' trilled Trinity. 'Until then I had no idea what a real man could do in bed. I never realised just how good it could be. I'll never have to fake it again.'

'Er, that's great,' interrupted Zoe, seeing an un-affected grin pass Luke's handsome face. 'But it's not getting us anywhere with this scene.'

But Trin was on a roll now and a dreamy expression settled across her perfect features. 'That's what happens when you're as deeply in love as we definitely are! In fact, this morning he proposed to me over the phone.' She paused to let that sink in. 'And I said yes!'

'Blimey,' said Luke, suddenly looking serious. 'That's a bit quick even for Bonkers Bobby. Are you sure about this, Trin? Doesn't he normally give it at least six weeks between wives?' The grin returned.

Trin wagged a finger at him. 'Now, now! His decree absolute came through two days ago and we just can't bear to be apart, so why wait? I can't go a second without thinking about him and I know he feels exactly the same way about me.' Trinity screwed up her eyes and glared at Luke. 'It's not like when *we* were together, darling!'

'Clearly not,' said Luke. 'I have my own teeth and hair, for one thing!'

'He's such a tease,' said Trin to Zoe. 'Seriously, Luke has to be the most unromantic man on the planet. Not like my darling Bobby! Not a day goes past without him sending me some flowers or a piece of jewellery. I'm just the luckiest girl alive.'

Since Trin had to be almost forty – in spite of the press releases to the contrary and fantastic surgery – 'girl' was pushing it a bit, and Zoe had to bite her cheek so as not to giggle. Besides, it was so blindingly obvious that she was laying it on with a trowel in order to make Luke jealous. But Luke didn't seem bothered at all. In fact he seemed to find the whole thing hilarious.

'I can be romantic,' he said. 'I just have to be with someone I truly love, and Fate hasn't given me the opportunity yet . . . but when it does, well, I guess then I'll be the most romantic man in the world.'

As he said this he smiled at Zoe and she felt her cheeks grow warm. Oh Lord, did he mean her or was she just being paranoid? For a second or two the atmosphere grew really uncomfortable before Trinity snorted and broke the tension.

'Well, let's just hope she speaks Klingon,' she said tartly. 'Because I know your idea of romantic, Luke Scottman, and, believe me, not every girl would be happy to stay in and watch a *Star Trek* box set!'

A rap at the door announced Melody's arrival. 'Sorry to interrupt,' she stammered, 'but there's a guy from *Scorch!* magazine here.'

'Will they ever leave me alone?' Trinity rolled her eyes. 'All right, darling, I'll give him five minutes.'

Melody's face did a great impression of a ketchup bottle. 'Er, he actually wants to see you, Mrs Kent.'

'Me?' Zoe was shocked. 'Why?'

Poor Melody looked mortified and as she spoke her voice was little more than a whisper. 'He says he has some photos of Luke leaving your house in the middle of the night and he wants your side of the story?'

'Zoe!' Fern burst into the room like a small blonde tornado. 'There was some scumbag pap guy looking for you. I told him to push off. Hope that's OK?'

Zoe slumped into her seat. 'Very OK.'

'What did he want with you, anyway?' demanded Fern, helping herself to a handful of Luke's M&Ms.

'Luke stayed over and got papped leaving my house,' Zoe said. 'Now everyone thinks something happened. But *absolutely nothing* did.' She gave Fern an earnest look. After all this time she'd hoped the non-event had passed Fern by unnoticed.

'Don't worry, you've not missed out on much,' deadpanned Trinity.

'Shall I give Max Clifford a call? You can do a full exposé in the *News of the World*,' suggested Fern through a mouth full of chocolate. ' "Cheating Housewife Beds Hollywood Star!" '

'I'm not a housewife!' cried Zoe. 'And nothing, I mean *completely nothing* happened! God! Would everyone please stop going on about it?'

'Calm down!' said Fern, looking surprised. 'I'm only teasing.'

'Because I assure you, Luke and I slept in separate bedrooms and it was all completely innocent. It was the snow and—'

'I know, I know.' Fern looked quizzically at her. When Zoe looked around she saw that everyone else was giving her the same look. 'Jeez, Zo, why are you so worked up?'

Zoe knew that her over-the-top reaction was a step too far. She'd protested too much, and now she'd raised Fern's suspicions.

12

Although an evening in the editing suite with Rufus could never be called pleasant, Zoe was glad to be able to stop thinking about the Luke situation and her fear that Fern would discover their betrayal. Zoe knew it wouldn't matter a jot to Fern that it had happened years ago, and after Fern and Luke had broken up; her friend was fiercely loyal and she'd be hurt beyond belief if she ever learned Zoe and Luke had been lovers.

It's fair enough, Zoe thought sadly as she walked down the basement corridor. I'd be devastated if Fern and Steve had had a fling during the time we'd split up. Friends just aren't supposed to do that to one another.

She wished with all her heart that Steve was around. A hug from her husband always made Zoe feel better. He was out on location with some minor cast members but hopefully he'd be back soon. Maybe she'd stop off at the deli on the way home and buy the ingredients for that rocket tortellini he liked so much. She'd splash out on a bottle of Prosecco and make a special night of it. Spending time with her wonderful husband would soon make her forget all this other nonsense.

Then, as though thinking about him had forged some kind of link, her BlackBerry beeped to announce a message from Steve. Zoe opened it with a smile, which soon faded when she read: *Another crisis! Susannah needs me to stay. Sorry hon. Love u x*

She groaned. Honestly! How many crises could one film possibly have? She'd never known anything like it. Maybe they should take the hint and quit while they were ahead.

She pushed open the door to the editing suite and poked her head round.

'Aha! The creative genius! All hail, Zoe Kent!' cried Rufus when she joined him.

Zoe exhaled with relief. This hail-fellow-well-met act must mean that he was pleased with what he'd seen so far. What a relief! The thought of reworking her script for the four hundredth time was not a happy one and if she told Trin they'd have to reshoot today's work the actress would probably go into meltdown.

'How's it looking?' she asked, sliding onto the seat next to Rufus and squinting at the bright bank of screens in front of them where Luke and Trin were paused mid-snog. Part of her still got a little tingle of excitement too when she heard her words being spoken by actors. There was something really magical about seeing your thoughts and ideas brought to life.

'Bloody great!' beamed Rufus, leaning across and planting a smacker of a kiss on her cheek. 'I don't know what you did or said to that pair but whatever it was it was brilliant!'

Zoe sat on her hands to resist the urge to wipe off the moist imprint of his lips. 'Thanks.'

'The love scene looks fantastic and you could scoop the sexual chemistry up in a ladle.' He shot a sly look at Zoe from beneath his inky lashes. 'How do you feel about *that*?'

'I don't know what you mean. If you believe all that rubbish in the press then you're even more stupid than I thought, seeing as it was you who set me up in the first place.'

'Touchy, aren't we?' Rufus pressed play in slow motion and together they watched as Luke's hand tenderly caressed the curve of Trinity's cheek. Trin had her eyes closed in rapture and Zoe was impressed with their acting skills, seeing as only an hour before the take they'd been sniping at one another.

'They look so in love,' Rufus said idly. 'I wonder if you and Luke looked like that?'

'Rufus, I don't know what you're talking about.'

'When you were in Australia?'

Zoe was suddenly cold to the core. 'What?'

'Oh, come on, don't play dumb. I know all about it.'
Rufus's voice was dangerously playful and his dark eyes
bright with malice. 'Amazing what a few beers can do to
a guy when he's in training, isn't it?'

Zoe's mind was racing. 'I . . . I . . .'

'I must admit I was taken aback. A steamy affair
doesn't exactly sit with your Goody Two-Shoes image,
does it?'

Zoe's mouth was bone dry.

'I bet Steve was surprised?'

This was a threat and it snapped Zoe out of her
inability to speak. 'You're his best friend so you must
know I haven't told Steve. It was just one of those silly
on-set things. And besides, it happened years ago when
we were having a trial separation.'

'Which it sounds like you enjoyed to the full!'
Rufus laughed. 'Oh, don't look so worried, Zoe. I won't
tell your dearest hubby. I'm the last one to talk about
morals but I must admit it's made me see you in a
whole new light.'

'Yeah, you make it sound like a red one,' muttered
Zoe bleakly, but Rufus was too busy gloating to listen to
what she might have to say.

'You must admit, though, what fun it is to have you all
here together.' He laughed. 'This'll add so much drama
and spice to the film; I just know it! It'll be amazing!
There's Luke pining for you, Trin longing for him, you

having to juggle all the secrets, and Steve—'

'What about Steve?' Zoe asked, but Rufus's mouth had shut like a clam and he just shrugged.

'Let's just say it's a little love quadrangle!' Rufus jeered. 'What fun! I can't wait to see what happens next!'

Zoe was just on the brink of telling Rufus where he could stick his quadrangle when Susannah came in, wanting to know how the rushes were looking. Rufus was still sniggering like a malevolent Puck so Zoe clawed back her cool and professional work persona and told her boss that the day's shoot had been a huge success.

'Thank God for that,' said Susannah with great feeling. 'I was starting to get seriously concerned that this production only needed feathers and cranberry sauce to complete the turkey look. What a shame Steve isn't here to see the rushes. Where is he again? I hope everything's OK now?'

Zoe was confused. 'I thought you called him away?' she said.

Susannah was no stranger to the Botox needle but this question managed to make her frown.

'No. He told me there was a family emergency. He looked really upset before he left. He said if he didn't sort this out then everything was in jeopardy.'

Although Zoe's heart was now bouncing off her

diaphragm, somehow she managed to keep herself from looking flustered.

'You know Steve!' she said, forcing a laugh. 'I expect he's up to something. He just loves surprising me.'

'Or else he's having an affair,' said Rufus. 'Joke!' But there was a gleeful look in his eye that both infuriated and worried Zoe.

'I trust Steve one hundred percent,' she told Rufus coolly once she thought Susannah was out of earshot. 'Trust is what you have to have in a marriage, Rufus. Not that you'll probably ever find out because I can't imagine anyone would be insane enough to take you on.'

Rufus shuddered theatrically. 'Marriage is for mugs. No man wants to be tied down to one woman. No wonder married men have affairs.'

'Stop this fighting now, children!' shouted Susannah. 'Honestly, Zoe, I thought—'

But Zoe couldn't help herself when it came to defending her husband. 'Steve would never have an affair!' she snapped.

'Of course not, I forgot. He's just like you,' Rufus said mildly. 'Of course he wouldn't. Silly me. After all, you guys tell each other *everything*, don't you?'

And with this parting shot he left Zoe with Susannah in the edit suite, staring at Trinity and Luke's frozen kiss, and with a horrible sense that things were about to go very, very, wrong.

'Sorry, Susannah,' Zoe said, feeling like a child who'd finally come down from a tantrum.

'Don't worry about it. It's just Rufus being a dick. I'm sure everything's fine.'

'Exactly,' said Zoe with a firm nod.

But why had Steve lied to her?

A few days later, Zoe was feeling far less pessimistic. Steve had explained why he'd been away, saying it was just something he'd had to sort out. He wouldn't be drawn as to what this was, but she had accepted his reason and had told herself she didn't need any further reassurance. This was Steve, after all; her reliable, genuine husband!

She had been worried that Rufus was going to tell Steve about her brief fling with Luke and had toyed with telling Steve herself. But every time she tried to psyche herself up, the thought of how hurt and disappointed he'd be hit her like a punch in the solar plexus. Try as she might, she just couldn't bring herself to say anything. Why hurt Steve unnecessarily? she reasoned. After all, they weren't together when she'd been with Luke and it wasn't as though the relationship had actually meant anything serious. Some things were just better left in the past, weren't they?

They were back on set and Rufus, it seemed, had

taken his mind off annoying Zoe and was focusing on the film at last. And it was paying off! This scene they were shooting now, in which Trinity's character confessed her feelings of dismay to Osmond's daughter, Pansy, brought tears to Zoe's eyes. Even though she had written every word and knew exactly what was coming next, the convincing way the actors delivered their lines made it as fresh and as meaningful as Henry James could have hoped.

That take was certainly great, Zoe thought with a surge of pride. Trin is acting her Jimmy Choos off today.

'I loved him so much,' Trinity was weeping, one slim white hand rising to dab her eyes with a lace handkerchief. 'So very much. But his egotism lay hidden like a serpent in a bank of flowers.'

'And cut!' called Steve. 'That was excellent. Well done, everyone! Especially you, Trinity,' he added giving the actress a thumbs up. 'That was awesome!'

Trinity beamed at him. 'It was good, wasn't it?'

'The best,' Steve assured her. 'OK, take a break, everyone. Back here in fifteen, please.'

Once the actors and crew had wandered away Zoe crossed the set and wound her arms around her husband's neck. 'Great work, Mr Hot-Shot Director.'

Steve lowered his head and kissed her tenderly, a kiss as soft as the brush of a butterfly's wings but so full of promised passion that her stomach turned a cartwheel.

'Why thank you, Mrs Kent,' he murmured into the crown of her head. 'Maybe we should sneak off to my office and celebrate just how well this is going?'

Zoe's heartbeat accelerated. 'Are you suggesting what I *think* you're suggesting?'

Her husband took her hand and, turning it over, grazed the inside of her wrist with his lips. 'I guess that depends on what you think I'm suggesting!'

Hand in hand and laughing, Zoe and Steve made their way to his office. Zoe couldn't remember when she'd last felt so carefree and so happy. Before they'd started filming *Portrait*, that was for sure.

Steve closed the office door behind them and then reached out to cup her face, pulling her close for a kiss that began softly before blossoming into something deeper and far more demanding. Giddy with longing Zoe forgot everything except the fact that all she wanted to do was touch and taste her husband before making love to him right there and then.

'I love you so much,' she told him.

Steve smiled down into her eyes. His own were smoky with desire.

'God, I love you too,' he said hoarsely. 'I've missed you so much, Zo.'

This was the point where, if they were in a movie, he would take her hand, lead her to the battered old sofa in the corner and kiss her until she was a puddle of desire.

Then he'd make passionate love to her and they'd hold
each other close until their racing heartbeats started to
slow. But unfortunately Zoe was living in the real world
rather than in a Mills & Boon novel, and just as Steve
reached for her hand there was a massive thump at the
door and a voice cried, 'Bollocks! Ouch! That hurt!'

Zoe and Steve looked at each other in resignation.

'Libby!' groaned Zoe.

'Is there no escape?' sighed Steve.

'Steve? Zoe?' Thud! Bang! 'I know you're in there!
Why's the door locked? Come on, open up!' Then there
was a pause and the chink of pennies dropping. 'Oh!
Sorry, guys! I'll come back!'

Steve ran his hands through his hair and pulled a
rueful face. 'The moment's kind of passed now, Lib.
Hang on, we'll let you in.'

Zoe unlocked the door, hoping that her hair wasn't too
messed up and that her lipstick wasn't half-way down her
chin.

'Sorry, Libby, we were just – um – going over the
script,' she bluffed as she opened the door.

'Yeah, right, you were shagging,' said Libby cheerfully. 'Don't look so worried, sis! I think it's great you still
do it at your age.'

Steve nearly choked in his outrage. 'I'm thirty!'

'And that's OK,' said Libby, but the pitying expression
on her face said it all. 'Anyway, never mind all that right

now. Trinity's having hysterics in her dressing room and I need you to help me calm her down. She's in floods of tears and I just can't get through to her.'

Confused, Zoe glanced at Steve. 'But the last take was fantastic.'

Steve nodded. 'It was and I told her so. What's the matter with her?'

'No idea,' said Libby. 'She was sobbing so hard I couldn't understand a word she was saying.'

'I'll go and speak to her.' Steve was almost out of the room in his haste to get to his leading lady before Libby grabbed his arm, stopping him in his tracks.

'Don't be daft. This is women's stuff!' she told him. 'Whatever it is that's wrong Trin won't want to discuss it with a man she hardly knows! Me and Zoe will go to her.'

That quickly put poor Steve in his place and he stepped back to let the two girls through.

A few minutes later, though, Zoe was desperately wishing her husband had gone to Trin rather than her. The actress was sobbing so hard that they could only make out the odd word. Her face was blotchy and her eyes so swollen it looked as though she'd been punched.

'Bobby!' Sniff. '. . . the wedding!' Sob. '. . . all over!' Howl.

'But he only proposed a few days ago,' Libby said, perplexed. 'You guys were so happy and excited. What's changed?'

Trinity opened her mouth to reply but only managed a wail. It was only when she passed a red-top tabloid to Zoe that the reason for her distress became apparent.

'Portrait of a Love Rat!' screamed the headline, and below was a grainy picture of Trinity clad only in a tiny baby-doll nightie waving farewell to a man at the doorway of her plush suite at Claridge's. Although the picture was poor it was clear that the man was leaving in the small hours, and from the way he was staring down at the floor and had a baseball cap pulled low over his face he had absolutely no right to be in Trin's suite.

No wonder Bobby Roberts was furious! Zoe didn't blame him one little bit. She was feeling pretty upset herself.

The picture might be grainy and the image of the man blurred, but Zoe would know the set of those slight shoulders anywhere. The cap was something of a giveaway too. She'd bought it herself. She clutched the newspaper so tightly that her knuckles glowed chalk-white through her flesh.

There was no mistaking this figure caught sneaking out of Trinity's room. No matter how hard Zoe tried to deny it the facts were there right in front of her.

The man leaving Trinity Duval's suite in the middle of the night was Zoe's very own husband!

14

As Trinity continued to sob and choke out her fears that Bobby Roberts would never speak to her again Zoe tried her hardest to quell a rising tide of nausea. Why had Steve been visiting Trinity late at night in her hotel room? She glanced down again at the paper she was still clasping in her trembling hands just in case her mind had been playing tricks, but no such luck: the figure sneaking out of the room was definitely Steve.

'Please, Trin, don't cry,' Libby said. 'It'll be all right.'

'No it won't!' Trinity wailed, tears dripping from her chin and splashing onto the carpet. 'Bobby will never believe that nothing happened.'

Hearing this was a relief, Zoe had to admit, because even though she trusted Steve with all her heart, seeing the grainy incriminating picture had shocked her horribly. There were probably a thousand reasons why he'd been to see the actress in the middle of the night but she couldn't think of one good reason why he would fail to mention it to her. And this was what made her stomach churn.

'Bobby just needs to hear you explain things,' soothed Libby, passing Trinity a wad of tissues. 'Besides, if he loves you then he should trust you. If he doesn't then perhaps you shouldn't be getting married after all. What's the point of a marriage without trust?'

As Trinity blew her nose Zoe reflected that Libby was right. She should trust Steve and not jump to conclusions. There was bound to be a perfectly rational explanation.

'Libby's right,' she told Trinity, suddenly feeling better. 'If Bobby loves you then he should believe you. If he doesn't then he isn't worth having.'

Trinity nodded, blotting her tears with the tissues before giving the sisters a watery smile. 'I know. But I really want this marriage to work. I *need* it to work. Otherwise I'll feel such a failure.'

'Because things didn't work out with Spotty Luke Scotty? Don't beat yourself up. Everyone knows he can't settle down,' scoffed Libby. 'He's hung up on some mystery woman; it's the worst-kept secret in the business.'

Zoe gulped. It was starting to seem that Luke really meant what he'd said to her and she felt terrible. She'd never intended to hurt him so badly. She wished she'd never taken that runner's job in Queensland.

'It's not that,' Trinity said, and glanced around, looking for any walls with ears. 'Not many people know this,' she whispered, 'but I was married once before and it didn't work out. I rushed into it, didn't think it through at all, and of course we split up. I've always felt such a failure.'

'Oh, you shouldn't. Our dad's always getting married!' said Libby airily. 'He's on his fifth wife now, isn't he, Zo?'

'Our dad isn't exactly a role model,' Zoe pointed out. She sat next to Trinity and put her arm around the actress's trembling shoulders. Zoe totally empathised with her dilemma; after all, how shaken up had she been on the hen night when Angela had predicted she'd be married twice? 'There's no shame in wanting to be married only the one time, Trinity. I feel exactly the same way. Marriage should be for life.'

'I do want to marry Bobby,' Trinity sniffed. 'I know everyone laughs because he's old and has been a bit of a hell raiser, but he really gets me and he makes me happy. After being with Luke it's such a relief to be with a man who actually wants to commit. I swear to God that nothing happened with . . . the guy in that photo.' She shot Zoe a guilty look. 'We just had something that we needed to sort out.'

Something that we needed to sort out. Zoe shivered because this was almost an exact echo of what Steve had said. But what had been so urgent that they'd had to sort it out in secret and in the middle of the night? She believed Trinity when she said that nothing untoward had taken place but nevertheless Zoe had the strongest gut feeling that something was very wrong.

'Call Bobby,' she advised. 'Tell him exactly what you've just told us. It's the best way. Starting a marriage with secrets and lies is a recipe for disaster.'

Trin gave her a weak smile. 'Thanks, Zoe. I'll do that and hopefully he'll listen. You and Steve are so lucky to have each other.'

Did Trin say that because she knows I know, thought Zoe, or because she wants Steve?

'Yeah, yeah, Zoe and Steve are an example to us all,' said Libby, not picking up on the looks between Trinity and Zoe. 'Come on, let me fix your hair and makeup. Then you can Skype Bobby and sort this out.'

Leaving Trinity in Libby's capable hands Zoe made her way back to the set. Catching sight of Steve setting up some test shots, she made a beeline for him. They had some serious talking to do and this time she wasn't going to be fobbed off with vague excuses. No, this time she wanted to know what was really going on!

'Hey, gorgeous wife, thanks for sorting Trin.' Steve smiled, abandoning the camera and stepping forward to take her in his arms. 'You know how highly strung these actors can be. You're such a talented fixer.'

But when Zoe didn't return his embrace her husband's smile soon faded.

'You've got some explaining to do,' she said in a low voice, not wanting the rest of the crew to hear. 'What were you doing visiting Trinity's hotel room the other night?'

'Babe, it isn't what it looks like!' Steve protested, looking so horribly guilty that instantly Zoe began to fear it was *exactly* what it looked like. 'It was just something that we needed to sort out.'

That phrase was so well worn it was starting to get holes in it. Zoe clenched her fists to contain her irritation.

'That's not enough,' she said. 'This time I need a proper explanation.'

Steve frowned. 'Are you saying you don't believe me? Have you any idea how insulting that is?'

Zoe stared at him in disbelief. '*You* feel insulted? My God, Steve, that's rich! How do you think I feel? There's a picture of you leaving Trinity's suite splashed all over today's tabloids!'

'You're kidding?' Steve sounded shocked. 'How on earth did they know I was there?'

'No idea, seeing as your wife didn't!' snapped Zoe. 'What's going on?'

'Keep your voice down!' Steve urged, placing what he thought was a calming hand on her shoulder. 'Everyone's looking. Can we speak about it later?'

This dismissal was enough to make Zoe really lose her cool. Enraged, she shook his hand off.

'No, Steve! I need to know now! Are you having an affair with Trinity?'

Unfortunately for Zoe, just as she said this, the music from the next studio stopped and her words rang out loud and clear. Suddenly she became aware that the cast and crew of *Portrait* were watching open-mouthed. Zoe was mortified and felt herself blush to the ends of her blonde hair.

'For God's sake, Zoe! What's the matter with you? Get a grip!' hissed Steve furiously.

'I will when you tell me the truth,' she shot back.

They glared at each other.

'Not now,' Steve said firmly. Then turning to everyone else he said, 'The show's over folks. Places for the next take, please.'

'So that's it? This is all you've got to say?' Zoe was stunned at being dismissed like this when as far as she was concerned their entire marriage was in crisis.

Steve sighed and his head fell. 'Of course not. I'm sorry.' He took her arm and gently guided her away from the set. 'Sweetheart, we can have this discussion later. It's all a huge misunderstanding anyway. I'd never ever cheat on you. I love you.'

Zoe felt her anger deflate like a popped party balloon.

This was Steve, after all! Her loyal, dependable, predictable Steve, the man who loved routine and habit, and who hated change and couldn't even alter his choice of curry, let alone lover. And the best thing about being predictable was that she knew they would make up after this row and everything would be fine between them. Better than fine. After all, they were each other's one true love; it would take more than a silly tabloid headline to get in the way of that.

It was past eight in the evening and the entire cast and crew of *Portrait* had taken over the Haven Arms in White City, a dive of a pub but very popular with the BBC employees who couldn't afford trendy wine bar prices. After a hideous day – the row with Steve just the tip of the iceberg – Zoe really needed a drink. Trinity had refused to come out of her dressing room, which had totally wrecked the shooting schedule, Fern had gone home with a migraine, leaving a junior to dress the set and Luke had ruined yet another wig. More script changes from Rufus and a long call from her sister-in-law, Charlotte, had set Zoe back even further, and now her head was thumping in time with the beat of the music booming from the jukebox.

Zoe scanned the bar but she couldn't see Steve anywhere. He'd sent her a text saying he'd meet her in the pub and that they could go for dinner afterwards to talk, and Zoe was holding him to this promise if it was the last thing she did. She was starting to feel that lately her husband had let her down far too often. She ordered herself a large class of Pinot Grigio and wove her way through the crowd, desperately searching for his sandy head. Being tall and lanky, Steve was usually easy to spot. Surely he was here?

'Have you seen Steve?' she asked Melody, who was drinking something vivid blue and nasty-looking from a bottle. Closer inspection revealed that the rest of the junior cast members were doing the same and Zoe glanced at her white wine rather sadly. Lord, she must be getting old!

'He's in the garden with Rufus, doing shots,' Melody informed her.

Zoe couldn't have been more taken aback if she'd been told her husband was wearing a basque and performing burlesque.

'That can't be right,' she said. 'Steve never does shots!'

'Steve never does shots? Yeah, right! That's a new one on me,' shrilled Trinity, who was leaning against the bar and clutching a bottle of Moët in her red-taloned hand. From the glazed look in her eyes and the way she was clutching the bar for support it was obvious she was more than a little tipsy. That must have been how they coaxed her out of her dressing room.

'Steve can drink more shots than anyone else I know,' Trinity drawled, before taking another swig from the neck of the bottle. 'He's the Tequila King!'

'Right . . .' said Zoe, feeling confused. Either Trinity was super drunk and getting Steve totally confused with someone else, or they'd had a major drinking session the other night – which would explain why he hadn't come home. Her spirits lifted at this thought.

'He'll be outside chatting to someone,' she said, 'or, knowing my husband, he'll be asleep on a bench!'

But Trinity shook her glossy blonde head. 'He'll be playing beer pong. They'll be nine glasses on each side of the table and another in Steve's hand and he'll be losing . . . on purpose.'

Was that glazed look just alcohol or was Trin on something? It would certainly explain this nonsense she was spouting.

'You don't believe me, do you?' said Trin. 'I bet you five quid I'm right.'

Zoe laughed. 'Since we're not betting Prada bags, you're on.'

Their good-natured rousting had attracted a crowd and everyone followed Zoe and Trinity outside to see who would win. The smart money was on Zoe – she was married to Steve, after all – but Trinity's smug face spoke volumes and several people decided to take the long odds.

But once outside Zoe was totally lost for words because the scene was exactly as Trinity had described it: a makeshift ping-pong table had been constructed from a picnic bench; copies of the script were being utilised as bats; glasses were lined up on the table and there was Steve with a drink in his hand and a silly grin on his face.

'Five pounds, please,' said Trinity with her hand extended.

Zoe shook her head in amazement. 'Are you psychic?'

'Maybe I am,' she slurred.

Zoe was just on the brink of demanding to be told exactly what was going on when Steve spotted her and came lolloping over to fold her into a beery bear hug. Zoe couldn't help laughing at her silly husband. 'Isn't thirty slightly too old for student drinking games?' she teased.

Steve shrugged. 'I'm losing too, but not necessarily by accident!'

'Oi! No hugging on court, that's a penalty!' yelled Rufus.

Steve spun round, then swayed from the movement. 'You just made that rule up!' But he walked over to the table and downed another shot anyway.

'I've never known you like this,' Zoe said, taken aback. She wasn't scolding him – Lord knew, Steve worked hard and she liked to see him kick back a little –

but this was a version of her husband that she'd never seen before.

'That's because you never knew Steve in the good old days,' replied Rufus, sloshing more tequila into the glasses. 'Seven-Shots Steve lives again. Woo hoo!'

'Seven-Shots Steve?' Zoe raised an eyebrow. 'That's your nickname?'

'One of them, eh, mate?' Rufus laughed, clapping him on the back. 'You never knew the old Steve, Zoe. Man! He was mental! That was the real Steve, the one I liked. We were always off doing crazy things back in the day, weren't we? What was the craziest thing you ever did, mate? Can you remember?'

A rather strange look passed between Trinity and Steve. Zoe couldn't quite make it out but it made her feel really uneasy. She felt as though she was the outsider.

Excusing herself she made her way to the ladies where she locked herself in a cubicle. Maybe I just don't know Steve as well as I thought I did, she told herself sadly. I had him pegged as sensible and predictable but that isn't the case at all! A cold hand squeezed her heart as Zoe realised that it no longer felt like she knew the man she'd married. Her Steve was an open book but this new Steve kept secrets and told half-truths. She'd thought she'd known her husband inside out but this evening another women had proven to everyone that she knew him even better. What on earth was happening to them? Tears blurred her eyes. Had she tried too hard to change Steve to fit what she'd thought she wanted from a man? He'd wanted to go away and get married but she'd said that she wanted a traditional wedding so they'd done things her way and at home. There was a spontaneous streak in Steve but maybe she'd forced him to quash it? Had she made him boring? Was he tired of their married life together?

This thought was too much and the tears fell in earnest. Zoe didn't often cry – she was normally the strong one who held everybody else together – but locked in the small cubicle she sobbed her heart out.

There was a soft knock at the door of the ladies and a hesitant voice called, 'Zo, you in there?'

Luke.

'One minute,' she called, pulling her hair out of its customary ponytail and freeing it to fall in gold ripples down her back. Hopefully the long locks would fall across her face and hide her flushed cheeks. She emerged from the cubicle, checked her face in the mirror – *Argh!* – and pasted a megawatt smile onto her face. There.

'This is a reversal, isn't it?' she said brightly as Luke peeped round the door. 'Men using the women's loo. Don't tell me you have a queue?'

'Stop it.' Luke cut straight through her façade and, striding forwards, pulled her into his arms, wrapping his around her and holding her close. 'You don't have to pretend with me. I saw what was going on out there and I know you're hurting.'

Her eyes filled. 'Please don't be nice to me. You'll make me cry.'

'Oh, Zoe.' His arms tightened and she felt his lips press against her hair. 'I'm so sorry. You don't deserve it. Steve's an idiot to treat you like that. Any guy lucky enough to be with you should be paying you attention and telling you how special you are all day long.'

Zoe tried to laugh but the sound that emerged had more in common with a sob. For a minute or two she allowed herself to relax in his arms, enjoying the feeling of being held and comforted by her friend.

'I'm sorry,' she said finally, stepping backwards and breaking the embrace. 'It's just been a seriously bad day.'

'For what it's worth,' Luke said, his sexy down-turned blue eyes crinkling at her, 'that dickhead Rufus has got poor Steve out of his skull on tequila. I don't suppose your husband even knows what day of the week it is by now! But one thing I do know, angel, is that Steve loves you.'

'You think so?' Zoe wasn't so sure any more.

Luke tenderly pushed a lock of golden hair from her face and tucked it behind her ear.

'I know so. God, how could he not? You're so beautiful, so much fun and so sweet. The guy would have to be crazy not to worship the ground you walk on.'

Zoe suddenly had a mental image of herself strolling along a red carpet while Steve prostrated himself before her. It was so funny that she started to giggle.

'That's better,' smiled Luke. 'I can't bear to see you cry.'

He's just being kind because he's a lovely guy, Zoe told herself. There was no hint of anything inappropriate. Luke was her friend. Granted, he was a stunningly gorgeous movie star to boot, but at the end of the day he was still her old uni buddy. They'd cooked spag bol together, bunked lectures to watch *This Morning* and lived on toast when their grants ran out.

For a split second she saw again that small cabin in Queensland and shivered as she remembered how he'd pulled her closer than words, saying nothing but holding her tightly and trailing quicksilver kisses along her collarbone, then lower and lower . . .

But that was a lifetime ago. She was married now to Steve, and Luke Scottman was just her friend.

So if memories of their time together in Australia were starting to seep back into her consciousness it didn't mean anything at all. Did it?

15

Zoe was feeling pretty fragile at work the following morning, and in between takes and rewriting she gulped Evian like it was going out of fashion and swore she'd never drink again. But last night had been fun! She had even ended up playing beer pong and she and Steve made more than a few public displays of affection.

Rufus, however, along with his many other faults, was one of those annoying people who didn't suffer from hangovers.

'Zoe! Hi! Come on in!' he beamed as he sat at his desk. 'Wow, may I say that you're looking particularly stunning today?'

Like the Greeks and their gifts, Zoe distrusted Rufus the most when he was being nice to her. And anyway, he was talking nonsense. She looked the antithesis of stunning this morning with her pale hung-over face, minimal makeup and her unwashed hair pulled back into a ponytail. Even her clothes matched the way she felt: black jeans, low pumps and a muted taupe sweater. Her suspicions were instantly alerted. What on earth was he after now?

'Look, babe, I really want to apologise for last night,' Rufus said, shutting the door behind him and perching on the edge of his desk. He was wearing leather trousers so tight they made Zoe wince.

'There's nothing to apologise for,' she said firmly, dragging her eyes away from the horrible sight of his groin and focusing instead on his glittering dark eyes.

'No, there is. I was a really bad influence on Stevie-boy last night. It was totally my fault he got so drunk.' Rufus shook his dark curly head. 'What can I say? It won't happen again.'

Talking to Rufus was like walking through a minefield. There was always something dangerous lurking beneath the surface and instinct told her that he was waiting for her to put a foot wrong.

'It's fine, Rufus, not a problem at all,' she said so sweetly that her teeth started to ache. 'We had* fun. Besides, old friends always revert to type when they get together.'

'You're a good sport, Zoe,' he said warmly. 'I was wrong about you.'

Talk about a backhanded compliment!

'Thanks,' she said.

Rufus leaned forward so that his sharp-cheekboned face was just inches from hers. She could practically feel the rasp of his designer stubble. Zoe caught a whiff of his heavy spicy aftershave and recoiled slightly.

'I mean it,' he said hoarsely. 'You're all right. Steve's a lucky bastard.'

Goose bumps rippled across Zoe's arms. Suddenly she was gripped by a hideous sinking feeling that she recognised only too well.

Rufus reached out and ran a stubby finger along her cheek. 'Steve's a nice guy but you need a real man.'

Zoe was frozen with horror. Rufus was so close now that she could see herself, small and pale, reflected in his inky pupils.

'Steve and I have always been good friends,' he continued huskily. 'Such good friends that we share everything. We've never held grudges when one of us borrows something that belongs to the other.'

Grabbing Zoe's hand, Rufus pulled her up hard against his hungry body. Through those tight leather trousers she could feel exactly what he had in mind and she was speechless with shock.

'I've always wanted you,' Rufus said, staring down at her with those hypnotic dark eyes. 'I wanted you the first time I saw you that day when Steve brought you to the film set and I've wanted you every day since. So how about it?'

He pushed his crotch against her and the sudden movement jolted Zoe from her stunned state. Yanking her hand away from his, she stepped back so violently that she almost fell and had to grab the chair to steady herself.

'Are you out of your mind?' she hissed.

Rufus crossed his arms and regarded her through narrowed eyes. 'You're making a big mistake.'

'You're supposed to be Steve's best friend!' Zoe cried.

Rufus snorted. 'Oh, please! Don't you think we've shared women before? Besides, you weren't so unwilling the last time, were you?'

Zoe felt sick. The incident Rufus was alluding to had happened on her wedding day. Half-way through the reception Rufus, the best man, had come to find her to offer his congratulations. Before she'd even had time to reply he'd pushed her into a dark corner and sunk his hard red lips onto hers. It was like being kissed by a sink plunger and Zoe had shoved him away with all her might and planted a sharp kick onto his shin. She'd tried hard to tell herself that Rufus had drunk too much champagne but somehow she'd always known deep down this wasn't the case.

'And you never told Steve either,' Rufus added. 'I wonder why? Was it because you were hoping for more?'

'I didn't tell Steve because you're his best friend and I knew he'd be hurt beyond belief, you moron!' Zoe said. 'And I thought you did it because you were drunk.' She pointed her finger at him with a warning. 'If you ever try anything like this again I swear to God I'll have you up on sexual harassment charges.'

Rufus's face turned red. 'Are you threatening me?'

'Bloody right I am!' yelled Zoe.

They glowered at each other. Then Rufus shrugged and wandered back to the other side of his desk. Sitting back down and hoiking his Gene Hunt-style crocodile cowboy boots onto the desk, he sighed.

'What a shame you didn't reciprocate. That would have been the perfect excuse for Steve to leave you.'

She stared at him. 'What?'

'Oh, face facts, Zoe! You're no good for Steve. You've stifled him and suffocated him from the first moment he met you. You've changed him for the worse. He's no fun any more. Last night was just a glimmer of what the real Steve used to be like.'

Zoe stared at him. She knew Rufus was trying to cover her rejection by hurting her but his cruel words were horrible echoes of some of her own recent thoughts.

'Steve used to be the wildest beast around,' continued Rufus, getting into his stride now. 'It's only a matter of time before he starts to look for a way out of his cage. I was just being a mate and trying to give him a head start.'

'By making a pass at his wife?' She shook her head. 'You need help.'

'You think? Well, I know things about good old Steve

that would make your hair curl,' sneered Rufus. He paused, enjoying every minute of dropping what he presumed would be a bombshell. 'Did you know, for example, that he's been married before?'

Now it was Zoe's turn to smirk at Rufus. 'Of course I did. As if Steve would marry me and keep a secret like that! You've got a lot to learn about adult relationships!'

Rufus's face was black with fury because now the wind was well and truly taken out of his sails.

Zoe regarded him pityingly. 'It's time you accepted that people grow up and move on, Rufus. Perhaps the reason Steve doesn't see you so much isn't because he's under my thumb but because he's outgrown you?'

He stared at her open-mouthed.

'Steve loves me and I love him,' she finished. 'Which means an idiot like you could never, ever split us up.'

And with this parting shot she stalked out of the office with her head held high, leaving Rufus fuming.

Zoe went back to her office but after the row with her producer there was no way she could focus on any work. Although the logical part of her knew exactly what nasty little game Rufus was playing, his words kept buzzing through her mind like bluebottles and soon she was starting to fret that there might be a grain of truth in them. Had she stifled Steve and forced him to become somebody he wasn't?

I have to fix things, she thought, powering down her laptop and snapping the lid shut. I can't go on like this!

Unable to focus on anything else for a second longer, Zoe abandoned her work and made her way to the set where Steve was directing a take.

'That's fantastic,' he was telling Trinity, smiling his sweet dimpled smile at the actress. 'You're doing a great job. Shall we take it from the top and roll?'

Not if Zoe had anything to do with it! Taking it from the top would mean hours could pass before Steve was free and she needed to talk to him *now*. If she had to wait then she'd probably drive herself insane.

Luckily Steve caught sight of Zoe and, seeing the worried expression, went straight to her side.

'Is everything OK?' he asked tenderly, taking her hand.

Zoe sighed. 'Not really. Steve, we need to talk.'

Without so much as even asking a question Steve told the cast and crew that they'd be breaking for an hour, even though they were in the middle of the shoot and to stop at this point would cost thousands. It spoke volumes about his feelings for her that he wanted to make up for not talking to her properly yesterday, and in spite of all her worst fears Zoe's heart lifted.

Together they headed to a nearby Café Rouge. After finding them a quiet table in the corner and ordering croque monsieurs, Steve switched off his mobile and leaned back in his chair. 'OK, Zoe. You have my full attention. What's going on?'

For the first time in their relationship Zoe felt fluttery with nerves. This was it: truth or bust.

'I need you to level with me,' she said softly, picking up a fork and twirling it thoughtfully. 'I need you to tell me the absolute truth, no matter how difficult that may be or how much you think it will hurt me.'

Steve looked puzzled. His kind hazel eyes behind the metal-framed glasses were gentle as they met her gaze. 'OK, I promise.'

Zoe exhaled shakily. 'Do I stifle you? Have I stopped you being the person you really want to be?' She paused for a moment and, thinking back to the strange moment in the pub where Trinity had seemed to know her husband better than she herself did, added, 'And is there something going on between you and Trinity?'

'What?' Steve almost choked on his Diet Coke. 'Where the hell did you get that from? Seriously, babe! Of course not! Are you still drunk?'

'Don't patronise me, Steve,' Zoe warned. 'I'm not in the mood to mess about and I'm not an idiot. You were in her hotel room the other night. She knows things about you, and you're always whispering together.'

'I'm her director,' Steve said patiently. 'Of course I talk to her.'

But as he spoke her husband started to pick at the skin around his thumbnail, an old nervous habit that warned Zoe about his state of mind. Zoe said nothing further. Instead she gazed pointedly at his hands before glancing back at him and raising her eyebrows.

'Zoe, this is really difficult for me,' Steve said finally. He removed his glasses, massaged his forehead with the heel of his hand, and then replaced them. Reaching out, he took her left hand and folded it between his, tracing the hard gold of her wedding band. 'I do love you. And whatever you may think now and later, I've never loved anyone more. You don't stifle me and you don't hold me back or any of the other things that you're worrying about.'

She squeezed her fingers. 'That's good. And Trinity?'

Steve paused and Zoe suddenly had the hideous sensation that the earth was giving way beneath her. If Steve told her he'd been having an affair with Trinity then she knew her heart would break.

'It's complicated,' he said slowly. It was as though he had to gear himself up before he could continue. 'You know how I got married in Vegas all those years ago?'

Zoe nodded.

He gripped her hand so tightly that it almost hurt. 'The woman I married . . . was Trinity.'

'What!' Zoe's eyes widened and her mind raced as

this news sunk in. 'But . . . but . . . I thought you said her name was Jane Smith?'

'It is. Trinity Duval's her stage name. She was just another wannabe actress when I met her in Vegas.'

He stopped his narrative as the waitress delivered their food and made a big show of grating black pepper everywhere. Task complete, she wished them *bon appétit* and left Zoe and Steve staring down at their food. Shock, Zoe discovered, did a great job of robbing a girl of her appetite. Maybe somebody should market it as a new diet plan.

'And you didn't think to mention this?' she said finally.

Steve looked miserable. 'I wanted to forget it. Zoe, I swear to God I never felt anything for her. Rufus and I were in Vegas celebrating the end of the first year of our film degree and things got pretty crazy. You know how Rufus can be.'

More than you realise, Zoe thought grimly.

'We were hammered,' Steve continued. 'We met a couple of girls in a bar and the next thing I remembered was waking up next to Jane who had a ring-pull on her finger and a marriage certificate in her handbag. I know I should have told you the truth but I didn't want to upset you.'

'I've been more upset thinking you were having an affair,' Zoe said. 'Especially when you were visiting her hotel room at night.'

Steve groaned. 'That was only because she was having a major panic. When Bobby Roberts proposed Trinity wanted to double-check that our marriage really was annulled. I went to reassure her that it definitely was. I did the paperwork myself.'

'So that was what you had to *sort out*!' Zoe couldn't believe how relieved she was.

Steve should have told her but she understood why he'd tried to protect her by keeping his ex-wife's identity a secret. She was so sensitive about his first marriage and it wasn't a topic that they readily discussed.

'I'm so sorry,' Steve said. He looked so pale and drawn that Zoe's heart went out to him; he must have been under so much strain. She leaned across the table and touched his cheek. 'It's OK, Steve. I understand.'

'No more secrets. That's a promise.' He turned his head and brushed her hand with his lips. 'What did I do to deserve you?'

'Seven-Shot Steve may not know when to stop but sensible Steve knows how to marry well,' quipped Zoe.

'I don't think we'll be seeing Seven-Shot Steve again. Hangovers are far too painful when you hit your thirties.'

'Shame, he sounded like a popular guy,' she teased, but Steve shook his head.

'No, believe me, he was an idiot.'

Relief restored both their appetites and they tucked into their food, chatting easily about the production. In the taxi back they snuggled up and kissed like teenagers, and Zoe could hardly wait to get her husband home. They had some serious catching-up to do!

'What brought on all this stuff about stifling me, anyway?' Steve wanted to know, and in between kisses Zoe told him all about Rufus placing doubt in her mind, making comments about Trinity and finally how he'd made a pass at her that morning.

'He did what!' Steve was furious. 'How dare he? Right, I'm through with him! I'm going to make sure you're OK, babe, and then he and I are going to have serious words. Like we said, no more secrets.'

Zoe gulped. The only secret she had left was her fling with Luke. She'd have to tell Steve now if they were going to stand a chance of putting their marriage back on the right foot. As the taxi drew up outside Television Centre and Steve paid their fare she psyched herself up to tell him. He'd be hurt and probably angry but it was the right thing to do.

'Steve—' she began, but was interrupted by the shrilling of his mobile.

'Sorry,' grinned Steve. 'I knew switching it back on was a mistake, but I'd better take this. It's the mighty Susannah.'

Zoe busied herself sorting out her hair and makeup – oh Lord, was that a stubble rash blooming across her cheeks? – but when she turned back to her husband she was horrified to see that he was ashen. Something awful must have happened!

'What's wrong?' she asked.

Steve looked down at her and his eyes were dark against the pallor of his skin.

'It's the production,' he said in a stunned voice. 'It's going to be shut down. We're being sued!'

16

Susannah paced up and down her office. Smoke wasn't yet coming out of her ears but if she carried on with this furious pacing it would soon be rising from the floorboards. Unlike Steve, who was pale and shocked, Susannah was crimson with rage and looked ready to explode at any moment. Her language threatened to turn the air blue too. Thank goodness the rest of cast and crew were locked out! If they saw their usually ice-cool co-producer in this state they'd be really worried, and the last thing Zoe needed was a panicking team.

'That little shit Rufus,' she said for the umpteenth time. 'I am going to wring his scrawny neck for this.'

Zoe's eyes slid to meet Steve's gaze and in spite of everything he winked at her.

'Get in the queue,' he told Susannah.

'So what's happened?' Zoe asked. 'Who's suing us?'

Susannah halted mid-pace. 'That idiot Rufus has been slagging off our previous stars, the ones that pulled out. The press has run with it and now they're suing us.'

She threw a sheaf of papers at Steve, who started to scan through them.

'But that's not our fault,' Zoe cried. 'We're not responsible for what Rufus says.'

Steve slumped against the desk. 'But we *are* responsible for changing their contracts.' He held up the contracts for Zoe to see. 'Their pulling out could be construed as our fault.'

'Rufus was in charge of the contracts,' Susannah snapped. 'I've just been examining them and it seems Rufus altered every one so they contained ridiculous caveats. There was no way any self-respecting actor would *not* pull out.'

'So all those diva-ish demands Rufus said they were making was just lies?' Steve shook his head in disbelief.

'He's up to something.' Susannah dashed her fist against her hand in frustration. 'But what?'

'It was all part of a big ruse to get publicity for the film,' Zoe explained. 'Once the original actors had quit he flew in two stars who have history with each other, *and* the director and scriptwriter. And if it breaks Steve and me up in the process then so much the better because that way he gets his friend back to himself.'

'That sounds exactly like the way he operates,' fumed Susannah. 'He's such a little weasel. But what I don't understand is why he thinks Luke being here should bother you, Zoe? You don't have history with Luke, do you?'

'No, nothing like that,' Steve answered for Zoe. 'Luke and Zoe were friends at university.' Zoe gulped. She really needed to tell Steve the truth about her and Luke. Preferably when their boss wasn't in the room, though.

'I'm going to find Rufus and see what the hell's going on,' Steve decided. 'We need to make some decisions soon.'

'Don't hit him,' said Susannah. 'That's my job.'

While Steve went to find Rufus, and Susannah went to see the Head of Entertainment, Zoe perched on the desk and read through the letter from Rufus's lawyer. Relief flooded through her veins. Closer and calmer reading seemed to indicate that it was Rufus personally who was being sued rather than the production company. As far as she could tell, the filming should be able to continue once they'd sorted out Rufus's mess. If she explained all this to the crew it would allay their fears and hopefully things would calm down a little. They were bound to have noticed the gaggle of reporters outside the studio and by now rumours would be flying.

'What's happening?' Melody asked as soon as Zoe emerged from the office. 'Is it true, the film can't go on?'

Zoe placed a calming hand on her shoulder. 'It's going to be fine, Mel. I promise. If you'd be a star and get everyone gathered on the set I'll tell you what I know.'

A smile stretched across Mel's face. 'I knew you could

fix this, Zoe! Everyone's in such a panic. We're all terrified we'll lose our jobs.'

'That won't happen, I promise. Now go!' Crossing her fingers behind her back, Zoe made her way onto the set. Standing on a chair, she waited until everyone was assembled. Telling herself this was no different from being Head Girl all those years ago and there was no need to be nervous, she smiled at her colleagues and began.

'Thanks for giving me a few minutes, everyone. I know that you've all heard some pretty wild rumours that filming's being axed.'

A few heads nodded and somebody called out, 'Are they suing us?'

Zoe held up her hands for hush. 'There is a lawsuit, that much is true, but it's not against the production company so there's no need to worry. Everything is going to be fine. We just need to get our heads down and press on with production, ignore this lawsuit and most of all ignore the paparazzi. We have a fantastic production here and that's all we need to focus on. BAFTAs, here we come!'

There was a cheer at this and a ripple of applause. Then Nick, the assistant director, called for the cast members of the next scene and things went back to normal. Or rather as normal as they could while both producers and the director were missing. Heaving a sigh of relief that meltdown had been avoided Zoe escaped to her broom cupboard and sank onto her desk. She was exhausted. This was turning out to be the day from hell.

When Luke knocked on her door, holding a bottle of Scotch and two glasses, Zoe felt like her prayers had been answered. Whatever she'd said just a few hours ago about never drinking again, she needed one now.

'You look like you could do with this,' Luke said cheerfully, sloshing a generous measure of whisky into a tumbler and handing it to her. 'That was some speech you just made.'

'Has it done the trick?' Zoe wanted to know. As a member of the cast Luke was a good barometer of how everyone was feeling.

'They've all calmed down a treat,' he said. 'But what's really going on?'

'Rufus has only landed himself with a writ. The man's a liability. How he's got this far in the industry is beyond me.'

Luke shrugged. 'It's not what you know but who you know, isn't it?'

'He certainly seems to know all about our business,' Zoe said. 'Honestly, Luke, what were you thinking, telling him our history? He's only gone and used that little gem to try and get more publicity for the film.'

Luke stared at her. 'What?'

'That's why he got rid of the previous stars and hired

you and Trin; he wanted to cause friction and he had some weird notion that something would happen between you and me because of our past.'

He said nothing but two bright spots of colour stained his high cheekbones.

'What are you looking so guilty for?' she demanded.

Luke drained his drink. 'I'm going to level with you, Zoe. I was kind of hoping for that myself.'

Zoe felt an unexpected flutter of butterflies in her tummy. 'What?'

'I'm not going to lie about it,' Luke said slowly, his eyes as blue as bright-burning gas flames as they met hers. 'I only took this job because I saw you were working on the film. I turned down a really lucrative movie deal.'

His soft low voice and that intense gaze held her spellbound.

'I don't know what to say,' she whispered.

'Don't say anything,' he said with a wry smile. 'There's nothing to say. No woman since has been able to hold a candle to you. It killed me when you left me in Australia.'

She hung her head. 'Luke, I'm so sorry. I'm not proud of how I behaved. I guess I wasn't quite myself. I'd only just split from Steve.'

'And I was your rebound fling?' Luke looked disbelieving. 'Sorry, but I don't buy that. What we had was real. I know it and I think that deep down you do too. Zoe, I love you.'

For a moment they were both silent, both thinking about the long hot nights and the limb-melting kisses. Then Luke sighed. 'I'm not being fair. You're happily married to Steve, I know that, and I shouldn't even be having this conversation with you. I'm glad you're happy and Steve's a great guy.'

Zoe felt terrible. 'Luke, I—'

'No, seriously, Zoe, I'm glad you're happy. I just wish it could have been with me. That's why I didn't come to your wedding. I could have put off my filming commitments. But I couldn't have borne seeing you walk down the aisle with another man. I only hope Steve knows just how lucky he is. I'd give up all my fame and wealth in a heartbeat to change places with him. Even for a few moments.'

Luke placed his glass on the desk, then ducked his head and gave her a feather-light kiss on the cheek.

'I'm with Steve,' she whispered.

'I know, and I will never get in the way of that,' Luke promised, his smile not effective at hiding his pain. 'But if Steve ever lets you down then I'm always there for you, just remember that.'

And then he returned to the set, leaving Zoe lost in thought at her desk, one hand touching the place where Luke's lips had grazed her cheek while his declaration of love spooled round and round in her mind like an edit-suite malfunction.

Luke Scottman was in love with her. But she loved Steve! She really, really did. There was no doubt of that in her mind whatsoever, but Luke's feelings for her and Rufus's knowledge of them were starting to make her feel very nervous.

The sooner she told her husband the truth about her past relationship with Luke, the better.

17

Feeling unsettled after Luke's declaration, Zoe needed nothing more than the sound of Steve's voice. She also knew she had to tell him the truth about Luke – that confession was well overdue!

Her fingers hovered over the keys of her BlackBerry for a second. Then her resolve hardened and she pressed the speed-dial key. This had to be done. Steve had to hear the truth from her before somebody else told him.

But when Steve answered it was soon clear his mind was still occupied with Rufus.

'I can't find Rufus anywhere,' was the first thing he said to her. 'He won't answer his phone. He's not at his flat. I've no idea where he is.'

'I have,' she said. 'The Haven Arms. Where else?'

'Will you come with me?' asked Steve. 'I might need you to stop me from wringing his neck.'

Half an hour later they were in the Haven Arms. At a table in the back Rufus was slumped onto his shoulder with a row of different-sized glasses lined up in front of him. Empty glasses.

His black gypsy curls were lank with sweat, his face a horrible pea green and he looked like he'd spilled a drink down his crimson shirt. Even the tight leather trousers were looking rather sorry for themselves, being scuffed about the knees from a tumble onto the pavement.

'Rufus.' Steve's voice was stern.

Rufus swung round to see them and his face fell. Then his body fell and he clung to Steve like a drowning man would to a life raft.

'Steve, it's over, man! I'm going to be sued! No one will employ me ever again. After all I've done for the business, the business just spits in my face when I make one tiny . . .'

With every drunken word he uttered Zoe felt herself growing more and more furious. How typical of Rufus that he was only worried about himself. He didn't give a monkey's that his shady dealings could have jeopardised the entire production and cost countless people their jobs. Nor did he seem bothered that he'd been doing his best to split her and Steve up.

Steve and Zoe took either side of him and walked him back to the studio. All the while, Rufus was complaining about the unfairness of his situation. By the time they arrived back at Television Centre, Zoe was ready to throttle him. She just hoped she could resist long enough to deliver him to Susannah. The older woman's wrath was legendary in the industry. She didn't shout but paced like a tiger sizing up its prey before springing in for a deadly attack. Personally Zoe couldn't think of anyone who deserved the treatment more than Rufus.

'What the hell were you thinking, risking the reputation of the BBC by altering contracts after they'd been signed?' was her opening gambit when Steve marched Rufus in. Springing up from her chair, she began her famous pacing while firing off a volley of questions each of which was more pointed and probing than the last. As she spoke and paced, the cast and crew on set crept closer to see what was happening.

'Maybe we should go into my office?' suggested Rufus nervously. He was starting to sober up as the true seriousness of the situation sunk in, and his dark eyes slid longingly to the office door.

But Susannah wasn't having this. 'There's nothing I'm going to say that can't be said in front of our colleagues,' she told him coolly. 'Besides, I think quite enough has gone on in secret behind that door.'

'So this is the thanks I get for raising the profile of this shitty film, is it?' Rufus's top lip curled into a sneer. 'Do you really think Luke and Trinity would have signed if it wasn't for me? You can't buy that kind of publicity, you know.'

'We can't afford your kind of publicity,' hissed Susannah. 'This lawsuit could cost thousands. But the damage to the BBC's reputation is even more costly.'

Rufus shrugged, then swayed dangerously. Automatically Steve was at his side to steady him.

'Cheers, mate,' Rufus slurred. 'At least I still have you on my side. I only did all this to help you.'

Steve shook his head in confusion. 'Rufus, how was a lawsuit supposed to help me out?'

'Not the lawsuit! Duh, sometimes, mate, you are so slow.' Rufus clutched Steve's shoulder and put his face so close to Steve's that Zoe thought it a miracle her husband wasn't asphyxiated by alcohol fumes. 'I wanted to set you free. I thought if Trin was here you might start remembering how good things were in Vegas and how much fun we had back then.'

Steve was perplexed. 'Rufus, I hardly remember anything about our time in Vegas. That was the whole problem!'

'No, *she's* the problem,' hissed Rufus, pointing at Zoe. There was such venom in his dark eyes that she recoiled. Whatever had she done to make him hate her so much?

'She's changed you! Since you met her you've become a right bloody nancy, with your nights in and your dinner parties!' Rufus spat.

'We always invited you,' Zoe said, hurt. 'You were always welcome to join us.'

Rufus rounded on her with such fury that she stepped back. 'As if I wanted to spend my time with you and your pathetic friends! I wanted my wingman, Steve, back.'

'You're mad,' Steve said slowly. 'I've never heard anything so crazy in my life! Zoe's my wife, Rufus! I love her and I want to be with her. She hasn't forced me to do anything. It's all been my choice.'

Rufus glowered at him. 'Ten years of friendship and you chose her over me? Mate, if you knew what she was really like you'd be off like a shot.'

'This is insane,' Steve said angrily. 'I love Zoe and nothing you can say or do will change that or split us up. Can't you get that into your thick skull?'

'Really?' Rufus raised his dark eyebrows. 'Nothing?' His eyes, bright with malice, slid to Zoe and she froze. 'Not even if I told you she and Luke Scottman have been lovers?'

'What!' Steve looked stunned. Then he shook his head. 'Oh, no you don't. I know your game and I'm not falling for it, so just give up. Zoe and I don't have secrets, do we, babe?'

Zoe felt her face burn. Oh, no. Not like this, she prayed. Please God, don't let me have to tell him in this way.

'Babe?' Steve echoed when she failed to reply. A look of horror etched itself across his features and he suddenly seemed to age ten years in as many seconds. 'Christ, Zoe. Tell me he's making it up? Please?'

Feeling as though the room was revolving very fast, Zoe cried, 'It wasn't anything serious, Steve! You and I weren't together at the time and it only lasted—'

'What?' said Steve, sounding shocked and hurt in equal measure.

'What?!' A cry from the back of the crowd interrupted her explanation. Zoe's heart plummeted into her L.K. Bennetts. She knew that voice. Sure enough, seconds later Fern elbowed her way through to the front of the room. Her blue eyes glittered with tears and her small heart-shaped face was pale with shock. Even her jaunty ringlets seemed to droop. 'You and Luke were together? When?'

'Fern, it wasn't—'

'How could you?'

The betrayal in Fern's face felt like barbed wire being dragged through Zoe's insides.

'Fern, it meant nothing,' she tried to explain but Fern just backed away, her hands raised and tears now running down her cheeks.

'I don't want to hear it!' she sobbed.

Spinning on her heel, Fern pushed her way through the silent crowd. For a few seconds they could hear her sobs, then all was still. Zoe looked in despair from the empty space Fern had left to Steve and had never felt so torn in her life. Who did she go to first? Her husband or her dearest friend?

'Follow Fern,' Steve said in a cold voice. 'No, I mean it; go to her,' he insisted as Zoe hesitated. 'I don't want to be near you right now.'

Close to tears herself, Zoe set off at a sprint and finally tracked Fern down by following the distant sound of weeping. Arriving at a lavish nineteenth-century boudoir set she found Fern curled up on the bed and sobbing into a damask pillow.

Sitting down next to her, Zoe tentatively reached out and touched Fern's shoulder.

'Hey,' she said softly. 'I know you don't want to see me, but I really need to explain.'

Fern looked up. Her pretty face was blotchy with grief and the betrayal in her eyes was enough to break Zoe's heart.

'What's to explain?' she asked in a choked voice.

Zoe sighed. 'Everything, I think. Fern, please believe me when I say that I never meant to hurt you. The thing with Luke . . . well, it just happened.'

Fern sat bolt upright and shook her head vehemently. 'That's crap, Zoe. Sleeping with your best friend's boyfriend doesn't just happen!'

'But you and Luke had split up by then,' Zoe tried to explain. 'And Steve and I had broken up too. It was just after he'd told me about his first marriage. I was so hurt and so upset that I just took off. I went to Australia to work on a shoot and it was pure coincidence that Luke happened to be there too.'

Fern wiped her eyes on the corner of the cushion. 'So you thought you'd shag him, did you? I suppose you'd always secretly wanted him and all the time he was with me Luke had felt the same way? Isn't that how the script usually goes?'

'No, of course not! Luke had never meant more to me than just a friend. But I was so unhappy and confused and it was such a comfort to have him there. He listened while I talked about Steve. He was a good friend to me at a really awful time in my life.'

'And then you slept with him,' said Fern bitterly.

'It wasn't like that,' said Zoe helplessly. 'He was so sweet and so kind that—'

'Oh, please stop,' Fern snarled. 'I bet you both had a good laugh about me. Silly little Fern. Just as well she's on the other side of the world.'

Appalled, Zoe cried, 'We'd never have said that! In fact the whole thing barely lasted two weeks.'

'Two weeks?! It shouldn't have lasted two seconds!'

'I know! I couldn't live with knowing that I'd done something that could hurt you so badly, and realising how easy it is to make such whopping mistakes showed me that I had to forgive Steve. I quit the job, left Australia and I hadn't laid eyes on Luke until a few weeks ago!'

Fern raised her eyes, as blue and wet as rain-drenched bluebells, and the look of hurt and anger in them took Zoe's breath away.

'How dare you compare what you did to Steve's stupid, drunken Vegas thing! Steve was drunk whereas you knew *exactly* what you were doing. And besides, Steve told you about the wedding, didn't he? If Rufus hadn't have shot his mouth off just now you'd have kept your fling with Luke a secret forever! God! You make me sick! Some bloody friend you turned out to be! Luke was the love of my life!'

'That's not true,' Zoe shot back, stung. 'And you know it. You've found your soul mate.'

'Stop trying to wriggle out of it,' Fern said sharply. 'Luke was my first love. When we split up I thought I'd die of grief. If it hadn't been for you . . .' She choked up for a second, then managed to regain her composure. 'How ironic! All the time you were comforting me you were plotting to have him for yourself!'

'That's not true!' Now Zoe was crying too. 'Fern, I can't believe you'd think I could do that. Surely you know me better?'

But Fern just shrugged. 'I'm starting to think I don't know you at all.'

'But I'm your best friend!'

Fern curled her lip. 'One who runs off with the man I loved. Yeah, some best friend you turned out to be. I'll never forgive you, Zoe. Never. From now on just stay away from me. I can hardly bear to look at you!'

She leaped up from the bed and ran from the set, leaving Zoe staring after her in despair. Fern was famous for her fiery artistic temperament but this outburst felt entirely different. Zoe had a horrible feeling that this time Fern meant every word she said. Heavy with despair Zoe decided to give her friend the space she so clearly needed. It was time she went to try to explain herself to Steve. . . .

Unlike Fern, Steve was calm and collected, but the distance in that cool control was somehow worse than anger and Zoe found herself wishing he'd rant and rage at her instead. That night, after all the explanations were done, they lay in bed and rather than their usual smooch and curling around one another before drifting into dreamland, there was a gap between them. It was only inches wide but it may as well have been miles. Zoe knew that Steve was awake but she didn't dare try to speak again. Instead she too pretended to be asleep and they both stared up at the ceiling, aware of the huge secrets they'd been keeping from one another. In the silence and darkness Zoe's perfect relationship suddenly seemed very far from perfect, and tears slipped down her cheeks and soaked into the pillow. Steve must have heard her muffled sobs but made no move to comfort her. Instead he turned on his side, offering her just the view of his back, and leaving her bereft and lonely.

Zoe closed her eyes in silent despair. In spite of all her hopes and good intentions it seemed Angela had been right all along: maybe they were destined for the divorce courts after all.

18

At Anvil Hall the early morning drizzle had lifted to reveal the arrival of the vast contingent of Britain's celebs. The famous Gretna Green venue had never seen so many stars before, and camera flashes lit up the grey day like lightning as a myriad of A-listers sauntered from their stretch limos and into the assembly room. Trinity had decided to take advantage of the few unexpected days off that Rufus's shenanigans had granted them and get married on a whim. Somehow she'd managed to fly her Hollywood friends over. Watching them arrive, all Wotsit tans and dazzling white teeth, Zoe supposed that if you had a private jet then short notice wasn't really an issue.

'Oh my God!' Libby shrieked, clutching Zoe's arm so tightly that the nail marks would remain for days. 'It's only Brad bloody Pitt getting out of that limo with Luke! I'm going over!'

'You are not!' Grabbing her sister's arm, Zoe yanked her back. 'You're spoken for, remember?'

'But it's *Brad Pitt*!' grumbled Libby. 'And he knows Luke! Can you believe it?'

'Not really,' admitted Zoe, glancing over to where Luke, blond and heart-stoppingly gorgeous in a morning suit, was laughing with the world's most handsome man. Although Luke was serious competition.

Sensing her gaze, Luke looked across and their eyes locked. Zoe looked away hastily, hoping he couldn't tell what she was thinking. Something crackled in the air between them and her heart rate suddenly accelerated. Whatever it was, and however inappropriate it was, she knew Luke felt it too.

'Oh. My. God. They're coming over!' shrieked Libby, as sure enough Luke waved at the sisters and started to head in their direction with Brad in tow. Zoe felt faint but not because of Brad; in fact, he hardly figured in her tangled thoughts. All she could think was that if Steve caught her chatting to Luke it would confirm all his worst suspicions and also fuel enough rumours to sustain the cast for the rest of the shoot. She was relieved when Luke was diverted by another limo depositing the Bollywood superstar Dash Suri. Dash was an old friend of Luke's and had worked with Libby too and, poor Brad forgotten, Libby tore over to greet him, shrieking and hurling herself into his arms.

'This doesn't seem real, does it?' remarked Susannah, crunching across the gravel in spiky scarlet Manolos.

Pausing to adjust her enormous hat, she stood with Zoe for a moment and together they watched as more stars arrived and Bobby Roberts's burly security guards battled to hold back the press and excited onlookers.

'Total and utter madness,' the older woman continued. 'Still, as our dear friend Rufus would say, it's all good publicity for the production.'

'I feel like I'm in a virtual reality version of *OK!* magazine,' Zoe admitted as she watched Peter Andre climb out of a black BMW 4×4. 'I'll wake up in a minute.'

The whole day was starting to take on a rather surreal quality. From the movie stars decked in PVC macs with Gucci and Versace underneath, to the bevy of rock legends Bobby had invited, Zoe felt as though she was having a strange dream. Sharon and Ozzie had already sailed by to take their seats in the huge red-brick building, and Brian May was tuning up inside. Add to this the bizarre fact that Trinity had insisted Zoe and Libby were her bridesmaids and there you had it: one of the weirdest days of Zoe's life was underway.

'Isn't Dash lush?' Libby said, rejoining her at the door. 'Those eyelashes are so wasted on a guy! I had a class teenage crush, thank God, unlike some, who fancied Boyzone!'

'Mmm.' Tuning out Libby's chatter, Zoe glanced down at her list of who should be sitting where. To be honest it wasn't a list anymore but a highly sophisticated colour-coded spreadsheet that she'd made last night. Never one to take on a job half-heartedly, Zoe used her organisational skills to the full and now one glimpse of her clipboard told her who was with the bride or groom, who was a celebrity and who was press. Trin had especially requested that ugly people were seated behind pillars but this was a step too far even for Zoe's fixing talents.

So far things had gone pretty much according to plan but now the cast and crew of *Portrait* were arriving and the looks they gave Zoe were colder than the Scottish wind. Zoe knew that they'd closed ranks and were siding with Fern and, although she understood why, it still hurt. Biting her lip hard she pretended to be totally absorbed in her clipboard until they'd passed.

'Are you OK? I know they're giving you a hard time,' whispered Libby.

Zoe sighed. 'I'll survive. Anyway, today isn't about me. The other stuff will just have to wait.'

She was right; there was hardly a minute to think once the paps descended in style from *HIYA!* magazine and were snapping away and asking her to smile. This had to be the most exciting thing that had ever happened to Gretna Green. Helicopters packed with press buzzed overhead and somewhere just beyond the gate some paps were having a scrap with the security men.

'It's a bit different to your wedding, isn't it?' Libby

remarked as she signed the name 'Nicole Kidman' with a flourish in an autograph pad and handed it back to a delighted woman.

'My wedding was wonderful,' said Zoe wistfully. It really had been the happiest day of her life. How had things managed to go so wrong so fast?

'It was perfect, not like this bun fight,' agreed Libby.

'Perfection isn't everything,' Zoe said sadly, remembering what Steve had said. He'd been right too. If only she'd realised it then.

'Cheer up, dear,' said an old lady kindly as she tottered past Zoe on her way to the hall. 'Your turn will come. I'm sure a girl as pretty as you will be a bride one day.'

Libby laughed and Zoe joined in. She *should* be more cheerful. At least she had been a bride and had married a lovely man. Of course Steve was annoyed about the Luke thing. She should have told him, she knew that, but they'd work it out. Nobody ever said that marriage was easy. It was about commitment and hard work. That's what the 'for better for worse' line was all about. She and Steve would get through this. They'd been together too long and shared too much to throw it all away.

Zoe's train of thought was rudely interrupted by the arrival of the bright purple souped-up 1967 Ford Mustang Fastback. Bobby Roberts stepped out of the garish vehicle to rapturous applause looking every inch the rocker in his purple suit, snakeskin boots and shirt slashed open to the waist in order to display salt-and-pepper chest hair. Even though it was a cloudy morning his eyes were shielded by enormous shades and as he walked to the church he gave the cheering group the *rock out* hand signal.

'Lord,' hissed Libby in Zoe's ear, 'he looks like Iggy Pop's granddad!'

Bobby swaggered along the gravel path, shaking hands with the crowd and even planting a smacker onto the cheek of a doddery old lady who practically swooned with joy.

'He is perfect for Trinity,' giggled Libby. 'He overacts nearly as well as she does!'

Then the groomsmen alighted from the next car and, to Zoe's surprise, one of them was Steve. His tall rangy body was made for a morning suit and she swallowed, unable to stop thinking about the last time she'd seen him outside a church and dressed for a wedding.

'Wake up, darlin'!' Bobby Roberts snapped his fingers under her nose and jolted her from her reminiscences. 'Are they ready for Bad Bobby?'

'Ready and waiting,' Zoe assured him. 'Best of luck.'

Bobby didn't need luck, he was buoyed up by good spirits and (judging by his breath) a good slug of whisky too. Grinning like a Hallowe'en lantern he bowled on into the church, pausing in all the doorways to pose for the cameras.

Steve walked by in the procession and smiled at Zoe, a slow sexy smile that melted her insides like sunshine on a snowman.

'Hello there, wife,' he whispered.

'Hello, husband,' she whispered back.

Steve's hand slipped to caress her waist and he gave her a squeeze. 'It's going to be OK,' he said gently. 'We'll work this out.'

'Do you really mean that?' Zoe asked, her hopes soaring like a loose hot-air balloon.

'Listen, I'm not happy about what happened with you and Luke but I kind of understand why it did and I know we weren't together at the time,' he told her. 'We'll get through this.'

As the bride's limo drew up and the paps surged forwards Steve bent to kiss Zoe tenderly.

'I'll meet you afterwards,' he promised, 'and we'll talk – *really* talk. But right now, Chief Bridesmaid, I believe you have a bride to attend to!'

Five minutes later a harassed Zoe and Libby had managed to herd Trinity through the hordes of paps. Although she was wearing a dress so shockingly pink and full even Katie Price would think twice about it, Trinity still looked stunning. Her hair was a golden sheet down her back and her eyes sparkled even more brightly than the ten thousand Swarovski crystals that covered her wedding dress.

Together, they walked down the aisle. Zoe would have felt nervous but all eyes were on Trin. And when the bride joined Bobby at the altar Zoe couldn't help but well up. OK, so it wasn't really her kind of wedding, but it was romantic. When Bobby reached out and took Trinity's hand he looked at her with such adoration that any cynical thoughts she'd harboured about publicity stunts vanished. The service was short, ten minutes at the most, and finally the vows were exchanged and fifty grand's worth of diamond-studded eternity ring was nestling on Trinity's finger.

'I now pronounce you man and wife,' announced the celebrant. Then he grinned at Bobby. 'You may kiss the bride.'

The congregation broke into applause as Bobby swept Trinity into his arms and proceeded to stick his tongue down her throat like a teenager.

'Let's hope his false teeth don't come out,' giggled Libby, and Zoe had to clamp her lips shut to stop herself from laughing.

Out of the corner of her eye Zoe saw a man burst into the hall, running and yelling.

She nudged Libby. 'What's he saying?'

The congregation finally caught on to the disturbance at the back of the hall and went quiet.

'Stop the wedding!' shouted the man, who Zoe didn't recognise.

Racing to the front of the church, he paused next to the celebrant and flashed an ID card. 'Ricky Ellis, *Daily Record!*'

The celebrant, an old man who made Ian McKellen look sprightly, frowned and said, 'You'd better have a jolly good reason—'

Ricky Ellis looked smug as he interrupted him. 'This wedding is illegal!'

Coming up for air and releasing Trinity so quickly that she would have toppled over if her dress hadn't been so huge, Bobby roared: 'Fucking press! Get out, you scum!' and would have launched himself at the reporter if Steve hadn't swiftly moved to hold him back.

'Calm down, mate,' said Steve, but Bobby was beyond listening.

'Calm down?' he was yelling. 'That little rat interrupts my wedding and you're telling me to calm down? I don't think so, man.'

Ricky Ellis was backing away. Although a fit-looking man in his early thirties he wasn't about to stick around to witness first-hand Bobby Roberts's famous temper.

'I've been doing some digging!' Ricky said breathlessly. Delving into the satchel across his chest he pulled out a sheaf of papers, which he flourished gleefully.

'Trinity Duval, or should I say Jane Smith, is still married to someone else!'

A collective gasp of horror rippled through the congregation. There was a whooshing sound in Zoe's ears and the tiled floor suddenly seemed to pitch and roll like the deck of a ship. Oh dear Lord! If Trinity was still married, then it was Steve she was still married to.

'You what?' growled Bobby.

'She's married to another man,' repeated Ricky Ellis triumphantly. 'Trinity Duval's a bigamist and I've brought a policeman with me to arrest her.'

Trinity started to wail and screech. 'Bobby! Tell him it isn't true!'

'Don't cry, my darling,' cried Bobby, sweeping his bride into his arms and crushing her against his scrawny chest. 'We'll run away together and be fugitives like . . . Bonny and Clyde.'

'But I'm not married to anyone else,' sobbed Trinity. Her thick mascara had run down her face and her tears splashed onto the floor. 'I was married to that man.' She pointed across the room at Steve. 'He told me the marriage had been annulled,' she continued tearfully and a note of accusation crept into her voice. 'He promised it was fine for me and Bobby to get married.' She paused and looked as though she was working on a maths problem. 'It must be fine because he's married to *her*!'

Now the French-manicured finger was aimed at Zoe. The rushing sound in her ears grew louder.

'Have you signed the register yet, madam?' asked the policeman, who'd joined them.

Trinity shook her blonde head. 'Not yet.'

'In that case, you've no case to answer. You haven't officially married Mr Roberts,' the policeman said carefully. 'But you, sir,' he added, turning to the horrified Steve, 'I'm afraid you're going to have to accompany me to the station!'

Trembling, Zoe had no choice but to watch in silence as her husband was led away by the police.

19

'Look on the bright side, we can't ever call Steve predictable again,' Libby said cheerfully. 'I never thought I'd live to see the day he was carted off by the Old Bill!'

Zoe, who was slumped on the sofa, looked up at her sister and shook her head wearily. Libby was hugely excited by all the drama and although she was supposedly there for moral support, her continual wondering aloud whether Steve was being roughed up by a renegade cop or had been locked in a cell was starting to get very wearing. And as for looking on the bright side, well, that was easier said than done when your husband was being investigated for bigamy.

'This isn't an episode of *CSI*,' Zoe said. 'This is real life, Lib, and Steve could be in big trouble here. Bigamy's a serious crime, you know.'

'Sorry,' said Libby hastily. 'Can I do anything to help? Would you like another cup of tea?'

Zoe rolled her eyes and pointed at the four full cups

of cold tea lined up in front of her on the coffee table. 'I think I'm OK for tea, thanks. I probably have Earl Grey flowing through my veins by now.'

In the hours that had passed since Trinity's disastrous wedding Zoe had almost worn a groove in the slate floor as she paced up and down the kitchen, making tea and endlessly checking her mobile just in case Steve had called. The plane journey back from Scotland with Bobby and Trin had passed in a blur and now there was nothing to do but wait. For once she was faced with a situation she couldn't fix and it was driving her crazy. This had to be a mistake.

'I can't believe he's done this,' she said.

'I know! It's incredible, isn't it? Steady Steve's married to a Hollywood star! How cool is that?'

Zoe closed her eyes in despair. Libby adored danger and risk but seldom paused to consider the consequences. It was typical of her that she'd be over the moon at the idea of her sensible brother-in-law transforming into some kind of criminal Casanova.

Zoe took a deep breath. 'Lib, you don't understand: Steve's still married to Trinity.'

'Yeah . . .'

'Which means he's not married to me.'

'Oh.' Suddenly Libby looked as if she didn't find the situation as cool as she did before.

'Our marriage isn't legal.'

'Zoe, I'm sorry—'

'Not to mention the fact that he's committed a crime and could go to prison.'

Libby's eyes were big blue circles of horror. 'You and Steve aren't married?'

Tears blurred Zoe's vision. 'You've got it, little sis. Steve isn't my husband after all.'

Libby was speechless but she had enough of her wits about her to pull Zoe into a crushing bear hug. Since Libby was strong and muscled from all her extreme sports Zoe's ribs feared for their lives but the gesture of comfort and support was very welcome and she found herself crying.

'How could he do this to me?' she choked into Libby's shoulder. 'How could he be so stupid?'

'It's all got to be some kind of mistake,' Libby suggested, smoothing Zoe's damp blonde hair back from her cheeks. 'Come on, Zoe! This is Steve we're talking about. It's just a silly mix-up, that's all.'

But Zoe couldn't believe this, even though she desperately wanted to. The police didn't tend to take people away for questioning without serious grounds for an inquiry and besides, that journalist had clearly done his homework. As much as she tried to convince herself things would be fine she knew she was just hiding from the inevitable. She and Steve had never been married at all. Their beautiful perfect wedding, the happiest day of her life, had been nothing but a farce.

'There's no mistake,' she said bleakly. 'This is really happening.'

'You need a drink and I don't mean tea,' Libby observed. 'Actually, *I* need a drink. Sit on that sofa and don't move.'

Zoe slumped back onto the sofa and watched as her sister bustled around the kitchen collecting tumblers and the bottle of twelve-year-old Macallan Steve had been saving for a special occasion. Feeling sad, Zoe supposed this counted even though it hadn't been quite what she'd had in mind. She always hoped he'd crack that bottle open on the day they shared happy news. Her hand fell to touch her flat stomach and more tears filled her eyes. It no longer seemed likely *that* would happen any time soon.

The sound of the key turning in the lock of the front door made both sisters start. Libby sloshed whisky onto the granite worktop and Zoe's heart raced faster than Usain Bolt.

'Zoe?' Steve called.

'In the kitchen,' Zoe called back, and was amazed at just how normal her voice was. From the pounding of her heart and tightness of her throat she'd expected to sound like Minnie Mouse.

'What a day.' Moments later he was in the kitchen too, his ashen face and red-rimmed eyes a perfect reflection of her own. His suit was crumpled and he was minus his tie too, while his hair stood on end, making him look like a startled baby bird. Zoe knew that he would have spent most of the afternoon running his hands through it in distress. But right at this second that idea failed to move her.

'What's happened?' Libby wanted to know. 'It's all going to be OK, isn't it?'

Steve sighed heavily. 'God, Libs, I really hope so. I've got a court summons in two weeks' time but the inspector who questioned me seemed pretty confident that I won't be in too much trouble. He thinks, judging from what I've told him, that I'll probably just get a slap on the wrists. There's no real harm done.'

As she watched her husband fetch a glass and pour himself a generous measure it was Zoe's turn to be speechless.

Libby set down her glass and slipped her feet back into her Sketchers. 'I'll leave you guys to it,' she said. Libby had always said that although Zoe had a very long fuse, when she finally lost her temper it was best to be very, very far away. Giving Zoe's shoulder a squeeze she added, 'Call me if you need me, OK? I'll be at my boyfriend's.'

Once they heard Libby shut the front door Zoe and Steve stared at each other. The atmosphere in the kitchen was millstone heavy and she saw the whisky in

Steve's tumble swish with the shaking of his hands.

'*No real harm done?*' Zoe echoed Steve's earlier comment and shook her head. 'You're married to another woman. Our marriage is a sham. You think there's no real harm done?'

'Babe—' Steve began, but the look on his wife's face stopped him in his tracks.

'Don't you dare "babe" me!' cried Zoe, all the hurt and fears of the afternoon tumbling out as she rounded on him. 'How could you? How could you not do something as important as making sure our marriage was legal?'

'I did make sure it was legal! I know I signed those annulment papers!' Steve protested. 'That's what I've been telling the police all afternoon. When I find them I'll show you and them, and this whole ridiculous mess will be sorted. Of course we're married!'

She stared at him, not quite daring to feel relief yet. 'You're not really married to Trinity?'

'Of course I'm not really married to Trinity! Come on, Zoe! The whole thing's just a stupid misunderstanding.'

'So all you have to do is show the police the papers and everything's OK?'

Steve nodded. 'They said they couldn't find any records anywhere that the marriage had been annulled, which is weird. But all I need to do is locate the originals and present them at the police station and the whole mess is cleared up.'

'Thank God!' Zoe finally exhaled. 'Right, well, what are you waiting for? Once you get to the station Trin and Bobby can get married, I can be Mrs Kent again and we can all get on with our lives.'

Steve bit his lip. 'There's a slight problem. I don't know where they are. You know what I'm like with filing.'

Zoe did know. They'd almost missed their honeymoon because he'd mislaid his passport (which she'd eventually located in the airing cupboard, the safe place Steve had totally forgotten about). Rising to her feet she gave him an exasperated look.

'Come on then, let's get started. The sooner we find those papers, the sooner this is all over with. And then,' she added sternly, 'you can take me out for a very expensive meal.'

Steve laid his hand on his heart. 'After what I've put you through today a meal is the very least I owe you.'

But two hours later food and fine dining were the last things on Zoe's mind. They'd ransacked the house from top to bottom and now the place looked as though it had been burgled. Every cupboard door was open, drawers spewed forth their contents and even the freezer had been searched because Steve recalled hiding the emergency credit card there. All sorts of exciting treasures had been uncovered, from Zoe's first love letter to their degree certificates, but so far there was no sign of the annulment papers.

Zoe sat back on her heels and closed the bottom drawer of Steve's desk with a thud. Her husband was so exasperating! What she had originally seen as a cute quirk of his personality was fast becoming seriously annoying. *I don't care if it's interfering or me trying to fix things as always*, she decided firmly, *but I'm buying Steve a filing cabinet!*

'Aha!' she heard him cry. 'Found them!'

Steve was standing at the bookcase and brandishing the *Beano* annual from 1995 as though it was an Oscar. 'I tucked them in here. I remember now.'

Biting back a comment about his crazy filing system Zoe exhaled deeply. This whole thing had been just a misunderstanding after all. 'Great. Now who do you have to send them to to prove it?'

But a frown was pleating Steve's brow. 'Damn! This is just a photocopy of the paperwork I filled in. It's not the decree of annulment.'

Zoe felt like walloping him over the head with the *Beano* annual. 'Might you have tucked it in another comic?'

Steve was white, so white that even his lips had a bluey tinge. One of his slender hands clutched the bookshelf for support. 'Zoe,' he whispered, 'this is all I have.'

'What?' Zoe stared at him in disbelief. 'Are you telling me that there isn't an annulment document?'

Steve's hazel eyes met hers. They were bright with distress but at that moment she was far too livid to worry about how he was feeling.

'I just assumed that this was it,' he said quietly. 'I never actually thought to check about other forms or certificates.'

Anger surged up inside her. 'You have to be kidding? You never thought to actually check you weren't married? Who does that?'

'A person who trusted his best friend,' said Steve bleakly.

'You can't blame this mess on Rufus,' she told him. 'You married Trinity, not him. Getting the annulment was your responsibility, not his!'

'I know, I know.' Throwing the papers down in disgust Steve started to pace up and down the office. 'I promise you I filled in those annulment papers the day after I married Trin. I put them in the envelope and made sure they were signed by both of us. Then Rufus said he'd take care of the rest. He said he felt responsible for letting me get so drunk that I married her in the first place and that he'd post them and deal with the legal stuff. This is the envelope he gave back to me.'

'I can't believe you'd leave something so important to someone else!' Zoe was incredulous.

Steve buried his head in his hands. 'Rufus and I had always looked after each other. I really thought he'd posted those documents. Clearly he didn't.'

As she stared at the man who was most certainly no longer her husband Zoe suddenly felt weary beyond belief. To go from despair to hope and then to plummet back to despair again was more than she could take.

Stepping across the debris that littered the office floor, Steve took Zoe's hands in his and stared down at her. 'I'm so sorry, babe! I wouldn't have done this to you for the world.'

She slid her hands away. 'But you have, Steve.'

'Please, Zoe, don't look at me like that,' he pleaded. 'Come on, sweetheart. We love each other. We can get through anything.'

Could they? Once upon a time Zoe had really believed so but now she wasn't so certain. 'I don't know. It's all too much. We seem to be constantly finding things out about one another that we didn't have a clue about before.'

'But that's all part of being married!' Steve insisted.

'Except that we're not married, are we?' Zoe shook her head. 'We were going to work it all through when we were, because that's what you do when you are married, isn't it? But we're not married. Maybe we should take it as a sign?'

He stared at her. 'What exactly are you trying to say?'

Zoe's mouth was dry with fear. She knew that once these words were spoken she could never unsay them, but neither could she pretend for much longer that she still believed wholeheartedly in the illusion of Zoe and Steve, the perfect couple.

'That fortune-teller at my hen night told me I'd be married twice,' she whispered. 'What if she was right? What if you and I aren't meant to be after all?'

Steve stared at her. 'Since when did you believe in all that rubbish? You're starting to sound like Libby.'

She shrugged. 'I don't know. I'm just not sure any more.'

'Sure about what?' Steve folded his arms across his chest and fixed her with his searching hazel gaze. 'Are you trying to say you don't want to be with me? Is that it?'

'I think . . .' a Stonehenge-sized lump was in Zoe's throat, '. . . I think we need to take a break.'

Dragging herself into work the following morning had to be one of the hardest things Zoe had ever had to do. After Steve had left she'd cried until her face was raw and her breath came in sharp hard gulps. There had been no phone calls of regret made. No texts. Since they'd met, apart from their brief breakup, they had barely gone an hour without speaking. Now they both needed time to think.

Sleep had eluded her until the small hours when exhaustion rendered her unconscious. When the alarm shrilled at six fifteen she felt and looked as though she'd been in a cage fight and, no matter how much Touche Eclat she painted on the big black bags beneath her eyes, they still looked as though they could hold the contents of the weekly trip to Waitrose.

Sitting on set and pretending to be busy, Zoe knew that although she felt awful, taking a break from Steve was the right thing to do. She loved him but after everything that had happened recently she was starting to wonder whether she actually knew him at all. And there was also the matter of Angela's prophecy to consider. All the other hens were now with the men that Angela had predicted; disregarding her words seemed rather foolhardy. Maybe she and Steve were fated to end this way? Now that small room at the back of the house would never be anything more than an office.

I'll be married twice, Zoe recalled sadly as she doodled broken hearts onto the corner of her script. Next time she was going to make sure she got it right.

Steve was already on set running through the camera shots and shooting schedule for today's scene. He looked tired and his T-shirt was wrinkled, but apart from that he seemed fine. Every inch the professional, he'd nodded hello, run through the script with Zoe and the actors, and now he was preparing to direct the first take of the day. Every so often their eyes met across the set and Steve would nod awkwardly before turning his attention back to his work. Zoe sighed. Dealing with their new single status was going to be easier said than done. The fiasco at Gretna Green had been so public that of course all the cast and crew knew about Steve and Trinity, and consequently everyone was giving Zoe a wide berth, unsure of what to say.

Tears prickled her eyes and Zoe bit her lip hard, willing them away. How could she possibly have any more tears left when she'd already shed enough to cause a small monsoon?

'Mrs K— er, Zoe? Are you OK?' A small hand, the nails gnawed into stumps, fluttered to touch her shoulder. Looking up from her reverie Zoe saw that Melody had paused by her side on her way to the dressing rooms. Her face was full of concern, which really touched Zoe so, dredging up what inner reserves of strength remained, she gave her a warm smile.

'I've had better days, Mel, but thanks for asking,' she said.

Across the studio she saw Celina staring at them and gesturing to Melody. Aha. So Celina needed Zoe to do something but hadn't wanted to approach her and had sent Mel instead had she? That poor girl. Feeling protective and not wanting anyone to see just how unhappy she was, Zoe pasted a bright smile onto her face and asked Mel what she could do for her.

'Celina says there's a problem on the other set,' Mel said. 'Can you help?'

'I'll do my best,' Zoe assured her. Set issues were no problem, it was married husbands she couldn't handle. 'What's up?'

'It's the set design for the day room. Celina thinks it's totally wrong and she's had a big row about it. You know how she can be.' Mel pulled a face. 'Fern's going mental.'

Great. A bad day had just got a hundred times worse.

Zoe hoped that karma didn't exist because the thought of what she may have done in a past life to have earned all this grief was too horrific to contemplate.

'Now Celina won't talk to Fern,' Mel continued. 'She says seeing as you're in charge you can sort it.'

'Thanks, Celina,' Zoe muttered, making a mental note to add the stroppy floor manager to her list of people she'd never work with again. Now she'd have to talk to Fern, who hated her. But Zoe felt so numb that she could deal with anything right now – even a sub-zero reception from her former best friend.

The far side of the studio housed a collection of interiors for Isabel's house. In the furthest one, which was supposed to be a morning room, Zoe could see Fern sitting cross-legged on top of an ornate chesterfield with her arms folded defensively and her small pointed chin set in a defiant angle. All the assistants and interns looked terrified and Zoe couldn't blame them. Fern might only be five feet tall and weigh eight stone on a fat day but her temper could teach Krakatoa a lesson in how to erupt. Giving her a cheery wave, which was pointedly ignored, Zoe approached the set with a sinking heart.

'I suppose you've come to have a go too, have you?' was Fern's opening salvo. 'You like destroying stuff that's important to me so why should this set be any different?'

Zoe winced at the bitterness in her friend's voice.

'Fern, I couldn't be any sorrier. I know I've hurt you, even if I didn't mean to, and I'm not expecting you to forgive me yet, but—'

'Yet?' snorted Fern. 'Never, more like!'

'But,' Zoe continued, 'we need to be professional. You might have defriended me on Facebook but we have to work together in real life, so what do you say to leaving our personal issues behind?'

Fern shrugged. 'Whatever. The fact you've lied to me and betrayed me for *six years* won't affect our working relationship at all.'

'Good,' said Zoe, deliberately ignoring her sarcasm. 'So what's the problem with the set?'

Fern scowled. 'I don't think there is one. I've dressed the morning room in scarlet and crimson themes but bloody Celina has thrown a fit. Apparently it's totally inappropriate. Like she'd have a clue!'

Zoe swallowed nervously. Sure enough the set was a swirl of rich reds and burgundies, which was sumptuous and opulent but not at all what an Edwardian morning room would have been like. She was confused. Fern's research was usually meticulous and it was unlike her to make such a basic mistake.

'Well?' demanded Fern. 'What do you think?'

Treading carefully – she had no desire for her blood to be added to the colour scheme – Zoe said slowly, 'It's very striking, Fern, lovely. But historically I think it would have been far more usual for a morning room to be pale and floral. Blue or green, maybe.'

'Bollocks.' Fern tossed her curly hair. 'And anyway, how many of the viewers would care about that? It's perfect and I'm not changing it.'

The assistants gasped. Any minute now and they'd be selling ringside seats, thought Zoe. Well, there was no way she'd give them or Fern the satisfaction of seeing her lose her cool. Professional head firmly in place she said thoughtfully, 'That's true, but at the BBC we do pride ourselves on historical accuracy. What was the rationale behind the colour scheme?' Zoe hoped that by turning the question back on Fern she could make her think again.

Fern's big blue eyes glinted with challenge. 'I figured that Isabel is a right bitch, going off with one man when the one who really loves her is waiting at home. How selfish, eh? I thought the dark red reflects her cruel, nasty heart and the fact that deep down she's a bit of a slag.' Fern smiled and batted her eyelids. 'What do *you* think, Zoe?'

Zoe felt as though she'd been slapped. Her cheeks the same colour as the set and, her heart pounding, she said, 'I think that neither man is perfect. In fact, nobody's perfect, Fern. People make mistakes because that's all part of being human. Everyone deserves forgiveness.'

'Only if they own up to what they've done wrong,' Fern shot back. 'If they try and cover up what they've done and pretend to everyone that they're wonderful when in fact they're just liars then it's very hard to find sympathy for them . . . as characters.'

Zoe sighed. Today was going to be a long day and it was only eight a.m. Just as she was psyching herself up to pull rank and order Fern to redress the set Susannah appeared, took one look at the set and demanded that it was changed instantly. Leaving the seething Fern with no choice but to obey, Susannah swept Zoe into her office and kicked the door shut with the pointy toe of her spike-heeled boot.

'Firstly, let's address the Steve-shaped elephant in the room,' said Susannah, chisel blunt as always. 'I'm so sorry about what happened in Scotland. How are things now?'

Zoe pressed her hands against her throbbing temples. 'Tricky, to say the least. Basically, it turns out he never actually got the marriage to Trin annulled so he and I were never officially man and wife.'

'Bloody hell!' Susannah gasped.

'Quite,' Zoe nodded. 'So, to cut a long story short, Steve and I have decided to take a break for a bit. There's so much about him I don't know that it's starting to feel as though he's not the man I walked down the aisle with anyway.'

'Indeed,' agreed her boss. ' "His egotism lay hidden like a serpent in a bed of flowers," ' she quoted.

'Not egotism exactly, but yes, quite a few things were hidden like snakes,' Zoe said sadly. She glanced down at her wedding and engagement rings. She supposed she ought to take them off really since she had no right to wear them. The thought made her feel sick.

Susannah tutted loudly. 'Men, eh? Nothing but trouble.' She sighed and clenched her jaw. 'And talking of troublesome men; I hate to be the bearer of yet more bad tidings but I wanted to tell you before you found out some other way . . .'

'What is it?'

'Rufus is back.'

Zoe couldn't have been more gob-smacked if Elvis had strolled on through, demanding a salad. 'How on earth did he manage to pull that?'

'The boys' club, darling. Old school ties and all that,' said Susannah scathingly. 'Somehow the execs came to the conclusion that in spite of all his foul play, Rufus is an asset to this project.'

'Come again?'

'It seems his tactics of raising a media storm have worked. Apparently there's loads more interest in *Portrait* now, especially after the Bobby and Trinity marriage attempt hit the papers.'

Zoe winced. She hadn't dared to look at a paper yet but Libby had told her she'd made the red tops. Again. This was starting to become a habit, Libby had teased. Should Katie Price be afraid?

'I tried to talk sense into them,' Susannah continued, pacing now like a Prada-clad tiger. 'I said they were making the wrong decision and they'd regret it sooner rather than later but nobody was listening to a word I said. All I can say is sorry, Zoe. I did my best but it looks as if we're stuck with the little shit.'

Zoe was just about to tell her boss that she didn't blame her one bit when Melody rapped on the office door and told them that a cast and crew meeting had been called on the set. Moments later they'd joined the flow of bodies moving like syrup into the centre of the studio where Rufus was strutting about as large as life and channelling the Jack Sparrow look. All he needed was a parrot and a cutlass, Zoe thought as she watched him swaggering in his tight trousers and scarlet bandanna, and Disney would probably sign him on the spot. Sensing her gaze Rufus curled his top lip in the kind of sneer Mick Jagger would envy and pointedly turned his back on her.

'Right, you lot, put a sock in it!' Rufus hollered, leaping onto a faux Louis Quinze chair so that he towered above everyone. 'I'm back and there's going to be some pretty big changes. So shape up or ship out!'

Susannah groaned. 'I think I'm going to have to resign before I kill him.'

'Get in the queue!' Zoe whispered back.

'The powers that be missed the old Rufus magic and luckily for them they saw the light and persuaded me to come back,' he continued. 'But I said there was one condition. Any ideas what it was?'

'Sex with every woman on the set?' quipped some bright spark.

Rufus threw his head back and roared with laughter. 'Too late for that! No, seriously, there was one condition and they agreed it straight away. You're going to love this!' Rufus glanced round the room and his bright boot-button eyes lit up. 'Aha! Here he is! The new director of our production: the one and only Eastwood Jones!'

The crowd parted Red Sea style but the man who walked through to pump Rufus's hand was no Moses. Tall, muscled, tattooed and shaven-headed he looked like Arnie's bigger and tougher brother, and far more at home shooting a kick-ass action movie than period dramas.

Zoe glanced at Steve, knowing exactly what this meant for him. Some best friend Rufus had turned out to be! He'd lost Steve his wife and his career in little more than twenty-four hours. Surely that had to be some kind of record?

'You can't do that!' Zoe hadn't meant to say anything but there was no way she could look at Rufus's smug face and keep quiet.

'I think you'll find I can,' gloated Rufus. 'I wrote the contracts, remember?'

'As if we could ever forget,' muttered Susannah.

'So if you'd be so kind as to leave the studio without a fuss, Stevie, that would be great,' said Rufus. 'Unless you'd like me to have you escorted off, that is?'

Eastwood Jones cracked his knuckles and Zoe's stomach lurched. Libby had worked with the director and claimed he was a pussycat but Zoe wasn't convinced. He looked like he gobbled up slim bespectacled creative types for lunch and used their bones for stock. She was still mad at Steve but she couldn't bear to see anything bad happen to him.

But Steve just nodded and with quiet grace unfurled his long frame from the table he'd been leaning on. Every movement of his body screamed fury and indignation but somehow he managed to master his temper and walk across the studio with huge dignity.

'You'll be hearing from my lawyers,' he said coolly, and then he was gone, the only evidence he'd been there at all the swinging studio door and the stunned expressions on the faces of the cast and crew.

Unless Steve managed to hire himself a pretty amazing solicitor, it didn't look as though he'd be back in a hurry. So now, Zoe realised, she wouldn't see Steve at home *or* at work.

Was Fate trying to tell her something?

21

Heathrow airport was bursting with passengers. Queues snaked around the concourse, children weaved in and out of their parents' legs, and every few minutes the nasal whine of the Tannoy announced last-minute calls. Zoe checked her watch and sighed. Three hours to go until her flight.

The cast and crew of *Portrait* were heading off to Italy for a week's on-location shooting. Although a week in Florence might sound like a bit of a jolly, Zoe was under no illusions. It was going to be very hard work, especially now that the über-demanding Eastwood Jones was calling the shots. Already he'd decided that filming would start at six a.m. and had turned his nose up at the script, forcing Zoe to spend the last five nights writing frantically into the small hours.

'Overweight!' A frantic wail rose from the check-in desk. 'How dare you call my luggage overweight!'

It was Trinity, of course, and Rufus ran over to try to calm the star.

It was still really hard for Zoe to see Trinity and not think about Steve and how hurt she felt. But Trinity was just as upset as she was because Bobby Roberts's offer to run away with her seemed to have been forgotten and the on-set rumour was that Trinity hadn't heard from him since. It seemed Zoe wasn't the only woman broken-hearted, thanks to Steve's inability to secure the annulment.

Zoe hurried through to the departure lounge and, after a quick pat down from an overfriendly customs officer, she found the nearest Caffè Nero and ordered a huge vat of coffee.

'Can I join you?' Luke stood at Zoe's side, a shy smile playing on his sexy mouth and a huge mug of coffee balanced on a tray. 'I can't deal with these early starts now I'm getting on a bit!'

'Sure, but less of the getting on a bit stuff, please! We're the same age,' Zoe scolded.

'You don't look a day older than when I first met you,' declared Luke gallantly, which made Zoe splutter into her drink. 'Sorry! That was totally cheesy,' Luke said with a rueful shake of his head.

'Full-fat Cheddar,' Zoe agreed. Accepting a napkin she blotted the spilled coffee while Luke sipped his drink thoughtfully.

'How are things?' he asked eventually. 'I heard Steve's moved out.'

Zoe frowned. She hated people gossiping about her. 'I suppose you heard that on set? Well, it's true. I imagine you're pleased.'

'Hey! Despite how I feel about you, it doesn't mean I'm happy you've split up with your – with Steve. It must be awful for you.' He reached across and took her hand in his, curling her fingers inside his large strong ones. 'If there's anything I can do then you only have to say.'

Zoe glanced at Luke from beneath her eyelashes. He was so handsome with those ski-slope cheekbones, honey-warm skin and the dusting of cinnamon freckles across the bridge of his nose. Add to that those crinkly denim-blue eyes and a sculpted toned body and there you had it – the total package that any woman would be only too happy to unwrap! She swallowed. She was feeling so hurt and lonely that nothing would have been nicer and easier than falling into Luke's arms.

But that wouldn't be fair to either of them.

'That's really sweet, Luke,' she said carefully, slipping her hand from his, 'but what I really need right now is some space.'

Luke sighed. 'I understand.'

'I'm sorry if that isn't what you want to hear but that's the way I feel.'

'Don't worry, Zo. I'm not about to start stalking you or anything. I'll respect your feelings and keep my distance . . . if that's what you really want?'

Zoe looked away from him. Across the coffee bar she saw Fern sitting with some of the crew and looking every bit as miserable as Zoe felt. Feeling beyond sad, Zoe turned her attention back to Luke.

'Yes,' she told him firmly. 'It's what I really want.'

It was a relief finally to be boarding the plane. After their conversation in the coffee bar Zoe had headed towards Duty Free where she'd spent far too much money comfort shopping. Now she was a carrier bag heavier and a hundred pounds lighter but somehow the delicate smells of Chanel and Dior didn't soothe her heart in the way she'd wanted.

She'd hoped Fate might have seated her ex-best-friend next to her so that they would have no choice but to spend the flight talking things through.

But Fate, it seemed, had another plan.

'Oh dear,' Luke said as they exchanged an embarrassed look. He looked again at the ticket in his hand and saw that he was indeed in the right place. 'So much for giving you space. Do you want me to see if I can swap with somebody?'

For a split second Zoe was tempted to say yes, that was exactly what she'd like him to do, but then she reminded herself that this was still Luke, one of her oldest friends and also the star of her production. Asking him to move would only be a catalyst for even more gossip.

'Don't be daft,' she said. 'The journey's only for a couple of hours. I think I can bear it!'

'I'll try to keep my hands to myself,' teased Luke. He sat down and fastened his seat belt. 'Actually, you ought to be pleased it's me. Eastwood Jones was supposed to be in this seat. I swapped so he could go first class.'

Of course, Luke was in Steve's old seat and since Eastwood was now doing Steve's job she would have been stuck with him. Just the thought of having to sit next to the foul-mouthed director was enough to make Zoe shudder. No doubt within five minutes of the plane taking off she'd have chosen skydiving without a parachute rather than sitting next to him!

'I can always swap back,' Luke said.

'Don't you dare!' Zoe told him. 'Actually it'll be nice to have company. To be honest I'm not really looking forward to going back to Italy. Steve and I spent our honeymoon in Venice . . . if it was a honeymoon, that is. Can you have a honeymoon after a wedding that never was?'

Luke's eyes were soft with sympathy. 'I'm so sorry, Zoe.'

She shrugged. 'I'm just not sure how I'll cope with being back in Italy so soon after everything that's happened.'

He said nothing but his silence showed he under-stood. For a while they sat in companionable quiet, Luke flicking through the in-flight magazine and Zoe lost in thought. The plane took off and neither of them spoke, but it was a comfortable silence and Zoe managed to relax a little.

These thoughts were interrupted by an announcement. 'Good morning, this is your captain speaking. I'm afraid we've just had word from Peretola airport. It seems that there are storms in the area and they have advised us not to land there.'

A groan went up from the rows of passengers.

'What now?' Luke said to Zoe.

'This film is jinxed!' replied Zoe. 'What more could possibly go wrong?'

The announcement continued. 'We'll be diverting to Venice Marco Polo. From there . . .'

But Zoe had zoned the speaker out. Her heart sank. How could she bear to return to Venice without Steve? They'd been so happy there. Every square, every singing gondolier and every shady church would open a Pandora's box of bittersweet memories.

'It'll be OK,' Luke whispered, seeing the colour drain from her face. He took her hand in his and this time Zoe didn't pull away. Squeezing her eyes shut in a desperate attempt to stop the tears from flowing she held his hand tightly and made the most of his warm and comforting presence. Something told her she was going to need it over the next few days.

*

The production team set the cast and crew up overnight in a large hotel before they headed to Florence the following day. Zoe stayed long enough to check in and shower before changing into a white cotton smock top and denim Capri pants, and setting off into town. Instead of heading into the busy tourist spots she'd explored with Steve and dredging up painful memories, she went to the old city, wandering down narrow alleyways flagged with washing and emerging, blinking, into sun-drenched squares.

Although she was still heartbroken the beauty of Venice was hard to ignore and impossible not to enjoy. Bold splashes of geraniums tumbling from shuttered windows, cool courtyards fringed with dusty trees and surprising dead ends flanked by dark sluggish canals held her rapt for several hours as she explored the secret heart of the ancient city.

It was so different from her trip with Steve where she'd perfectly planned every detail of a packed itinerary to make sure they didn't miss a thing. Oddly enough, Zoe found she was enjoying her unchartered tour. She was seeing things she'd never seen before: shops selling rich cheeses and crusty rye bread, an old woman feeding an army of stray cats, the odd ramshackle church . . . This was the real Venice, Zoe realised with a tingle of excitement, rather than the gaudy version laid on for the tourists.

After an hour or so the mouth-watering aroma of rosemary and tomatoes led Zoe to a small restaurant set into the wall beside an ancient church. Several tables were outside and perfectly positioned to catch the buttery rays of evening sunshine. Each table sported a wax-encrusted Chianti bottle with a scarlet candle rammed into its neck and although it was only early, several Italian families were already tucking into bruschetta and olives. Perfect! She must have found the only restaurant in Venice without a tourist.

Zoe sat at a table, and a waitress came over and handed her a menu with a smile and some words she didn't understand. Finally the tension started to slip away and she found herself relishing the warmth of the sun and the delicious smells. When the waitress returned Zoe ordered, '*Una verra di Prosecco e pescare e l'insalata verte*', her best pidgin Italian for what she hoped was a fish and salad supper.

Maybe she should just make an effort to enjoy this time in Italy and put all thoughts of Steve to one side. If she spent any longer thinking about how he'd turned out to be so different from the man she thought he was then she'd go crazy. It was time to take a holiday from her brain and practise some of that positive-thinking stuff Libby was always on about. If she followed that philosophy to its ultimate conclusion maybe Steve being still married to Trin was Fate's way of offering her a no-fuss way of ending a relationship that was no longer working?

Argh! There I go again! She needed an off switch for her brain.

As her food arrived, looking every bit as mouth-watering as it had smelled, she saw something out of the corner of her eye. A figure, a gait she recognised; broad shoulders and long legs.

Luke.

Her eyes widened. What were the odds of Luke turning up at the quietest restaurant in Venice? How many more times could this man accidentally cross her path? If Fate was trying to give her a sign she felt she was being beaten over the head with it.

Then she laughed at herself. *For heaven's sake, Zoe! What's got into you? You sound like Libby!*

Spotting her, he waved but headed to another table, clearly respecting her wish to be left alone. Zoe speared some rocket thoughtfully before placing her cutlery down with a clatter. This was ridiculous! They shouldn't be sitting at separate tables in the same restaurant. Besides, she was a single woman again. She could eat dinner with whomever she chose.

She picked up her plate and crossed the restaurant to join him. ' "Of all the bars, in all the towns, in all the world . . ." ' she quoted with a smile.

'Zoe, I'm so sorry. I swear I'm not stalking you!' Ever

the gentleman, Luke rose to his feet when she joined him. 'There are hordes of fans outside the hotel and I just needed a quiet place to eat. I came here during the Film Festival and remembered it, but I'll go somewhere else if you'd rather?'

'That's really thoughtful but no, please don't. I'm sorry about earlier, Luke. It's not like you're contagious or anything.'

He smiled that heart-stopping smile. 'There's nothing to apologise for.'

With a look she saw that they had made peace. 'May I join you?' she asked.

'There's nothing I'd like more,' Luke said softly. Pulling out a chair for her and ordering a bottle of wine, he added, 'Well, actually there is but we won't go into that right now!'

Zoe rolled her eyes. 'I'm trying to eat!'

Luke laughed and any awkwardness between them vanished almost as fast as Zoe's fish. Over dinner they chatted easily about the film, mutual friends, Libby's latest stunts and their days at university. They both tried as hard as they could to steer around the subject of Fern but since she'd been such a huge part of their lives this soon proved to be easier said than done. By the time a copper-coin sun was slipping behind the church and their coffees arrived Zoe couldn't avoid it any longer.

'I wish Fern would forgive me,' she said miserably. 'I

know I've hurt her and I understand why she's so angry but I miss her so much. I'd do anything to make it right.'

'Zo, you haven't done anything wrong. Fern and I weren't even an item when you and I got together.'

But Zoe shook her head, glad that her long blonde hair fell over her eyes to hide the shimmering tears. Lord, she'd blubbed enough on Luke Scottman lately; it was a miracle the poor guy hadn't dissolved. 'This is different. She was in pieces when you guys broke up and for me to have a relationship with you and then lie about it must feel like the ultimate betrayal. We should never have got together, Luke.'

'What kind of flawed logic is that?' Luke said, looking perplexed. 'Are you saying I'm never allowed to be with anyone else because it might upset an ex?'

'No, no.' Zoe pushed her hair back behind her ears. 'Of course not. But what if—'

'What if you and I are soul mates and destined to be together? Do we have to stay apart because of a girl I dated when I was twenty?'

She stared at him. Then, flapping her hand as if to swat him away, said, 'Don't be ridiculous, Luke. We're not soul mates. Since when did you ever think that?'

The sun's last orange fingernail slipped into the canal. Luke's face was pale in the flickering candlelight but his eyes burned hotter than any flame.

'Since that first time in Queensland,' he said hoarsely.

'That was when I knew we were meant to be together. From the second I first held you, Zoe, that was when I knew for certain. I loved you from that moment and I've loved you every moment since.'

The intensity of his gaze and the passion in his voice made goose bumps rise up like sunflowers over Zoe's limbs. Luke might be an amazing actor but she knew every syllable, every word of this speech was sincere.

'I don't know what to say,' she whispered.

'Don't say anything,' he suggested, pulling his gaze away from her and staring at his hands. 'I don't want to pressure you or make you feel awkward, but I do want you to know how I feel. I can't keep it to myself any more.' He looked up and into her eyes again. 'Just know that if you ever need me I'm there for you. And if you ever want to be with me, then I'm waiting. All you have to do is say.'

Zoe was speechless but her heart was skidding about like crazy. Just as she was struggling to find an answer an Italian man joined them at their table. His paint-spattered smock and the canvases rolled up and tucked beneath his arm suggested he was one of the street artists who made their living from sketching tourists or knocking up quick watercolours of Venice. Sure enough, he was unrolling a simple sketch of her and Luke smiling into one another's eyes across the table. Pencil Luke was gazing at Zoe with a lovestruck look, while pencil Zoe looked down at the table, a mysterious smile playing across her lips.

'You like?' asked the artist hopefully. 'I call this picture for you *Gli amanti!*'

'*Gli amanti*?' echoed Luke. 'Sorry, mate, but my Italian's pretty ropey. *Il conto, per favore* is about my limit.'

'*Gli amanti*. It means . . .' the artist paused, searching for the English equivalent before beaming when he found it, '. . . it means "The Lovers"!'

Zoe was dismayed and Luke's expression was equally aghast.

'So much for being discreet,' he groaned. 'I am so sorry, Zoe!'

But the humour of the situation had suddenly hit Zoe. Before she knew it she was laughing, and then Luke was too. A strange feeling seemed to build up within her, making her feel giddy and lighter than air. For a moment Zoe was confused before she realised what it was.

For the first time in weeks she was happy.

22

The Hotel Maria in Florence was pretty enough, set around a cool and shady courtyard with a little fountain playing in the middle, and as Zoe unpacked her small case, the trickling sound of water soothed her frayed nerves. So it wasn't quite the Grand Hotel Baglioni where Trinity, Luke, Eastwood and Rufus were staying in five-star luxury, but it suited Zoe just fine. When she flung open the shutters she gasped because the view of the city was absolutely stunning. Plump citadel spires rose up into a cloudless blue sky and terracotta roofs tumbled higgledy-piggledy as far as the eye could see.

It's perfect, thought Zoe with pleasure. The long hot bus ride from Venice to Florence had been worth it for this view alone. Maybe things were starting to look up at last.

After showering off the grime of the journey and smothering herself in the Jo Malone body lotion she'd liberated from Libby, Zoe wrapped herself in a fluffy white robe and lay on the bed – which in true Goldilocks style was just right! Closing her eyes she drifted off, only to wake with a horrible jolt a couple of hours later. She'd better get moving if she wasn't going to be late for the sunset shoot. Still, the powernap had done her the world of good and suddenly Zoe felt ready for anything.

She sat up and stretched luxuriously. Mmm, siestas were certainly the way forward. She even felt creatively inspired. That one line she'd been wrestling with had just popped into her mind with such ease that she laughed out loud.

Determined to write it down before the muse slipped away she opened the drawer in the bedside table, hoping to find a pen to scribble it down. Unusually, though, instead of the usual monogrammed cheap biro the drawer contained an expensive Parker fountain pen. This struck a chord with Zoe because she'd once had one, a far less costly version, but one that she had great sentimental attachment to. Picking it up and turning it round in her hands, she admired the glittery emerald-style stone set into the tip of it and the engraving that read 'Behold the light of day'. What a fancy pen for a three-star hotel! Maybe somebody had left it there by mistake. Or maybe it was a secret message between star-crossed lovers. Pondering this idea, Zoe jotted down the line onto a notepad and then replaced the pen in the drawer.

Now she'd really better get her skates on if she wasn't going to be late.

Emerging into the corridor Zoe blinked as her eyes adjusted to the sunlight, jumping when she saw she wasn't alone. Fern was standing by the door next to hers, frantically kicking the base with her platform-booted foot and stabbing the keycard into the lock.

'Bloody, bloody thing!' Fern hissed, timing each kick with an expletive. 'Let me in, you bastard!'

'Do you need a hand?' Zoe asked nervously.

Fern spun round and for a moment the two women stared at each other, Fern visibly bristling. Then the fight seemed to drain from her slim body and she bumped her head despairingly against the door.

'I've had a nightmare day!' she wailed. 'For a start they gave me the wrong key to the wrong room and I walked in on a couple who were definitely on honeymoon! I seriously thought the guy was going to throttle me. Now they've given me a key to this room and it doesn't work. I'm going to be really late. Eastwood Jones will rip my head off and make it into a prop!'

Zoe couldn't help laughing. 'Oh, Fern! You are classic!'

Luckily Fern was laughing too. Hostilities seemed to have been suspended, noted Zoe with relief. Taking the card from Fern's small ring-covered hand Zoe slid it into the lock, waited for the required ten seconds and then opened it.

'Blimey!' said Fern in awe. 'Is there really anything you can't fix?'

The mess that is my life? Zoe thought sadly as Fern dashed inside, dumped her suitcase and shot out again. But perhaps it wasn't too late to fix their friendship?

'Shall we share a cab to the set?' she asked tentatively. 'If you want to, that is?'

'OK.' Fern nodded, her springy curls bouncing. 'It makes sense, I guess. And anyway,' she added with a cheeky grin, 'I haven't got a blooming clue where it is!'

Once their cab was speeding away from the hotel and out into the Tuscan countryside Zoe found herself apologising to Fern all over again.

'I must've been crazy to go with Luke,' she said sadly. 'I knew how devastated you were after the break-up and also I knew how much he meant to you. There's no excuse for what I did, Fern, but I was really messed up back then. I'd never have betrayed you otherwise.'

Fern looked out of the window at the blur of olive groves and vineyards. Her shoulders were so stiff that they were practically hunched up to her ears.

'I'm so, so sorry,' Zoe whispered, her throat tight with tears. 'I wouldn't have hurt you for the world.'

There was a long sigh, as though Fern was letting go of something heavy. Turning round, and with tear-filled eyes, she said, 'I know you wouldn't, Zoe. Of course I do.

The Luke thing wasn't really a huge surprise, if I'm honest. I guess deep down I'd always suspected there was a connection between you guys. Sometimes I used to think you'd be much better suited to Luke than I was.'

'That's rubbish!' protested Zoe, but Fern shook her head vehemently.

'No it isn't. You've got much more in common with him than I ever did. I suppose that's why it hurt so much when I heard about you guys getting together. It confirmed everything I'd always worried about.' Fern looked at the floor. 'All the time Luke was with me and I thought we were so happy, was he secretly longing to be with you?'

Zoe wanted to deny this but Fern wasn't prepared to let her speak.

'It doesn't matter now, and anyway, that wasn't the thing that hurt me the most,' she continued. 'I always thought we were best friends and that you'd tell me the truth about anything, no matter how hard. Yes, I'd have been gutted to learn about you and Luke but I'd have got over it and accepted it. Now I'm just wondering what other secrets you've got. Can I ever trust you again?'

'Oh, Fern! Of course you can!' Zoe cried.

But Fern just shrugged. 'It doesn't feel like it. But things change, I guess, don't they? People move on and all that bollocks. If you want to give it a go with Luke then don't let me hold you back. I think you should go for it.'

Zoe stared at her, shocked by the hard note in her friend's voice. 'But what about our friendship, Fern? You can't just throw that away over a guy!'

'Why not?' said Fern, the bitter tone creeping back into her voice. 'You did.' And with this parting shot she popped in her iPod earphones and busied herself scrolling through tracks while Zoe hung her head in shame.

Filming was taking place in an ancient Tuscan villa, all crumbling alabaster-white stone smothered in vines and wisteria. Zoe and Fern were quickly swept into the action and it was a good four hours later that they ran into each other for a second time. On this occasion, though, it was Fern who sought Zoe out, finally tracking her down in the makeshift canteen where she was sipping a coffee and going through her notes for the next scene.

Please don't let her pick up where we left off, Zoe thought with a sinking heart. She felt upset enough about Fern already and didn't think she could face another guilt trip, not when she still had a return ticket for the last one.

Fern did a fake knock on an invisible door. 'I'm not disturbing you, am I?' she asked.

Zoe put down her pen. 'I was just checking the lines

I've rewritten for Trinity's scene, but it can wait.'

'Cool.' Fern slid into the seat opposite. 'Look, this might sound weird but Luke's just been pouring his heart out to me and asking *my* permission to date you!' Her small nose crinkled. 'It's like this is the nineteenth-century and I'm your dad or something.'

'I've already told you, Fern, I won't go out with Luke. Not ever,' Zoe said firmly. 'In spite of what you think of me right now your friendship is much more important.'

Fern flapped her hands impatiently. 'Yes, yes. I know all that, but what if I'm the one who's at fault and Luke really is the love of your life? What if I'm being selfish and keeping two soul mates apart?'

Zoe pulled a face. 'I hardly think so. It was all a very long time ago.'

'So?' Fern said excitedly. 'You could still be destined to be together! What if Luke's the one? You have to find out, Zo. You can't live for the rest of your life always wondering *what if.*'

'You've changed your tune,' said Zoe, taken aback.

'Luke's a pretty persuasive guy,' Fern told her, a sad smile set on her face. 'Anyway, apart from the fact he's a Trekkie, he's a great guy and totally into you, just like my brilliant new man is into me. Luke Scottman isn't my other half . . .' she gave Zoe a pointed look, '. . . but he could be yours.'

Zoe's head was spinning. 'I always thought Steve was my soul mate.' Zoe and Steve hadn't spoken since he left that night. She had expected him to call, and when he didn't, and she tried to lift the phone to call him, she'd lost her nerve. What did that say about a happy reunion?

'Steve's lovely, but he's married to Trin,' Fern said. 'Which is odd. I really thought all Angela's predictions would come true but she got yours totally wrong. It doesn't look as though you and Steve will be together forever after all.'

Zoe sighed and realised it was time to confess. 'That wasn't my prophecy.'

'What?'

'You guys just assumed it and I didn't correct you.'

Fern's jaw dropped to her chest. 'But . . . well . . . um . . . so, what *was* your prophecy?'

'Angela actually told me I'd marry twice.'

There was a moment of silence as the information sunk in.

'Blimey,' said Fern, shaking her head in shock, 'that's not exactly what you want to hear the week before your wedding.' Her eyes widened as a thought occurred. 'Maybe she means that you're going to marry Luke?' Zoe heard the catch in Fern's voice. 'He must be the love of your life after all.'

Zoe wasn't convinced but she could see Fern was.

'And if that is the case what happens to our friendship?' she asked softly.

Fern bit her lip. 'I don't know,' she said eventually. 'It's not about Luke anymore, is it? It's about the fact that you're not the person I thought you were. You lied to me, Zoe. That's what I can't get my head around. Maybe the damage has already been done.'

Fern left it at that and walked back to the production designer, who was calling her back to the set.

Zoe decided there and then she'd do whatever it took to make things right between them again. As Susannah joined her, cigarette in one hand and espresso in another, Zoe had a flash of genius that would have given Stephen Hawking a run for his money.

'Hey, Zoe,' said Susannah wearily, all but collapsing next to her. 'I hope your day's going better than mine. That idiot director of ours only wants a graphic sex scene now. Trinity's stormed off because nudity isn't in her contract and God only knows where Luke is – on the starship bloody *Enterprise* as usual, I suppose.'

Zoe laughed. Eastwood's crazy demands were the least of her problems.

'There are some sane people on the crew, though,' Zoe said, putting her plan into action. 'Actually, I wanted to have a word with you about one of the set designers.'

'Oh, no, they're not causing problems, are they?' Susannah groaned.

'Nothing like that,' Zoe reassured her. 'But I think one of them may have been rather overlooked, thanks to the good old boys' club again.'

Her boss bristled visibly. 'Tell me more.'

'**M**ay I leave a message for Luke Scottman?' Zoe asked the beautiful receptionist at the Grand Hotel Baglioni. 'I'm a friend of his.'

Zoe had a horrible feeling the thing she was about to do next was really going to hurt Fern, no matter what her friend might say to the contrary.

But if Luke Scottman really was her soul mate then there was only one way to find out . . .

The receptionist regarded her coolly. 'I'm afraid you're mistaken, Signora. We have no one by the name of Luke Scottman staying here.'

Duh! Of course they didn't.

His mobile was off; he'd been working elsewhere and now he had a code name for his room. So near and yet so far! Was this a sign that she was making a mistake?

Then Zoe had a brainwave.

'Sorry! Silly me,' she said. 'I meant to say, may I leave a message for James T. Kirk?'

'Of course, Signora,' smiled the receptionist, instantly clicking the mouse with her beautifully manicured fingers. 'What would you like the message to say?'

Zoe thought for a moment. Actually, that was a question that a member of Mensa might struggle to answer.

What did she want to say to Luke? Deciding brevity was best, she said, 'Could you tell him, "Zoe says, OK. This evening." Please?'

The receptionist repeated this cryptic message as she tapped it into the computer.

Zoe had barely left the cool of the hotel's reception and crossed the square when her BlackBerry buzzed. Fishing it from her bag she smiled when she saw Luke's name flashing across the screen. Wow. Talk about keen!

'Hello, Captain,' she teased, taking a seat on a stone bench shaded by plane trees. 'You got my message then?'

'I sure did,' Luke replied, and even though she couldn't see him Zoe knew he was smiling. Closing her eyes she could imagine the cute dimple in his cheek and the way his eyes would crinkle. A lovely fluttery feeling rippled through her as though a thousand butterflies had taken flight inside.

'This evening, then,' Luke said softly. 'Shall we go somewhere quiet and just talk? Maybe have dinner and some wine in a taverna?'

Although his voice was quiet and calm he wasn't able to totally disguise his excitement and Zoe felt a wave of tenderness.

'That sounds perfect.'

'Great,' said Luke, and then there was a brief silence as they both struggled to adjust to this new path that their friendship was taking. He was still Luke, her dear lovely friend, but now there was something else there too, a little frisson of something new that made her shiver.

'Zoe, this is just dinner and conversation,' Luke said eventually. 'I'm not expecting anything else tonight, and I promise that I won't put any pressure on you. Much as I might want to! You're pretty hard to resist.'

Zoe had to smile. If he could see her now in her frayed denim cut-offs, ancient gypsy top and scuffed Timberlands he might think differently! 'Thanks, Luke. That's very sweet.'

'Sweet? Yuk!' She knew he was grimacing at that. '*Cosmo* put me at number two in the World's Sexiest Bachelors and you describe me as *sweet*? I can see I'm going to struggle to impress you!'

'You don't need to impress me,' pointed out Zoe. 'I know you, remember? We shared a student house. I know all your grotty habits!'

'In that case I really have my work cut out,' he sighed. 'I'd better get my thinking cap on. I'll meet you at your hotel at about seven, if that's OK?'

'Seven's fine,' fibbed Zoe, panicking slightly because this gave her only an hour to transform herself from dusty bag lady to consort suitable for a film star. 'Where are we going? Can I do anything to help?'

'Absolutely not,' said Luke firmly. 'I'm organising everything. I insist! All you have to do is get ready and meet me.'

Easier said than done, thought Zoe once they'd said goodbye. Hailing a cab to her hotel she then shot up to her room and dived into the shower, where she plucked and scrubbed and exfoliated as though her life depended on it. She knew that nothing was going to happen – in fact, she was determined to make sure that nothing happened. But even so, a girl had standards!

My first new date for years! Zoe perched on the edge of the bed and smothered herself in vanilla body lotion. *And it's with a world famous movie star!* No wonder she felt nervous.

Rummaging in her wardrobe, she settled on a jade maxi dress, lacy bolero and jewelled flip-flops. Her long blonde hair she allowed to dry naturally so that it fell in golden waves down her back and scooped back from her face by two glittery slides. Her skin was lightly tanned from the Tuscan sunshine so she decided to keep her makeup simple, settling for a dusting of bronzer, a touch of mascara and a slick of clear lip gloss. The sparkle in her blue eyes and pink blush across her cheeks were totally her own in delicious anticipation of the evening ahead.

Now, what jewellery should she wear? Normally with this dress she'd plump for the emerald earrings but since these had been a wedding gift from Steve, wearing them on a date with another guy just felt wrong. Priya would have snorted that this was ridiculous – they were just stones, after all – but Zoe suddenly had such a vivid image of Steve tenderly hooking each emerald into her ears before trailing delicious kisses along her collarbone.

The emeralds were staying behind.

With a sigh she put the earrings into the drawer then made her way down to reception where Luke, and maybe the next chapter of her life, was waiting.

'Hey, Zoe! Over here!' he called as she stepped out into the glare of the evening sunshine.

Blinking, Zoe pulled on her shades and there he was, dressed in faded Levi's and a simple white linen shirt, and grinning at her from a mint-green Vespa.

'Come on,' Luke said, holding out a second helmet. 'Let's go!'

'Just as well I didn't spend hours on my hair,' laughed Zoe as she did up the chin-strap. 'Where are we going?'

He tapped his nose with a forefinger. 'Now that's my secret!'

'Only I was reading in the guidebook that the Bar Ricchi is supposed to be amazing and—'

'Er, Zoe,' said Luke patiently, 'has anyone ever called you a control freak before? Just hop on the moped and enjoy yourself!'

She blushed. Perhaps it was time she learned to step back and let other people have a turn?

'That's it, sit behind me and hold on tight,' instructed Luke.

Zoe, for once, did what she was told.

'No, sit sideways in that lovely dress and wrap your arms around my waist.'

'Aye, aye, Captain,' she teased, hopped on the bike and hugged him tight.

'Ah! Perfect!'

Zoe swatted his shoulder. 'That's a cheeky trick, young man! I thought you said you didn't expect anything?'

Luke looked a picture of innocence. 'I just don't want you to fall off. Now, hold on. I'm a bit of a boy racer on these things!'

Zoe put her arms around him again and was touched to feel him tremble. Luke was nervous! This was a guy who regularly saved the world – in movies, anyway – and she found it really endearing that he was on edge too. As they pulled away and wove through the evening traffic it wasn't actually that much of a hardship to hold on to him.

The firm muscles of his back rippled beneath the linen shirt and her fingers grazed against a six-pack.

Eventually Luke pulled up outside a small restaurant on the outskirts of the city.

'Grouchos,' read Zoe. Hmm. That one certainly hadn't been in her guidebook. It looked more like someone's house than the sort of five-star restaurant frequented by Hollywood A-listers.

'You are so in for a treat,' Luke told her as, hand placed in the small of her back, he guided her inside. 'This place is one of the best-kept secrets in Italy. I met Groucho's son when I was travelling and believe me, they do the best pizza in Florence!'

'What do you mean, in *Florence*?' boomed a rotund man in his fifties. 'It's the best pizza in the world!'

Groucho, Zoe guessed, judging by his chef's apron and the way he was kissing Luke's cheeks as though greeting a long-lost son. As he led them to a secluded table, chattering away in machine-gun-rapid Italian, Zoe stood on her tiptoes and whispered into Luke's ear, 'I can't believe I'm on a date with a movie star and we've gone for pizza! I thought you guys only ate in The Ivy!'

Luke winked at her. 'Don't believe everything you read in *Heat*. And anyway, wait until you've tried this pizza.'

By the end of the evening, and with a stomach that

was fuller than it had been for ages, Zoe had to agree that Luke had been right. The pizza had easily been the best she'd ever tasted; the base crispy and light, the cheese melt-in-the-mouth gooey and the seafood topping so fresh it must have jumped out of the sea and onto her plate. Add to this several glasses of sharp sparkling wine and conversation that flowed just as easily as the drink and there you had it: an absolutely fantastic evening. She'd laughed and smiled so much that her cheeks hurt.

'Thanks for a great night,' she said as, farewells made to Groucho and his wife, Luke helped her back onto the Vespa.

'Hey, it's not over yet. If you're up for one more trip, that is?' Luke asked.

In the blues and greens of the warm Tuscan night his face was shadowed but his eyes seemed to shine every bit as brightly as the moon riding high above the higgledy-piggledy roofs.

To her surprise Zoe found herself nodding before even thinking about it and this time she didn't bother asking where they were going. Whatever Luke had in mind she knew it would be amazing, and she trusted him totally. As they rode back into the heart of the ancient city she found herself resting her cheek against the warmth of Luke's strong back. Whether it was the wine or just the result of a perfect romantic evening Zoe didn't know, but she felt so safe and so cherished that when they pulled up outside Giotto's bell tower she didn't want to move.

'Come on, sleepy head,' Luke said, lifting her from the scooter and clasping her close to his side. 'Time to climb the tower and work off all that dinner.'

Zoe smothered a yawn. The tower had been on her list of things to do while in Florence. Arm in arm they strolled through the shadows to the tower doors, which were very firmly locked. A sign hung on the door that read: *'Chiuso.'* Closed.

'If I'd been allowed to do a little research for this trip we'd have known this,' Zoe joked, but Luke just smiled.

'O ye of little faith. The tower might be closed to tourists . . . but I've made an arrangement,' he said, and as if by magic a young man appeared and unlocked the doors for them.

Zoe shook her head in wonder. 'Let me guess, you met this guy walking in the Andes? Building hospitals in Bratislava?'

'Sorry to disappoint you. He's just a massive fan,' Luke confessed. 'Hey, if I can't use my fame to impress a lady, then when can I use it?'

She laughed and ruffled his thick blond hair fondly. 'Fair point. Come on, then. Let's climb.'

The stairs seemed endless and, full of pizza, Zoe began to wonder if it really was such a bright idea. After all, she never hit the gym after a Sunday roast, but Luke was adamant, and when they reached the top of the Campanile she could see why: the view was breathtaking and awaiting them was a bottle of champagne on ice and two sparkling flutes.

'Luke!' Zoe gasped, flying to peer over the balcony and down at the twinkling lights of the city lying before them like diamonds sprinkled across black velvet. 'This is amazing. Thank you so much!'

Luke popped the cork and poured Zoe a foaming glass. 'No, thank *you* for coming out with me tonight. I've had such a great time.'

She turned to face him and her heart began to skitter as the atmosphere between them suddenly shifted from easy banter to something totally different.

'Me, too,' she whispered.

Luke took a step towards her. 'Has it been enough to make you think that maybe you could start feeling something more than friendship for me?'

Zoe swallowed. 'I don't know, Luke. Maybe.'

'There's one way we could find out,' Luke said softly as he stepped forward and pulled her close against his strong body. Then he leaned in and brushed his lips against her lips, a butter-soft moonlit kiss that melted her resolve and her limbs.

'Oh, Zoe,' he murmured as he pulled away, 'you have no idea just how long I've been dreaming of this.'

Zoe's bones had turned to melting ice cream. Suddenly she felt as if every fibre in her being was tuned into his, and as though under a spell she moved closer to him. His gaze was so intense that it seemed almost to sear into her soul. Who could possibly resist?

But I don't have to resist! Zoe realised suddenly. If I want to kiss Luke then I can!

It was about time she had some fun and, rising onto her tiptoes, she brushed her lips against his. With a moan Luke gathered her in his arms and kissed her back, a long and searching kiss that left them both breathless and wanting more.

Suddenly, a deafening sound ripped them apart. Zoe covered her ears with her hands.

It was the seven bells ringing just above their heads. Luke gave Zoe a pained expression, grabbed her hand and they both ran down the steps from the bell tower. They reached the doors to the campanile, ran through them, and laughed and laughed.

'Ouch!' said Zoe. 'I think I might be deaf.'

'What?' quipped Luke, then laughed some more, clutching his sides. 'Oh dear! That certainly wasn't part of the evening!'

But maybe just as well, Zoe thought to herself. Her heart was galloping and every cell of her body wanted him, but the bells had rung some sense into a desire-giddy brain.

*

Once back at the hotel Luke was every inch the gentleman. He walked Zoe to the reception, kissed her softly on the cheek and told her he'd see her on set the next day.

'It's late,' he told her, his warm mouth just brushing the corner of hers and making Zoe shiver with longing. 'And much as I'd love to sweep you into my arms and carry you upstairs, I need to get a good night's sleep.'

Up in her room Zoe recalled Luke's words and kisses, and smiled. It really had been the perfect romantic evening. Her fingertips rose to touch her lips, the same lips that only an hour ago had been kissed by his. She felt as though she'd been having a very strange and very lovely dream. Curling up in her bed and closing her eyes, she expected to drift off into a contented slumber but to her frustration, sleep refused to come. As she tossed and turned for about the five hundredth time she felt something sharp scratch against her arm. Reaching under her pillow she plucked out a sheet of the hotel's writing paper.

Clicking on the lamp and sitting up, she furrowed her brow as she read the words typed on it: 'Spring's sweet flower, month of May'. What on earth did that mean? She'd heard of hotels leaving chocolates on pillows, but poetry? Since when did that become the fashion?

Perplexed, she placed the paper on the bedside table and sank back onto her pillows.

Zoe yawned. Whatever. She was far too tired to worry about it any more. She had a busy day tomorrow and Luke would probably want a few definitive answers regarding her feelings for him. A mysterious line of poetry really was the least of her problems.

24

'I'm glad you came; I didn't know if you would,' Trinity said warmly when Zoe joined her at her table in the hotel's roof terrace.

To be honest Zoe hadn't been sure herself. When Trin had collared her at the end of the day's filming and invited her for a drink at the Grand Hotel Baglioni her first instinct was to decline. Why on earth would she want to cosy up with the woman who'd shattered her dream of a happy marriage and perfect relationship? But then curiosity had got the better of her. This was the woman that Steve had married, after all, and Zoe couldn't help wanting to know more. It was with some trepidation and reluctance that she found herself taking a seat and accepting a glass of Veuve Clicquot.

'I love it up here,' Trin was saying, gazing across the roofs flushed salmon pink by the descending sun. 'It's so peaceful after a day on set.'

It was a stunning view but Zoe wasn't in the mood to make small talk with the woman who'd single-handedly destroyed her world. Setting her glass down she said, 'What's all this about, Trin?'

'Look, Zoe, I'm really sorry about the way things have turned out. I feel terrible and I guess I want to clear the air.'

Zoe sighed. 'It's a mess – I won't pretend otherwise – but it isn't really your fault. Steve should have made certain your marriage was dissolved. If he hadn't just assumed everything was fine none of us would be in this mess.'

'He trusted Rufus,' Trinity said gently. 'Granted, that wasn't the most sensible of decisions, but the guy was his best friend.'

'Then Steve needs to improve his taste in friends!'

The actress nodded. 'Believe me, I'm not in the mood to join Rufus's fan club any more than you are. But surely you can overlook Steve's misplaced trust? Especially now he's secured the annulment?'

Zoe stared at her. 'What?'

'The annulment? I received the paperwork this morning. Steve's sorted it so we're all free to marry whoever we want.' Trinity paused and an expression of sadness flickered across her face. 'If Bobby still wants to marry me.'

Zoe was silent. Steve was free but hadn't contacted her to say so. Not even as much as a text. The sudden pain was so savage that it took every inch of self-restraint she had not to cry out.

'So what's this I hear about him moving out?' Trin wanted to know with all the tact of a bull rampaging through Harrods' china department. 'Surely you haven't broken up? Not when you're so perfect together!'

'Maybe we weren't so perfect after all,' Zoe whispered, and to her dismay she realised that she could no longer hold her misery back. Tears fell in earnest as she told Trinity that Steve had moved out and she hadn't heard from him since. Trinity listened sympathetically, her beautifully manicured hand reaching out to squeeze Zoe's before she topped up her champagne flute.

'You look like a girl in need of a drink,' she observed.

'Sorry,' Zoe croaked through her tears. 'I'm alright really.'

Trinity snorted. 'That's baloney! Of course you're not. You've had a terrible time. What you need is something to cheer you up.'

Zoe mopped her eyes with her sleeve. The way she was feeling she didn't think she'd ever cheer up again. The sooner she was drowning in her own duvet the better.

'We need to have a big cast and crew party,' Trin declared, with a toss of her blonde mane. 'That'll put a smile on your face.'

Personally Zoe couldn't think of anything worse than having to socialise and pretend to be happy. Then a thought struck her and she laughed; it was her birthday tomorrow. She'd completely forgotten. Some happy birthday this one would be. There'd be no Post-it notes, predictable tulips or meals in special restaurants this time, a thought that made her so desperately sad the tears threatened to fall again.

'What's wrong?' Trin asked, alarmed. 'Have I said the wrong thing?'

Zoe gave her a feeble smile. Libby was right: Trinity was actually quite sweet once you got below the plastic veneer. 'It's my birthday tomorrow.'

Trinity nearly bounced out of her seat with excitement. 'Oh my God! A birthday party! You'll be the guest of honour and the centre of attention and—'

'No,' Zoe said quickly. 'Absolutely not. This year I'm forgetting about my birthday.'

Trinity looked sympathetic; she was a woman who'd been forgetting her birthdays for at least the past five years.

'Ages can be tweaked, sweetie,' she promised. 'But no way are we forgetting your birthday. Don't look so worried. I'll sort out everything!'

'That's what's worrying me,' muttered Zoe, but Trin wasn't listening. She was far too busy planning Zoe's party and no matter how hard she tried Zoe just couldn't persuade the star that she really wasn't in a mood to celebrate.

*

The next night, a tired and saddened Zoe somehow managed to drag herself from her hotel room to the taverna that Trin had hired for her party. She was wearing a plain white angel-sleeved dress with simple jewelled flip-flops and had loosely piled her hair up onto her head, so she was dressed for a party even if she didn't feel like partying. The day's filming had been gruelling: Eastwood's endless bellowing had given her a pounding headache, Rufus had been even more diva-like than usual, and she'd checked her BlackBerry for messages from Steve so many times that her eyes were in danger of getting RSI.

Nothing.

She couldn't believe Steve hadn't contacted her, even if it was just to wish her a good day. It seemed that as far as he was concerned it really was over between them. I asked him to leave, Zoe reminded herself sternly as she paid the taxi driver and thanked him in her rapidly improving Italian. It was my decision; it was what I wanted. She just hadn't expected Steve to give up on them so quickly.

Crossing the piazza towards the taverna, Zoe gasped because Trinity really had gone to town. She hadn't just booked the restaurant, it seemed she'd hired the whole square because the entire place was decked out with twinkling pink and white fairy lights, matching balloons, and a live jazz band. The cast and crew sat at an array of tables and chairs chatting while Italian wine poured as though from one of the merry fountains.

Strange to be attending a birthday party I didn't organise, thought Zoe. Strange . . . but actually quite nice!

'It's Zoe!' Melody cried, and at once everyone started clapping and calling out, 'Happy birthday!'

Zoe flushed with pleasure. Although she still didn't feel in the party mood, it was lovely to see how many people had made the effort to come and celebrate with her. Accepting a drink from Melody, her initial pleasure soon faded when she realised that Fern hadn't shown up. She couldn't have made her feelings any clearer if she'd hired the advertising hoarding in Leicester Square and flashed up a message which read 'Zoe Kent and Fern Moss are no longer friends!'

'Hey, you,' said a soft voice from just over her shoulder. Luke. 'Penny for them?'

He was so close Zoe could feel the whisper of his breath across the nape of her neck.

Turning to smile up at him, she said, 'They're not worth that much!'

'Are you sure?' Luke replied. 'I'll pay more if I'm in them.' He paused, looking so vulnerable, that Zoe's heart contracted with tenderness towards him. 'Am I?'

The longing in his eyes darkened them to an almost navy hue, and sent a tingle of desire zapping through her blood stream. Luke looked every bit as gorgeous as she remembered and the memory of their passionate kiss almost threatened to overwhelm her. She ought to tell him she'd made a mistake and that she was too muddled and too hurt by everything that had happened to get involved with somebody new, but there was a part of her that couldn't resist Luke. If he stepped forward right now and took her in his arms she knew she wouldn't be able to push him away, in fact she'd probably take his hand and slip into the shadows where they could exchange intense and searching kisses to their hearts' content.

'A little bit,' she whispered. 'I had a fantastic evening.'

As an answer his hand rose to trace the curve of her cheek. 'Me too. The best of my life.'

She turned her head and kissed his strong hand. 'Thank you.'

Luke closed his eyes and took a deep breath as though gathering the strength to speak. When he opened them again she saw that they were bright with emotion, glittering just like sapphires. 'Zoe, there's something I need to ask you. Something really serious that I have to have an answer to.'

Her breath caught in her throat. What was it he wanted to know?

Luke exhaled slowly. 'Zoe, I—'

'Zoe! There you are!' Trinity swooped down on them, her voice screeching through Luke's words like nails down a blackboard. She grabbed Zoe and crushed her into a bony embrace. 'You look good enough to eat!'

Laughing, Zoe hugged her back, well aware that her Miss Selfridge outfit hardly compared with Trin's ravishing, scarlet Dior column dress.

'Now, I won't let you hog her all night,' Trin declared, wagging her finger at Luke. 'Zoe's the star tonight and everyone's waiting for her.'

Grabbing Zoe's hand, Trin dragged her into the taverna to a table where some of the cast members were already tucking into seafood risotto and garlic bread. Her heart sank when she saw that Rufus was with them, but luckily he was rendered mellow by a gallon of Prosecco and having far too much fun flirting with the waitress to be obnoxious to Zoe. Zoe allowed Trinity to pile her plate high with the delicious food and drank a glass of Granny Smith-sharp wine but as much as she tried to join in with the in-jokes and banter all she could focus on was Luke's interrupted question. What had he been about to ask?

'God, I love Prosecco,' Rufus said, draining his glass and reaching forward to top himself up again. To Zoe he added, 'I remember one time when me and Stevie-boy were in Trieste. We drank three bottles of the stuff and got lost on the way back to the hostel. Because of me we nearly died!'

'Now why doesn't that surprise me?' said Zoe drily, but Rufus was too busy laughing to hear her.

'What happened?' asked Trin, all agog.

'I saw a fence and I was convinced that if we climbed over we'd be back at the hotel in no time. Anyway, over we climbed and out of nowhere appeared a security guard yelling at us in Italian, with a bloody vicious dog ready to attack. So what do you think Steve did?'

Zoe had no idea. She was still taken aback to learn that Steve had ever got himself into such a scrape in the first place. More proof, she supposed, that she'd never really known him at all.

'He only charmed the guard by telling him how amazing the dog was,' Rufus wheezed. 'Somehow Steve persuaded him we were just a couple of stupid lost English boys rather than thieves out to rob his restaurant!'

She smiled. Now *that* sounded like the Steve she knew.

'By the time we left they'd swapped addresses and even played a game of cards!' Rufus concluded. 'Classic!'

They all laughed. 'Then there was the time we were at that fancy-dress party and Trin thought she'd had her handbag stolen.' Rufus was nudging Trinity. 'Steve took charge and organised a massive search and then you found the bag under a pile of coats. But the funny thing was that while he was ordering everyone around, Steve was dressed as a giant banana!'

Everyone at the table creased up at this, except for Zoe, who just felt desperately sad. Steve might have had a wilder side when he was younger but he was still the same man underneath, the man she'd fallen in love with. Maybe she shouldn't have doubted how well she knew him after all.

Lost in thought Zoe barely touched the delicious tiramisu when it appeared for dessert. Her appetite had well and truly vanished, and although surrounded by her friends and colleagues all she could see was the heartbroken expression on Steve's face when she'd told him to leave.

Oh dear God, what had she done?

'Hey, birthday girl, I've got a present for you,' Trin announced proudly, delving into her Chloé bag and plucking out a beautifully wrapped parcel. 'Happy birthday!'

'You shouldn't have!' Touched by the gesture, Zoe took the present and unravelled the intricate tangle of ribbons and paper to reveal a jewellery box. Popping the lid open she gasped to see a stunning emerald brooch nestling on a bed of white velvet. 'How did you know I like emeralds?'

Trin looked confused. 'I didn't. Emerald's your birthstone. Didn't you know that?'

Zoe shook her head. She'd had no idea. She'd never had any interest whatsoever in birthstones, prophecies or psychics. Until recently.

'You must know the old rhyme,' Mel chipped in from

the far end of the table. Features contorted into an expression of deep concentration she quoted: ' "Who first beholds the light of day/In spring's sweet flower month of May/And wears an emerald all her life/Shall be a loved and loving wife." ' She ground to a halt as she just realised what she said. 'Oh my God! Sorry!'

Something really weird was going on. That was the exact line from the poem in her hotel room. Zoe smiled at Mel. 'It's fine,' she said. Mel hadn't done it on purpose but she had made Zoe even more perplexed.

When Trinity placed a pile of cards in front of Zoe she was still in a daze as she tried to work out what was happening. Almost automatically she worked her way through the cards, laughing at the jokes and holding up the rude one (Rufus's, surprise, surprise) until she reached the last one. Just a plain white envelope. Inside was a thick piece of plain white card. On the card was printed four words: 'Will you marry me?'

There was no signature or any other mark that would identify the sender. It had to be from someone at the party because it was hand delivered. Who could have sent it?

Luke.

Zoe glanced down to the far end of the table where Luke was chatting to one of the gaffers. Sensing her gaze he looked up and waved shyly. She felt that spine-tingling pull of desire and looked away hastily. So that was the question he wanted to ask her! After just one date? But then they knew each other so well and the chemistry between them was undeniable, so what was there to wait for? Every time their eyes met she half expected one of them to combust with desire. But was desire enough to base a marriage on? What about love? She liked Luke but she was pretty sure she didn't love him yet. She'd loved Steve from the minute they'd first met.

Yeah, well, look how that had turned out. Love at first sight was definitely not to be trusted. Whereas longing and passion . . . well, those were different issues altogether.

Zoe put the card face down on the table and bit her lip. The proposal had now raised a whole question all of its own, but there was one question that would drive her crazy unless she found an answer fairly soon.

How on earth should she reply?

25

'I can't work on this pathetic excuse for a movie a second longer, God dammit!' Eastwood Jones's bellow could be heard right the way across the film lot. Cast and crew alike held their collective breath as the director flung his megaphone onto the ground and stomped off set. Hot on his heels was Rufus, who was also shouting at everyone, from the assistant director to the guy who made the coffee. Trinity was in tears; Luke's sculpted clean-shaven face was rigid with fury, and poor Mel was white and shaking, having just had a strip torn off her.

'I can't work like this any longer,' Trinity said, dabbing her eyes with the sleeve of her elaborate costume. 'All he does is roar at me. I thought he was a monster in Thailand, but he's a million times worse here.'

'Too right,' agreed Luke. He put his arm round Trinity's trembling shoulders and gave her a hug. To Zoe he said, 'You can tell our illustrious producer that if this carries on Trin and I are walking; contract or no contract.

No one treats Trinity like that.'

Zoe sighed. Since Luke had accused her of being a control freak she'd been really working on stopping her fixing compulsion so it was ironic in the extreme that he was now asking her to make it all better. Promising the disgruntled actors she would do her best to sort things out, Zoe reluctantly set off in pursuit of Rufus, who predictably was smoking a cigarette in his trailer while Eastwood Jones puffed furiously on a fat cigar.

'You've really upset Luke and Trinity,' she told Rufus.

'An actress who's upset,' said Rufus as he threw his hands in the air. 'So what's new?'

'I'm serious. They're fuming. Luke was talking about walking.'

'He can try,' sneered Rufus. 'I'll sue his arse to kingdom come.'

Zoe wanted to grab him by the lapels of his silly purple crushed-velvet jacket and shake him.

'Luke won't care about that. He's got his own lawyers and enough money for a hundred law suits,' she snapped. 'But it will mean the end of the movie if he quits. We've already recast once and we're hideously over budget. You need to go over and apologise. Both of you!'

'Whatever,' Rufus said, looking like a teenager who'd just been told to tidy his room. 'Anyway, if we're playing the blame game then maybe you ought to start looking at yourself!'

'Me?' Zoe stepped backwards as his bony digit sliced through the air just beneath her nose. 'What have I done?'

'You wrote the goddamn script!' boomed Eastwood.

Zoe felt cold all over. Had all her recent problems been affecting her work? She hadn't thought so, but maybe she'd been kidding herself.

'What's wrong with my script?' she whispered.

'It's a heap of shit, that's what!' yelled Eastwood, his face scarlet with fury. 'There's no sex, no explosions, no guns! Who in their right mind would want to watch a piece of junk like that?'

She goggled at him. Explosions and guns in a period piece? He had to be kidding?

'Who the hell wants to watch a movie that doesn't have a decent car chase in it?' So, he wasn't kidding. 'We'll go straight to DVD before you can say "boring crap".'

'*The Portrait of a Lady* is a literary classic,' Zoe tried to explain. 'As a novel it's stood the test of time.' But Eastwood wasn't listening.

'How about we beef this up? I got an idea: what if Isabel decides she's had enough of Osmond and his bitch? So she gets a gun.' Rufus nodded along thoughtfully. 'They did have guns then, right?'

'Right,' Zoe agreed faintly.

'Right!' said Rufus, leaning forward and getting enthusiastic.

'So she grabs a gun and goes on a shooting rampage!' Eastwood said excitedly.

'Um . . .'

'That's brilliant, Eastwood,' said Rufus.

'What if her daughter joins in too?'

'You're a genius!'

They're joking, Zoe told herself. At any moment they'll shout 'punk'd' or something!

'I like it,' Rufus said slowly. 'It could be a mother-and-daughter shooting spree. A keep-it-in-the-family version of *Bonnie and Clyde*—'

'Or *Thelma and Louise*,' said Eastwood, equally enthused.

Rufus turned to Zoe with his eyes wide and wild. 'It'll be right up your street, Zoe, being a feminist. Feel free to burn your bra any time.'

Zoe stared at him. Something in her snapped and she knew that she couldn't tolerate another second of working with Rufus. He was an arrogant, misogynistic, ignorant pig – those were his good points – and no career was worth putting up with him for. For years she'd tolerated him because he was Steve's friend, and then because he was her producer, but she wasn't suffering his stupidity any longer.

'Killing men isn't feminism, you moron,' she said icily. 'And it takes more than guns and car chases to make a narrative work. If you had any talents other than getting drunk and harassing women then you'd know that! I've no idea how you've made it this far in the industry because you are totally ignorant and lacking in any judgement and integrity. Seriously, Rufus, you have to be the worst producer it's ever been my misfortune to work with.'

Rufus was crimson with rage, with the exception of his cruel lips, which had turned bloodless. For a second Zoe really thought he was going to thump her because his hands bunched up into fists. After seven years the gloves were finally off and they eyed each other with mutual loathing.

Then Rufus started to laugh, a harsh sound and not joyous in any way. 'You're right.' But he didn't look like a person who was seeing her point. 'And a person with "integrity" would never sack someone for just speaking her mind.' He threw her a cruel smile. 'But as you were only too happy to point out, I don't have any integrity, so guess what Zoe? You're fired!'

She stared at him. 'What?'

'You heard me,' sneered Rufus. 'You're fired. Sacked. Let go. You are the weakest link, goodbye. Well, go on then. What are you waiting for?'

Zoe didn't want to give Rufus the satisfaction of seeing her cry so she bit her cheek hard and squeezed back the tears that threatened to fall. She loved her job, prided herself on her career. She'd never been sacked in her life.

'Cheerio, Zoe,' sneered Rufus, loving every minute of his victory. 'Make sure you collect your P45 on the way out.'

Reeling with shock, Zoe stepped out of the trailer and slowly made her way across the film lot. Rufus's mocking laughter rang in her ears until she was a fair distance away and only when she could hear him no longer did she allow herself to cry. Yes, the job had turned into something of a nightmare, but she'd slaved over the script and had really been proud of what she'd created. And now it was all for nothing, all those pages of carefully crafted language massacred into some insane action movie. She was shaken to discover just how much Rufus hated her.

Dashing tears away with the back of her hand, Zoe reached into her bag for her BlackBerry. It was only when Steve's answer machine message kicked in that the horrible realisation dawned anew: they weren't together anymore. But Steve was the only person she wanted to speak to. He was the one person who knew her best and who understood just how precious her scripts were to her. She needed to talk to Steve. No one else would do. Luke didn't even come close. Yes, he was fun and a dear friend and she was flattered by his attention but when the chips were down she didn't want Luke, did she? She wasn't in love with Luke. No matter how hard he'd tried to convince her, she knew deep down that he wasn't her soul mate.

That place belonged to another. It was Steve's; it always had been and always would be. There was no one else for Zoe.

'Steve,' Zoe began her message tentatively, wondering why she felt so nervous about something so simple. 'It's me, Zoe. Oh, why aren't you here? I need you!' Her voice caught and then before she had a minute to stop herself the words were just tumbling out. 'Oh, Steve, please, please call me. I've made a huge mistake; I know that now!' Her tears were falling fast and this time she didn't even bother attempting to stop them. What was the point? She really was at rock bottom. All she needed was a pickaxe and she'd be ready to dig. She took a shuddering breath. 'I know we're not together anymore but I wish so much that we were. I'm not saying that because I'm like Isabel and think I ought to do the responsible thing, but because I have the freedom to choose, Steve, and I do! I choose you! I love you and I miss you and us and the way things used to be. I know this is the right thing and the right choice. If you want me back, that is.'

That last sentence brought her to a standstill. He didn't want her back.

'And, well, that's it. OK, well, bye.'

She hung up. Steve would probably just erase her message straight away. And who could blame him? She hadn't exactly been sympathetic to him lately. When he'd tried to protect her she'd accused him of lying and when he'd levelled with her she'd rejected him. So much for 'for better for worse'. She should have paid more attention to that one.

Zoe had well and truly blown it.

Two hours later, when she had almost finished packing her bags, Zoe was still crying. It was as though someone had flicked an internal switch and try as she might she just couldn't wipe her tears away fast enough. Even when she went to answer the knock on her door she was still sobbing.

'Bloody hell! You look like shit!' cried Susannah when Zoe answered the door.

'Thanks. I feel so much better now.'

'I heard what that little arse did and, believe me, I'm spitting chips too. But seriously, Zoe, it's not worth crying over.' Susannah's face was dark with anger. 'From what I'm hearing you've probably had a lucky escape. This film is jinxed, especially now that Rufus and Eastwood have written in a gun fight. I've resigned in protest.'

Zoe was touched. 'Thanks, Susannah, I appreciate your support.'

'Good,' said the older woman briskly. Delving into her Marc Jacobs bag she plucked out a wad of Kleenex.

'Now dry your eyes and stop snivelling. There'll be other films, I promise. No one will take any notice of what an idiot like Rufus might say.'

Zoe took the tissues and wiped her eyes. 'I'm not really that upset about the film.'

Susannah looked doubtful. 'So what's with the puffy frog look then?' she asked, gesturing to Zoe's swollen eyes.

'Steve,' Zoe said miserably. Just saying his name made her sob. 'I can't get hold of him and I'm missing him so much. I've got a horrible feeling he's ignoring me and doesn't want to talk. Breaking up was a really bad idea.'

'Well, we all knew that, you silly girl,' said Susannah, giving Zoe a hug, then pulling back and looking her in the eye. 'Anyone can see that you and Steve are made for one another. Now tell me, does Steve have an agent?'

Zoe nodded.

'Right. Well, this is the plan: I call the agent and get her to contact Steve about a new film. He's not working at the minute so he won't turn that meeting down. We'll say he needs to come to Italy to see me and then you can meet him instead. You can talk things through, and bingo! You rekindle your love in beautiful Tuscany and everyone's happy. Am I not a genius?'

Zoe laughed through her tears. 'A total genius. But what if he doesn't believe it?'

The expression on Susannah's face said that in her

book failure wasn't an option. 'Then we have to make it believable. We'll make it a real film offer.'

'Huh?'

'I'll find a screenplay,' Susannah said airily. 'We'll pitch a film. Steve will come on board. We'll make the film. Steve'll be delighted and you two will live happily ever after.'

Zoe sank onto the bed. For the first time in what seemed like ages she felt a small glimmer of hope. 'Ironically, I do have a screenplay,' she said, thinking of the manuscript locked safely away back in Richmond. 'It's a rom com. And if we could get the finances, Steve would be the perfect director.'

'Great!' Susannah settled onto the bed next to Zoe and kicked off her Jimmy Choos. 'So pitch it to me!'

Zoe closed her eyes and dragged her mind back to a sultry July evening that felt like a lifetime ago.

'It all starts in a small quiet street in Richmond,' she began. 'A group of girlfriends are celebrating a hen night and have organised for a clairvoyant to read their fortunes.'

'Mmm, I like it,' Susannah said thoughtfully. 'We've got friendship, men and that paranormal stuff that's so trendy right now. How does it end?'

Zoe smiled and her stomach flick-flacked with excitement. 'I'm not sure yet but do you know what? I think I have the perfect idea!'

'Zoe!'

Luke looked thrilled when he opened the door of his hotel room. His honey-blond hair was ruffled from sleep and he swept a pile of clothes from a canvas chair and motioned for her to take a seat. 'Excuse the mess. We've been filming some crazy hours and my body clock's screwed, I'm afraid. I was just catching forty winks.'

'You look tired,' Zoe observed. Luke's usually merry blue eyes were bloodshot and bruised with purple shadows, and a sprinkling of golden stubble dusted his strong jawline. As he leaned against the table and smoothed down his crumpled white T-shirt he yawned widely.

'I'm shattered. Eastwood's a bloody slave driver. I was only water-skiing by moonlight last night.'

Zoe's eyes widened. 'Water-skiing? In a Henry James adaptation?'

He grimaced. 'Don't ask. The whole thing's a disaster.

Just be glad you escaped before it was too late. If my reputation survives this it'll be a bloody miracle.'

Now that she was over the humiliation of being ordered off set Zoe was actually very glad to have escaped. She felt as though ten tons of concrete had just been lifted from the top of her head. It was a relief to be getting out of the whole thing.

But first she had to talk to Luke.

Luke perched on the counter and crossed his arms across his strong chest. 'But enough shop talk,' he said slowly. 'Something tells me this isn't just a social call. Am I right?'

Zoe nodded.

'And something tells me I'm not going to like it. I'm right again, aren't I?'

Even all crumpled from sleep Luke was still the most gorgeous man she'd ever laid eyes on. He was every bit as sexy now as he'd been the other night when he'd kissed her in the bell tower. Luke Scottman had it all. Except for one thing: he wasn't Steve.

'The other evening, at my party, you wanted to ask me something,' she said slowly. The card with 'Will you marry me?' lay folded in the bottom of her bag. She had looked at it a hundred times as she tried to decide what to do for the best.

Luke shrugged his broad shoulders. 'Hey, forget it. I have.'

She stared at him. 'Really?'

He gave her a heart-meltingly sad smile. 'No, not really but I know I'm wasting my time. Let's face it, Zoe, I don't need to ask you how you feel about me any more, do I? Not when deep down I already know.'

Zoe couldn't speak.

'You still love Steve,' Luke said gently. 'I know you do. There's no point kidding myself any longer. It doesn't matter how much I wish you didn't or how much I love you because it won't make any difference. You've always loved Steve and I think you always will.'

'I'm sorry,' Zoe whispered, unable to bear the hurt in his voice.

'Hey, hey, I'll live,' Luke murmured, stepping forwards and folding her into his arms. Unlike the other evening, though, this embrace wasn't passionate and limb-meltingly sexy, but rather regretful and tender and warm.

He's my dear friend, Zoe reminded herself as she rested her head on his shoulder and closed her eyes, and I wish him all the happiness in the world.

'These things happen on set,' Luke said. 'Crushes, flirtations. It's never real, just a way to pass the time or the inevitable consequence of people having to work so closely together.' But the tremor in his voice belied the robust words, as did the way he trembled as he held her close. Zoe's heart broke for him.

'Go and find Steve,' Luke ordered, dropping a kiss onto the crown of her head and then releasing her. 'And be happy, or I might just come looking for you again!'

'And you be happy too.' Zoe blinked away tears.

Her eyes rested on the wedding band and emerald engagement ring that still nestled on her finger and her heart skipped a beat. She was fond of Luke and, if she were honest, flattered by his attention, but she didn't love him and never had. He was right: Steve had always been the one.

'Don't you fret about me,' Luke said gruffly. 'I'll probably find some beautiful, big-boobed actress and live happily ever after.'

And that was when Zoe had a flash of psychic genius that would have given Angela a run for her money. Who adored Luke? Who had he been protecting so furiously from the wrath of Eastwood Jones only the other day? The answer was so blindingly obvious that it was all she could do not to laugh out loud!

'Do you know what? I think she's a lot nearer than you think!' Zoe told him as she reached up onto tiptoes and brushed a sisterly kiss onto his stubbly cheek. 'Take care, Luke, and be happy.'

Once she was gone Luke stared sadly after her, his fingers resting on the spot where, only minutes before, her lips had rested. Then with a heavy sigh he picked up his bag of DVDs and went to find Trinity . . .

*

Luisa de Ruissano's office was located in the heart of Rome, not much more than the flip of a penny from the Trevi Fountain. Although the sun beat down outside onto the baked pavements and hordes of excited tourists flowed though the streets, Zoe shivered and pulled her lacy cardigan against her. Luisa de Ruissano was renting Zoe her office for Steve's pretend interview, and the woman liked the air con set to *freeze*. Or maybe Zoe was shivering because she was so nervous? She was shaking so much that her teeth were chattering.

Actually 'nervous' seemed a bit of an understatement for this seething, churning sick feeling that was see-sawing in the pit of her stomach. As she paced the office, pausing only to peer out of the window, Zoe thought that she'd probably never felt more anxious in her life; more than her first date with Steve and a million times more than their wedding day. This time she knew with every cell of her being that Steve was the man she wanted to spend the rest of her life with. There were no *what ifs* or nagging fears about the psychic's predictions now, only a firm and unmovable certainty that she was doing the right thing. The rest of her life depended on what Steve decided he wanted, and for Zoe, the Fix-It Queen, that was a pretty tough thing to come to terms with.

Where was he? He was supposed to be here an hour ago. Steve was never late anywhere, not unless there was a very good reason. His punctuality was one of the things that made him so dependable. Surely he wouldn't be late for a potential job.

Crossing the office for the umpteenth time Zoe started to despair. He wasn't coming. She had to face the truth: her plan to get Steve back had failed. Common sense was telling her that she should just give up and at least keep her dignity but her inner voice was screaming over and over again that she loved Steve and wanted him back.

Glancing at her watch again her heart plummeted into her glittery flip-flops. That was it. He wasn't coming. Game over.

No show :(

Zoe texted Susannah, who immediately answered with a stern command to keep her chin up. If that didn't work they'd come up with something else. In spite of feeling so miserable Zoe couldn't help but smile. Even when it came to organising people's love lives Susannah still had to crack the whip.

Deciding to leave a note, on the Victoria Beckham-slim chance Steve might still turn up, Zoe scribbled something down using the emerald pen from the hotel. What could she say? She'd need more paper than the large-print copy of *War and Peace* if she were to put into writing everything she needed to tell him. For a second the fountain pen hovered over the paper, then she started to write, the words flowing as fast and as smoothly as the ink.

> *Dearest Steve,*
>   *You're probably not coming but if you have and get this note, you'll have recognised my hand-writing by now and are probably wondering why you've been dragged here under false pretences. The reason is that I wasn't sure whether you'd come if you'd known I wanted to see you. We didn't exactly part on good terms and I'm so sorry about that. I'm sorry about everything. I made a really big mistake ever doubting you and our relationship. I just wish I'd had the sense to realise it earlier.*
>   *Zoe x*

Locking the office and returning to reception, Zoe handed the note to the receptionist. Now she needed to consult her *Rough Guide* and find her way to the bar where Susannah was waiting. She could seriously do with a large glass of Pinot.

'Zoe?'

Zoe froze. The arctic conditions in that office must have done something to her brain because that dear voice, as comforting and as warm as tomato soup on Bonfire Night, sounded just like Steve.

'I see you got the pen I sent you,' he continued.

Turning around slowly, hardly daring to believe it was true, Zoe saw that Steve really was there.

Dressed in a rumpled linen suit, powder-blue shirt, and with his shades perched on top of his head he looked every bit as surprised as she felt.

'Steve?' she gasped.

'Hi.'

His opening words only just sunk in. '*You* left the pen for me?'

Steve gave her a wink, the same secret wink he used to give her across the studio or the edit suite, and her stomach somersaulted. 'You've been working out my clues far too easily lately so I decided it was time to make things a little more challenging!'

'So it wasn't just a coincidence! It *was* there because I used to have a Parker pen!'

Steve nodded. 'I've never forgotten. You had that pen when we first met and you used to tap it against your teeth while you were deep in thought. I was mesmerised! I think that was when I started to realise that my feelings for you were more inappropriate than a mentor's ought to be!'

'And it had the emeralds in it,' Zoe said excitedly as she started to piece the clues together. 'You always buy me emeralds because of the green flecks in my eyes!'

'That's not why I bought you emeralds.' Steve stared

at her and then started laughing. 'I bought you emeralds because that's your birthstone, you wally!'

'Hey, watch who you're calling a wally!' Zoe grinned.

He grinned back. 'And that poem I sent you – "And wears an emerald all her life/ Shall be a loved and loving wife" – it's going to apply to us from now on.'

Steve dropped to his knees. Zoe could not dare to believe what was happening.

'If you'll let it, of course,' he said.

'Steve!' cried Zoe. 'What are you doing?'

'What I wanted to do ever since the first time I saw you,' Steve told her. Delving into his pocket he pulled out a small box and, opening it with a flick of his wrist, revealed a perfect solitaire ring. 'I was going to play it safe and leave you to decide,' he continued, smiling shyly up at her, 'but instead I thought it might be more fun to leave a few clues to remind you of what we had, then come out and win you back. Did you get my special birthday note? The one that said, "Will you marry me?"'

Zoe's eyes were wide. That was Steve? She felt like leaping up and down with relief and happiness!

'Zoe?' Steve prompted. 'I hate to rush you but being down on our knees is a bit painful for us poor old thirty-somethings! So? Will you? Marry me? Again?'

'Yes, yes, yes!' cried Zoe, dropping down to the floor and flinging her arms round him. As if there could ever be any doubt! She knew that she loved this man with all her heart.

And when he kissed her, a soft kiss that contained the depth of his feelings for her, Zoe knew they'd never be apart again.

Steve was her rock, her best friend and her whole world. In his arms Zoe knew that she had finally come home and that this time she was there to stay.

27

'Your carriage awaits, my lady,' said Steve to Zoe as they exchanged the cool of the offices for the blast furnace heat outside.

Zoe's hands flew to her mouth, for parked right outside the door was a white stretch limo, complete with tinted windows and a uniformed chauffeur already holding the door open for her.

'This is for us? You have to be kidding!'

Steve took her hand and squeezed it. 'I kid you not!'

Zoe didn't need to be asked twice. Although the car was horribly ostentatious she had always secretly longed to ride inside one, while sipping champagne and listening to music. Steve had used to tease her and said she'd obviously watched too many episodes of *Girls of the Playboy Mansion*, so she was totally taken aback by this gesture. Two huge surprises in one day? This was a new and spontaneous side to Steve, and one she was really starting to like!

But inside the limo was yet another surprise:

Susannah was seated on the far side, reclining against the white leather and sipping Bolly from an elegant flute. But Susannah was supposed to be in a bar the far side of the city! Zoe had only spoken to her a few minutes ago.

Susannah looked sheepish when Zoe asked her what she was doing there. 'I'm afraid I haven't been totally straight with you. Here,' she added, passing Zoe a glass of champagne. 'You look as though you could do with a drink.'

Zoe took the glass and settled down opposite. Wow! The leather was soft and the champagne delicious. This really was the way to travel.

'I'm sorry I put you through all that rigmarole, but Steve had sworn me to secrecy,' Susannah explained. 'He recruited me to the cause of winning you back pretty much as soon as you two broke up. It hasn't been easy, though! It would be easier to smuggle drugs than to get that bloody pen and poetry into your room! I'm sure the concierge thought I was a stalker!'

Zoe shook her head in disbelief. 'I was starting to think I was going mad!'

Susannah laughed. 'No, I think I'm the mad one for agreeing to all this in the first place. I've been head-hunted many times but never to arrange a wedding before!'

Zoe's mouth fell open. 'What?'

Steve slid into the seat beside her and pulled her

close against him. 'I asked Susannah to help me plan the most amazing, unpredictable surprise wedding there's ever been. I hope that's all right with the bride-to-be?'

She flung her arms around his neck. 'It's more than all right, Steve! It's fantastic! I can't think of anything that would make me happier than being Mrs Kent. For real! And as soon as possible!'

'Phew!' Steve mimed mopping his brow as he caught Susannah's eye. 'That's a relief! There'd be a lot of explaining to do if you'd said no.'

Zoe glanced out of the window. By now they had sped through the outskirts of the city and the limo was winding its way up into the Apennine Mountains.

'Where are we going?' she asked, but Steve just smiled and silenced her with a kiss. Minutes later the limo rounded a corner and paused before two enormous wrought-iron gates, which swung open without so much as a whisper. Ahead lay a thick gravel path leading like a cream ribbon to the most beautiful villa Zoe had ever seen.

As the car scrunched along the drive Zoe saw that on the main lawn staff were busy setting up an arbour made of ornate white metal work, which was threaded with plump pink roses and white ribbons, which drifted lazily in the warm breeze.

For a second the view shimmered because she felt so overcome. Steve had planned all this for her?

'Do you like it?' he asked.

'Do I like it?' Zoe shook her head in wonder. 'Steve, I *love* it!'

Steve smiled his sweet curly smile and kissed her. 'I'm so glad. This is just where and how I wanted to get married the first time around, but I knew you didn't like surprises.'

She touched his cheek and smiled up into those honey-warm eyes. 'I'm not the same person I was back then. I love surprises now, especially ones as wonderful as this.'

'Thank God!' Susannah exclaimed with feeling. 'Because there are plenty more surprises to come. Now let Steve go for a minute. Everything's arranged for your big day – all you need to do is sit back, relax and enjoy every minute!'

This was crazy and the last thing she would ever have expected from Steve. To be honest, she felt as though she was in a weird dream. The door to the limo was opened and Steve ran off to get ready.

Things got even more weird when Zoe realised that the man who opened her door was no chauffeur. It was her dad!

'Steve flew me over,' Mike Forster explained after hugging and kissing his daughter. 'He's thought of absolutely everything.'

Looking around at the villa, the arbour, and the

countless stunning flower arrangements, Zoe's heart contracted with love for Steve. There wasn't a tulip in sight!

'I wouldn't have missed this for the world,' Zoe's dad beamed. 'I can't wait to give my beautiful daughter away.'

There was a snort from Susannah at this. 'Outdated patriarchal practice!'

'Dad, meet Susannah,' Zoe said hastily. 'My boss, friend and feminist.'

Mike's bluey-green eyes swept over Susannah, drinking in every inch of her gym-sculpted body, shown off to perfection in a clinging olive-green dress and her sleek mane of ebony hair, and he smiled.

'Delighted to meet you,' he said, taking her hand and raising it to his lips. 'And may I say that you are the most beautiful feminist it's ever been my pleasure to meet?'

Zoe winced and waited for Susannah to wallop Mike over the head with her Marc Jacobs bag, but to her surprise the older woman was laughing. Was that a blush spreading across her cheeks? Zoe groaned inwardly as she watched her father work his usual magic. Surely he wasn't already on the hunt for wife number six?

'Sorry to interrupt,' she said, stepping between them and laying her hand on Susannah's arm, 'but there's something I've just thought of and I can't possibly get married unless it's sorted.'

'Right!' Snapping straight back into efficient work

mode, Susannah fished out her BlackBerry. 'What do you need?'

Zoe exhaled slowly and wearily. 'It's not a case of what. It's a case of whom. Susannah, do you think you could get Fern here?'

Susannah's face fell. Stroppy directors and moody actors were no problem but the angry and hurt Fern was another matter entirely. 'I'll get Fern to the villa if I have to enlist the local Mafia to kidnap her,' she said.

But it was clear from the look on her face that she didn't hold out much hope. And nor did Zoe.

Two hours and much pampering and champagne drinking later, Zoe stood in the villa's vaulted hallway waiting to walk through the double doors and into the golden-syrup sunshine of a perfect Italian evening. With her were her bridesmaids, Libby and Priya, dressed in jade silk, with white roses woven into their hair. Although Charlotte hadn't been able to make it, being about to give birth at any minute, she had phoned to wish her soon-to-be sister-in-law all the happiness in the world.

Zoe shivered with delicious anticipation, hardly able to wait before she became Steve's wife for the second and final time.

'You look stunning, Zo,' Libby said with satisfaction as she adjusted Zoe's tiara and tweaked a ringlet into place.

'She does,' agreed Zoe's father, squeezing her hand proudly. 'Steve's a lucky man.'

Zoe smiled. 'I think I'm the lucky one. Look at all this! And after I was so quick to give up on what we have.'

'You're both lucky,' Priya told her, in full bridesmaid mode as she straightened the train of Zoe's dress and then handed her the bouquet of pink and cream roses.

Libby raised her eyebrows. 'You've got soppy in your old age! What's brought this on? You are seriously loved up with your guy. Aren't you?'

Shyly Priya rested one hand on her flat stomach. 'I wasn't going to say anything but . . .'

'Oh my God!' Zoe's hands flew to her mouth and then she and Priya were hugging and crying while Libby frantically dabbed at Zoe's running mascara with a tissue. As Zoe kissed her friend she couldn't help thinking how strange it was that everything Angela had said on that long-ago hen night really did seem to have come true, if not quite in the way that they had anticipated! That night was so fresh in her memory that if she closed her eyes she could almost see Angela, with her kindly round face and soft grey curls . . . except, wait a minute! This wasn't her imagination! It couldn't be? This was impossible!

'Surprised to see me, my loves?' Angela chortled as the three girls stared at her in disbelief.

Libby's face was a picture of amazement. 'Oh my God! You were able to predict when and where Zoe and Steve were getting married? That's amazing!'

'That *would* be amazing, if it were true!' Angela chuckled. 'No, sweetheart, that lovely Steve invited me. He thought I should be here to see how it all ended.' She glanced at the three girls and smiled. 'I think maybe now you all believe that the spirit guides really do know best?'

Zoe kissed her cheek.

'Well, it doesn't take my psychic gift to predict that you – all of you, in fact – are going to be very, very happy.'

'Can I ask you one thing?' Zoe asked Angela quietly, as she heard the string quartet start to play 'Pie Jesu' and her bridesmaids rushed off to take their places. 'I'm going to be casting a film next month and I think there's a part in it that would be perfect for you.'

Angela smiled, her warm eyes crinkling. 'I'd be honoured.'

As she scuttled off Zoe stared after her. For a second she contemplated calling her back to ask whether or not Fern would ever forgive her. But did she really need to be told? After all, the Fern-shaped hole in her wedding made her feelings pretty clear.

Zoe sighed. Angela had gone and with her any chance of knowing what the future held, which was probably a good thing. Angela's predictions hadn't made her very happy in the past.

'Right, we're ready.' Mike Forster let himself into the hall and offered Zoe his arm. The doors swung open and Zoe took a deep breath. There at the end of the aisle and turning to face her was Steve. Her Steve, his face alight with love and smiling from ear to ear. Marrying him again was the best decision she'd ever made – and she knew she'd marry him a thousand times more if that's what it took to make it stick. If Steve was the groom, Zoe knew she was always the bride.

'OK, Dad,' she whispered, reaching up to kiss his cheek, 'let's get this show on the road.'

'Wait! Wait! Wait!'

The shout from the far end of the hall was so loud that Zoe's feet literally did leave the floor. Turning round, she saw to her delight that it was Fern. Fern, running across the tiled floor, her hair in disarray, a jade bridesmaid's dress hoiked up at the side and still wearing her purple platform boots. Susannah, who was clutching a posy and a tiara, which she was trying her hardest to wedge into Fern's curly mop, closely followed her.

'Susannah! You did it!' Zoe cried in delight while Fern hurled herself into her arms, gabbling away nineteen to the dozen.

'I'm sorry, I'm sorry,' Fern said over and over again. 'I've been such an idiot!'

'Me too,' Zoe told her, tears of happiness threatening to ruin her perfect makeup. 'I never meant to hurt you.'

'Shush!' Fern said. 'We all make mistakes. I have, you have, Steve has, and bloody Rufus makes millions of 'em!'

'What did Susannah say to change your mind?' she asked, pushing Fern's crazy curls back from her flushed cheeks and securing the tiara.

'Susannah? What's she got to do with it?' Fern smoothed the silk skirt over her slim hips. 'I was coming anyway. I wouldn't miss my best friend's wedding for the world. It was just that I lost my watch, and then I got the shower gel and the moisturizer muddled and then I lost my train ticket from Tuscany and then I had to—'

Laughing, Zoe held up her hands. 'OK, OK! I get it! Another Fern-tastrophe!'

Fern laughed. 'I'll never change.'

'Do you know what?' Zoe laughed as she pulled the long skirt from Fern's knickers. 'I hope you never do. You're my best friend, Fern, and I wouldn't want you any other way.'

'Best friends forever?' asked Fern.

Zoe kissed her cheek tenderly. And then she picked up her bouquet, nodded at her father and stepped down the aisle and into the rest of her life.

Epilogue

'And that's a wrap!' Steve cried out to everyone on the set of his latest movie. 'Well done, everyone!'

Immediately the film lot rang with the cheers and whistles of the cast and crew, and the popping of champagne corks filled the air. On set, Luke, Trinity and Angela clapped and beamed, unable to believe that the past four months of hard work were finally over. Handing the film to Melody, Steve said, 'Take it to production, please, Mel. *Hen Night Prophecies*, Final Scene. We've finished it!'

'That was the most fun I've ever had on a shoot,' Luke declared, his blue eyes shining. His arm reached around Trin's tiny waist as he hugged her excitedly. 'I've got a feeling it's going to be a huge success.'

'I *know* it is,' Angela said with confidence. 'My guides told me so ages back!'

'Of course they did. And how could it be otherwise when my beautiful, talented wife wrote every single word?' said Steve proudly. 'Come on, Mrs Kent. Don't hide away. This is your moment too.'

Blushing, Zoe took his outstretched hand and when Steve pulled her close and kissed her there was another cheer, and none louder than that from Fern. As the fully fledged production designer, Fern had really blossomed on this shoot, as had her relationship with her new man. Seeing them together now, laughing and teasing one another, Zoe didn't need to ask Angela whether another wedding was on the cards anytime soon. She'd never seen Fern so happy.

'How about we all go out to celebrate?' Steve was saying to Fern's partner. 'I know a great Indian. I can't promise we'll get what we order but we'll have a fantastic time.'

But Fern wound her arms around her man's neck in a possessive gesture and shook her head. 'Sorry, boss, but I think you've had more than your fair share of our time. We're going home for a private celebration!'

'Get a room, you guys!' laughed Zoe. Turning to Luke she said, 'Are you up for it? Angela, my dad and Susannah are coming.'

'And me,' chipped in Priya, from her seat in Steve's director's chair where she was taking the weight off her feet. 'Unless lowly documentary makers and their boyfriends aren't included?'

'You can come, but no gross-out pregnancy stories,' teased Zoe. 'I want to eat my curry without vivid descriptions of your varicose veins!'

'Irresistible as this sounds I'm afraid I'll have to pass,' Luke pulled a mock sad face. 'As it happens I've got a date of my own.'

'Quick, ring *Heat*,' said Fern, her eyes like saucers at this tasty morsel of gossip. 'Who is she, the poor cow? Does she know about your smelly socks and *Star Trek* obsession?'

'She does actually, and she doesn't care,' Luke told her with a grin. 'Oh, come on, guys, surely you've worked it out by now?' Turning to Zoe said, 'You hinted at it months ago!'

'Trinity?' asked Zoe, delighted. *Like, duh*, as Libby would say. Trin and Luke were perfect for one another. You didn't need to be Einstein to figure that much out.

After the disastrous almost wedding, Bobby Roberts had quickly turned his attentions to an *X Factor* finalist and Trinity had been surprisingly blasé about it all. She'd given interviews wishing them well and had then posed for *Playboy* to show Bobby exactly what he was missing. Or rather Zoe had assumed it was Bobby this had been aimed at but now of course the truth was glaringly obvious. They'd been out before. Trin had always adored Luke and he adored her too, he'd just needed to get over his unrealistic dream of Zoe as his idealised woman in order to see what was under his nose.

'Of course it's Trinity,' Luke said with a grin. To the

actress he added, 'Looks like our secret's out, babe.'

'Good,' said Trin with a toss of her blonde extensions. 'And for anyone who's not convinced, this should really set the record straight.' She wound her arms around Luke and kissed him, a long passionate and pure Hollywood kiss.

'I know it's awful of me,' Steve whispered to Zoe, 'but I think this is going to be great publicity for our film.'

She swatted him on the arm. 'You're starting to sound like Rufus.'

Her husband shuddered. 'That world-class prick? Never! When I start wearing tight leather trousers I'll know I'm in trouble!'

'Whatever happened to Rufus?' asked Zoe. 'He seems to have gone very quiet lately.'

'Haven't you heard?' Susannah looked surprised. 'I guess you've been far too loved up to listen to any of the industry gossip.'

Zoe and Steve exchanged a tender glance.

'It turned out he invested his own money in the new version of the film – what was it called again?'

'*Portrait of a Lady with Attitude*,' shuddered Zoe.

Susannah laughed drily. 'Yeah, well, with a title like that what a surprise it's gone straight to DVD. The critics have panned it and Rufus's reputation is in ruins.'

'What goes around comes around,' observed Angela.

'Is that another prophecy?' Zoe's father asked.

'Because if it is then I'd like to make a prediction too. I think another wedding's on the cards.'

Zoe rolled her eyes. 'Sixth time lucky, eh, Dad?'

Stepping forward, Susannah slipped her hand into Mike Forster's and kissed him softly on the cheek. 'I certainly hope so,' she said.

'A wedding, hey?' piped up Angela, fishing her diary out of her enormous handbag. 'In that case you'll be having a hen do. I'm available, if you'd like?'

'No, thanks!' chorused everyone instantly. They'd had enough of Angela's prophecies to last a lifetime!

Threading her arm through the psychic's, Zoe said, 'Sometimes it's just simpler not to know what the future holds. Maybe not as exciting, but much, much easier.'

And, still laughing, they walked down the road and into Steve's favourite restaurant. Zoe knew that even Angela wouldn't be able to predict what dishes they ended up with! But she had predicted that she'd marry again . . . and was she glad she had!

Pick up a *little black dress* – it's a girl thing.

NO ORDINARY GIRL
A.M. Goldsher
£6.99

Abbey Bynum never asked for her strange superpowers; she was born with them and man, does she hate them. But when super-handsome super-villain Jon Carson appears on the scene under the guise of a brilliant new defense lawyer at her work, Abbey knows she must embrace her 'weird stuff' to have any chance of thwarting his plans for world domination.

978 0 7553 5858 8

Quirky, straight-talking, feisty and able to fly – this is one superheroine you won't forget!

TAKING THE LEAD
Sarah Monk
£6.99

Theo is an artist with blue eyes and long chaotic hair. Jonas is half Swedish, tall, blonde and channels his own creativity into his woodworking business. They're made for each other, but as Jonas hurtles towards his marriage day, time is running out. Their paths are tantalisingly close, but it will take something dramatic to lead them in the right direction . . .

978 0 7553 4514 4

Another engrossing, heartwarming LBD romance set in a stunning location.

Pick up a *little black dress* – it's a girl thing.

SARIS IN THE CITY
Rekha Waheed
£5.99

When ambitious City analyst Yasmin Yusuf's hope for a traditional 'happy ever after' in the romance stakes is shattered she decides there's only one course of action: get smart, sexy and successful, and what better way to do this than saving a failing lingerie business?

978 0 7553 5613 3

A fabulous feisty novel – East meets West in Rekha Waheed's brilliant romance.

UNLUCKY IN LOVE
Jessica Fox
£6.99

Risk-taker Libby Foster wishes she thought things through more – maybe then she'd avoid being humiliated at work over her reckless romantic attachments. So it's just as well that she's swearing herself off men and escaping to a Thai island, where nothing could possibly go wrong . . .

978 0 7553 4960 9

The fourth novel in this addictive new series, THE HEN NIGHT PROPHECIES, focuses on Libby, *'A danger to men . . .'*

Pick up a *little black dress* – it's a girl thing.

978 0 7553 5441 2

VINTAGE MAGIC
Sally Anne Morris
£6.99

Her love life in tatters, Rose Taylor decides to run away from London and open a vintage dress shop in Bath. If anyone can appreciate the life-enhancing power of wearing the perfect dress, it's Rose, but it seems that the dresses in Viva Las Vintage! really do have a life of their own . . .

SHOULDER BAGS AND SHOOTINGS
Dorothy Howell
£6.99

Little Black Dress's favourite shop-aholic sleuth, the lovable (and fashion-crazed) Haley Randolph is in trouble again . . . Get ready for another thrilling and funny romantic suspense from Dorothy Howell.

978 0 7553 4733 9

Pick up a *little black dress* – it's a girl thing.

ABOUT TIME
Niamh Shaw
£5.99

Why is Lara so nervous about moving to New York with boyfriend Barry? Of course, there *is* the small matter of forgetting about socially inept super-geek Conn, who has an annoying habit of making repeat appearances in her love life. It's about time she put the past behind her. Although that's easier said than done . . .

978 0 7553 4857 2

HEN NIGHT PROPHECIES:
HARD TO GET
Jessica Fox
£5.99

Charlotte loves her job at the Arts Council – it's just a shame she has to share the office with her ex-husband, who also happens to be dating her boss. Fate, hope and charity influence Charlotte's romantic destiny as the third prophecy in the addictive HEN NIGHT PROPHECIES series is revealed: *'Love will come through hope alone.'*

978 0 7553 4959 3

You can buy any of these other
Little Black Dress titles from your
bookshop or *direct from the publisher*.

FREE P&P AND UK DELIVERY
(Overseas and Ireland £3.50 per book)

TO ORDER SIMPLY CALL THIS NUMBER

01235 400 414

or visit our website: www.headline.co.uk

Prices and availability subject to change without notice